Then Saul, who is also called Paul,* filled with the Holy Ghost, set his eyes on him, and said, O full of all subtilty and all mischief, *thou child of the devil, thou* enemy of all righteousness, wilt thou not cease to pervert the right ways of the Lord?

Acts, 13, 9-10

To drive, to hold, to run, to offend,
to hear and to see, to turn and to breathe,
to hate and to depend,
and to endure.

A group of infinitives which, in Russian, are exceptions to certain rules

Not a line in all the marked and singular lineaments of his face which was not, even in the most absolute identity, *mine own!*

Edgar Allan Poe, "William Wilson"

Savl and Pavel are the Russian forms of Saul and Paul. [Trans. note.]

A SCHOOL
FOR FOOLS

SASHA SOKOLOV

Translated by Carl R. Proffer

Introduction by D. Barton Johnson

Four Walls Eight Windows, New York

To the retarded boy
Vaitis Dantsin,
my friend and neighbor

Originally published by Ardis, 1977.
English translation copyright © 1977 Ardis.

Introduction copyright © 1988 D. Barton Johnson.

First Four Walls Eight Windows edition published 1988
by Four Walls Eight Windows, Inc., New York.

Library of Congress Cataloging-in-Publication Data

Sokolov, Sasha, 1943-
    [Shkola dlia durakov. English]
    A school for fools/by Sasha Sokolov; translated by Carl R. Proffer. —
1st Four Walls Eight Windows ed.
    p.   cm.
    Translation of: Shkola dlia durakov.
    Reprint. Originally published: Ann Arbor, Mich.: Ardis, © 1977.
    ISBN 0-941423-07-7 (pbk.): $9.95

    I. Title
    PG3549.S64S5513 1988   87-33009
    891.73'44 — dc19   CIP

Four Walls Eight Windows
P.O. Box 548
Village Station
New York, New York 10014

Printed in the U.S.A.

Sasha Sokolov's *A School for Fools* has been called "a neglected masterpiece." The late Vladimir Nabokov, a man not known for the generosity of his critical judgements (especially of his fellow Russian writers), hailed it as "an enchanting, tragic, and touching book."

"Neglect" is a relative state. Compared to Boris Pasternak's *Doctor Zhivago* or Alexander Solzhenitsyn's *One Day in the Life of Ivan Denisovich,* Sokolov's brilliant novella is little known to the American reading public. Nonetheless, it shares with them the distinction of being one of the very few Russian novels to remain steadily in print since its first publication in 1976. *A School for Fools* is eagerly read and discussed in university classrooms from New England to Southern California. In Europe, it is read in German, Dutch, Swedish, French, Italian, and Polish translations. Conferences and articles are devoted to its reclusive author who lives in rural Vermont and Canada. He has been Regents' Lecturer at the University of California where there is an archive devoted to his work. Sokolov has entered into the standard Western handbooks and histories of modern Russian literature.

Nor is Sokolov neglected in the Soviet Union, where he wrote *A School for Fools* before his emigration in 1975. His three novels, all banned although resolutely apolitical, are eagerly sought after by Soviet literary connoisseurs, and also by the authorities who carefully removed all copies of his works from exhibition at the 1987 Moscow International Book Fair — this, in the era of Gorbachev's *glasnost* when even Pasternak's *Doctor Zhivago* is finally being published in the land of its birth. Sokolov's works are broadcast to the Soviet Union where they are heard by thousands. They also make the journey in other ways. A recent issue of a Soviet film magazine contained a picture of a young screen idol being interviewed in his apartment. On the book-lined shelves in back of him, a Sokolov novel was (in)discreetly in view. In private conversation the better-read, "official" writers speak of him admiringly, and in 1981 the editorial board of the "unofficial" Leningrad literary magazine *Chasy* awarded Sokolov's second novel, the arcane *Between Dog and Wolf,* its annual Andrei Bely prize.

Sokolov has achieved his present enviable reputation in slightly over a decade without the international political scandals, best-sellerdom, and popular film versions that attended Pasternak's tragic love story and Solzhenitsyn's grim camp exposé. Unlike these works, both traditional realistic novels, *A School for Fools* is a quiet, intimately personal book written in the spirit of high modernism. Pasternak's and Solzhenitsyn's novels are a continuation of the great nineteenth-century Russian literary tradition; Sokolov's marks the beginning of a new one.

A School for Fools is a journey through the mental landscape of a nameless, schizophrenic adolescent which he relates with the assistance of an author figure who may be the boy's older self. Through the kaleidoscopic prism of the teenager's schizoid mind, we share his bizarre perceptions and attempts to come to terms with the surrounding world. The boy, who refers to himself as "we", perceives himself and several other characters as two distinct but related persons, each with his or her own name. Much of the narrative is an interior dialogue between the two halves of the boy's mind, or interior monologues ostensibly directed toward often unidentified characters. Nor can the boy perceive time, or events in time, in any fixed order; past, present, and future are random and intermixed. These aberrations determine the unorthodox form of the novella. There is, in the ordinary sense, no plot, but rather an ever swirling verbal collage.

The novella's characters, who flicker in and out of the boy's imagination, are aligned with the two halves of his personality. The main voice is that of his free fantasy, his delusions; the other, lesser voice is that of rationality which constantly intrudes, hectors, and accuses the first voice of fabrication, both trivial and fundamental. One character grouping represents the repressive, institutionalized forces of society that constrain the freedom and creativity of the individual. These include the boy's prosecutor father; Dr. Zauze, the psychiatrist; and Perillo and Sheina Trachtenberg, the school officials. All are creatures of the city. The positive characters, Norvegov and the Acatovs, are all associated with nature and the summer settlement in the Moscow countryside. They are the characters of spontaneity and freedom. It is Norvegov who counsels the boy to "live in the wind."

Most of the characters are "doubles" who exist in two variants, although they are not always easily identifiable. Pavel, who is also Savl, i.e., Paul/Saul, takes his dual name from the iconoclastic Biblical figure. A more obscure pairing is Veta's scientist father, Arcady Acatov, who appears in many scenes as Leonardo da Vinci, scientist and artist. Mikheev, the elderly postman whose beard streams behind him as he rides his bicycle, is also Medvedev, and, perhaps, the legendary "Sender of the Wind." The villainess, Deputy Principal Sheina Trachtenberg, often appears as the witch Tinbergen. Each of these "doubles," projections of the boy's schizophrenia, is a complex blending of elements from life and the boy's imagination.

A School for Fools can be read as a socio-political indictment, but this is far too narrow an interpretation. Russian literature has a tradition, largely associated with Dostoevsky, that links rationalism with political tyranny and artistic sterility. The irrational, on the other hand, is identified with social and political freedom, and artistic creativity.

Madness, the most extreme manifestation of the irrational (at least in its romanticized, fictional representation), permits Sokolov's hero freedom from drab, institutionalized reality. His madness and "selective memory" even free him from the laws of time. The hero can simultaneously be a snotty-nosed, crazy schoolboy and a suave graduate engineer courting Veta in his own car. Death, along with all else, becomes problematic. Norvegov can be simultaneously alive and dead. The boy and his idol Norvegov pay a high price for their freedom, however, since it puts them in conflict with society.

Sokolov is a brilliant stylist, a language-obsessed writer, who revels in witty, elegant word play. His novella is a whirlwind of language and sound that shapes the narrative and rushes it along. This irrational, free, creative force of nature is embodied in the mythic figure of the "Sender of the Wind" which inspires and defends the positive characters and threatens havoc on their enemies. Norvegov, its prophet, is nicknamed the "winddriver" and the "windvane." His schoolgirl mistress is the mortally ill Rosa Windova. The name of the boy's beloved Veta poetically derives from the Russian word for wind, *veter,* as do the names and sobriquets of all of the affirmative characters. They are quite literally "children of the wind" who emerge from the verbal hurricane of the novella's stream of consciousness passages. Such poetic devices are the essence of Sokolov's literary style.

Sokolov was born in 1943 in Ottawa, Canada where his father, Major Vsevolod Sokolov, was attached to the Commercial Counsellor's section of the Soviet Embassy. In fact, Major (later General) Sokolov was deputy head of the intelligence network that passed U.S. atomic secrets on to Moscow. Expelled from Canada, the Sokolov family returned to Moscow where their dreamy son drifted through an unsatisfactory career in the public schools. After graduation the teenage Sokolov worked briefly as a morgue attendant and lathe operator before entering the Military Institute of Foreign Languages in 1962. This educational venture ended in brief stays in jail for being AWOL and then in a mental hospital as a ploy to be discharged from his military obligation. His favorite rehearsed delusions, that he was an unexploded bomb or a taut drum with internal Aeolian harp strings, were fine metaphors for a developing writer. The ploy was successful. Sokolov had been extremely fortunate that an ill-fated attempt to cross the Soviet-Iranian border on foot had not been detected. In the mid-sixties Sokolov was part of Moscow's literary bohemia, before entering the journalism department at Moscow State University in 1967.

Receiving his degree in 1971, Sokolov took a job as a game warden in a hunting preserve on the remote upper Volga. It was here that he wrote *A School for Fools,* although there was little hope of publishing such an avant-garde, stylistic tour de force in the USSR. Rather than submit the work to a Soviet publisher, Sokolov adopted the dangerous course of sending the manuscript abroad. While the novel was making its way toward publication abroad, Sokolov renewed his efforts to leave the Soviet Union. The interest of the KGB had been aroused by inquiries at the Canadian Embassy about Sokolov's possible citizenship. Matters came to a head when Sokolov and the Austrian girl who had taken his manuscript abroad decided to marry. The issue of Sokolov's mental health was raised again, and his parents signed a document disavowing his actions. Other authorities entered the picture.

Introduction

If the writer were not in fact mentally indisposed, he still faced completion of his military obligation. When the fiancée returned home to Austria for a visit, she was barred from reentering Moscow. The couple decided to stage a well-publicized hunger strike: the bride-to-be in Vienna, and the groom in front of the Palace of Weddings in Moscow. Through the intercession of Austrian Chancellor Kreisky with Leonid Brezhnev, Sokolov was permitted to leave the USSR.

Sokolov emigrated in 1975. In response to an invitation from his publishers, Carl and Ellendea Proffer, the co-founders of Ardis Press, he arrived in North America where his Canadian citizenship was soon confirmed. While still in Russia, Sokolov had conceived a novel based on a murder he had heard about on the remote upper Volga. *Between Dog and Wolf* (1980) is a novel of startling originality, difficulty and daring. Its Russian title-idiom refers to twilight when the normally distinct becomes blurred, if not indistinguishable. *Between Dog and Wolf,* which has some claim to being the *Finnegans Wake* of Russian literature, was a quantum leap in Sokolov's literary development.

Sokolov, who had taught in Russian language summer programs in rural Vermont, found it an appealing place and settled there in 1981. There he wrote his third novel, *Palisandria* (1985). Known in English as *Astrophobia,* it is a comic, picaresque work that lampoons many popular genres.

Although too much the atopical, recherché stylist to attract a mass audience, Sokolov is the most critically acclaimed of the younger Russian prose writers to come to the fore in the late seventies and eighties. Together with his fellow émigré, poet Joseph Brodsky, the 1987 Nobel Laureate, Sokolov is writing a new chapter in the history of Russian literature.

D. Barton Johnson
University of California
Santa Barbara, California

CHAPTER ONE

NYMPHEA

All right, but how do you begin, what words do you use? It makes no difference, use the words: there, at the station pond. At the *station* pond? But that's incorrect, a stylistic mistake. Vodokachka would certainly correct it, one can say "station" snack bar or "station" news stand, but not "station" pond, a pond can only be *near* the station. Well, say it's near the station, that's not the point. Good, then I'll begin that way: there, at the pond near the station. Wait a second, the station, the station itself, please, if it's not too hard, describe the station, what the station was like, what sort of platform it had, wooden or concrete, what kind of houses were next to it, you probably recall what color they were, or maybe you know the people who lived in the houses near that station? Yes, I know, or rather I knew, some of the people who lived near the station, and I can tell something about them, but not now, later sometime, because right now I will describe the station. It's an ordinary station: signalman's shack, bushes, ticket booth, platform (wooden), squeaky planks, nails sticking up all over and you shouldn't go barefoot. There were trees around the station: aspens, pines, a variety of trees, you know, a variety. The station itself was a normal station, but what was beyond the station was regarded as something really fine and extraordinary: the pond, the high grass, the dance platform, the grove, the rest home and other things. Ordinarily people went swimming in the pond near the station in the evening, after work, they would arrive on commuter electrics and go swimming. No, first they would go their separate ways to their dachas. Weary, breathing heavily, wiping their faces with handkerchiefs, swinging briefcases and shopping bags. Do you remember what was in the shopping bags? Tea, sugar, butter, salami; fresh fish with whipping tails; macaroni, buckwheat, onions, prepared foods; more rarely, salt. They would go to their dachas, drink tea on verandas, put on pyjamas, and take walks—arms behind their backs—through the orchards, and glance into the fire barrels full of efflorescent water, astonished by the multitude of frogs—which were hopping through the grass everywhere—and play with children and dogs, and play badminton, and drink kvass from refrigerators, and watch television, and talk to their neighbors. And if it was not yet dark, they would set out for the pond in groups—to go swimming. Why didn't they go to the river? They were afraid of the whirlpools and main channels, the wind and the waves, the deep spots and bottom reeds. And maybe there just wasn't any river? Maybe. But what was it called? The river was called.

Basically, every path and trail in our district led to the pond. Poor, narrow, virtually nonexistent paths stretched from the most distant dachas situated at the forest fringe. They barely glowed in the evening, glimmering, while the more significant paths, pounded down long ago, trails so beaten that there could be no question of any weeds growing on them at all—trails of this kind glowed clear, white, and even. This is at sunset, yes, naturally, at sunset, only right after sunset in the dusk. And so, one merging with the other, all paths led in the direction of the pond. Finally, several hundred meters from the shore, they united in one excellent road. This road ran through some meadows before penetrating the birch grove. Look back and admit it: wasn't it nice in the evening, in the gray light, to ride into the grove on a bicycle? It was nice. Because a bicycle is always nice, in any weather, at any age. Take Pavlov, for example. He was a physiologist, he did various experiments on animals and rode a bicycle a lot. In a certain textbook—you of course remember the book—there is a special chapter on Pavlov. First come pictures of dogs with some sort of special physiological pipes sewn into their throats, and it is explained that the dogs got conditioned to receiving food when a bell was rung, and when Pavlov did not give them food, but just rang the bell for nothing, the dogs got excited and their saliva started to flow—quite amazing. Pavlov had a bicycle, and the academician rode around on it a lot. One ride is shown in the textbook too. Pavlov is old there, but hale and hearty. He rides along, observing nature, and there's a bell on the handlebar—like in the experiments, exactly the same kind. Moreover, Pavlov had a long gray beard, like Mikheev, who lived, and perhaps still lives, in our dacha settlement. Mikheev and Pavlov—they both loved bicycles, but the difference is this: Pavlov rode a bicycle for pleasure, at leisure, but for Mikheev the bicycle always meant work, that was the kind of work he did: delivering mail by bicycle. Of him, of the postman Mikheev— but maybe his name was, is, and will be Medvedev?—one has to speak separately, he has to be allotted some separate time, and one of us—you or I—will definitely have to do this. Incidentally, I think you know the postman better, since you lived at the dacha much more than I, although if one were to ask the neighbors they would surely say it's quite a complicated question and that it's almost impossible to figure it out. The neighbors will say, we did not keep very close track of you—that is, of us,—and in general what kind of weird question is that, why do you suddenly need to clarify something absurd, what difference does it make who lived there longer, that's frivolous, they'll say, you'd do better to get to work: it's May in your garden, and apparently the trees have not been spaded, and you surely like to eat apples; and even wind-driver Norvegov, they'll remark — even he's been digging in his little garden since morning. Yes, he's digging, we'll reply—one of us—or we'll say in chorus: yes, he's digging. Instructor Norvegov has the time for that, and the desire. Besides, he has a garden and a house, but us—we have nothing like that—no time, no garden, no house. You have simply forgotten, we haven't lived here in this settlement for a long time, probably nine years. We sold the dacha after all—up and sold it. I suspect that as the more loquacious, gregarious person you'll want to add something to this, to rehash everything, start explaining why we sold it and why, from your point of view, we did not have to sell, and how the point isn't that we *could* not have sold, but that we *should* not have sold. But we'd better get away from them, we'll leave on the very first train, I don't want to hear their voices.

Our father sold the dacha when he was pensioned off, although the pension turned out to be so large that the dacha postman Mikheev, who has dreamed of a good new bicycle all his life, but who cannot ever save enough money, not because he's a spendthrift exactly, he's simply thriftless—so when he learned from our dacha neighbor, the prosecutor's crony, the kind of pension our father was going to get, Mikheev almost fell off his bicycle. The postman was riding placidly past the fence around our neighbor's dacha—by the way, do you remember his name? No, can't recall like that all at once: a bad memory for names, but then what's the sense in remembering all these first names and last names—right? Of course, but if we knew his name it would be nice to tell it. But we can think up some arbitrary name, names—no matter how you look at it—are all arbitrary, even if they're real ones. But on the other hand, if we give him an arbitrary name people can think we're making up something here, trying to fool someone, delude them, but we have absolutely nothing to hide, this is about a man who was our neighbor, a neighbor everyone in the settlement knows, and they know that he was one of the prosecutor's cronies at work, and his dacha is ordinary, not very fancy, and it was probably just talk about his house being made from stolen brick—what do you think? Eh?—what are you talking about? What's wrong with you, aren't you listening to me? No, I'm listening, only it just occurred to me that there was probably beer in those containers. In what containers? In the big ones in the neighbor's shed, there was ordinary beer in them—what do you think? I don't know, I don't remember, I haven't thought about that time for a long while. And at the moment when Mikheev was riding past our neighbor's house, the owner was standing on the threshold of the shed and examining the container of beer in the light. Mikheev's bicycle rattled violently as it jounced over the pine roots sticking up through the ground, and the neighbor could not help hearing and recognizing Mikheev's bicycle. And having heard and recognized it, he walked quickly to the fence to ask if there were any letters, but instead—surprising even himself—he informed the postman: the prosecutor—said the prosecutor's crony—have you heard? He's gone on pension. Smiling. How much they give him? responded Mikheev, not stopping, but just braking slightly—how much money? He looked back in motion, and the neighbor saw the postman's suntanned face had no expression. The postman, as always, looked calm; the only thing was that his beard, with pine needles sticking to it, was waving in the wind: in the wind born of the speed, in the swift bicycle wind; and it would certainly have seemed to the neighbor—had he been only a little of a poet—that Mikheev's face, blown by all of the dacha crosswinds, itself emanated wind, and that Mikheev was that very person who was known in the settlement as The Sender of Wind. To be more precise, *who was not known.* No one had ever seen this person, possibly he did not exist at all. But in the evenings, after swimming in the pond, the dacha dwellers gathered on their glassed-in verandas, sat down in their wicker armchairs and told each other all kinds of stories, and one of them was the legend of The Sender. Some asserted that he was youthful and wise, others that he was old and stupid, a third party insisted that he was of middle years, but retarded and uneducated, and a fourth party that he was old and sagacious. And there was also a fifth party which declared that The Sender was young and decrepit, a fool—but a genius. It was said that he appears on one of the sunniest and warmest days of summer, rides a bicycle, whistles with a nut-wood whistle and does nothing but send wind to the locale through which he is riding. What they had in mind was that The Sender sends wind only into a locale where there are all too many dachas and dacha dwellers. Yes, indeed, and ours was precisely that kind of locale. If I'm not mistaken there are three or four dacha settlements in the area of the station. And what was the station called?—I just cannot make it out from the distance. The station did have a name.

This is zone five, ticket price thirty-five kopeks, the train takes an hour twenty northern branch, a branch of acacia or, say, lilac blooms with white flowers, smells of creosote, the dust of connecting platforms, and smoke looms along the track bed, in the evening it returns to the garden on tiptoe and listens intently to the movement of the electric trains, trembles from the rustling noises, and then the flowers close and sleep, yielding to the importunities of the solicitous bird by the name of Nachtigall; the branch sleeps, but the trains, distributed symmetrically along the branch, rush feverishly through the dark like chains, hailing each flower by name, dooming to insomnia the following: bilious old station ladies, amputees and war-blinded traincar accordion players, blue-gray linemen in sleeveless orange tops, sage professors and insane poets, dacha irregulars and failures—anglers for early and late fish, tangled in the spongy plexus of the limpid forest, and also middle-aged islander buoy-keepers whose faces, bobbing over the metallically humming black channel waters, alternately pale and scarlet, and, finally, the dockmen, who think they hear the sound of an unfastened boat chain, a splash of oars, a rustle of sails, and then, throwing over their shoulders buttonless Gogolian overcoats, emerge from their dock-houses and stride across porcelain shoreline sands, and dunes, and grassy embankments; the faint, still shadows of the dockmen are cast on the reeds and the heather, and their home-made pipes gleam like maple stumps, attracting astonished moths; but the branch sleeps, flower petals closed, and the trains, lurching across switches, will not awaken it for anything, will not brush from it a drop of dew—sleep sleep branch smelling of creosote wake up in the morning and flower make the profusion of petals bloom into the eyes of the semaphores and dancing in time to your wooden heart laugh in the stations sell yourself to passersby and to those departing weep and keen naked in the mirrored coupes what's your name I'm called Vetka I'm Vetka acacia I am Vetka of the railroad I am Veta pregnant by the tender bird called Nachtigall I am pregnant with the coming summer and the crash of a freight here take me take me my blossoms are falling and it costs very little at the station I cost no more than a ruble I am sold by tickets and if you wish travel without paying there will be no inspector he is sick wait I will unbutton myself see I am all snow white so shower me shower me all over with kisses no one will notice the petals they are not visible on white and I am sick of it all sometimes I seem to myself simply an old lady who has spent all her life walking across red-hot engine slag on the roadbed she is aged appalling I don't want to be an old woman dear no I don't want to I know I will soon die on the rails me me it hurts me it will hurt me let go when I die let go these wheels are covered with oil your palms what are your palms in can those be gloves I told a lie I am Veta chaste white branch I flower you have no right I dwell in gardens don't shout I'm not shouting it's the train coming tra ta ta shouting what's this tra ta ta what tra who there ta where there there there Veta willows willows branch there outside the window in that house tra ta ta tum of whom of what of Vetka oars of wind tararam trailer tramway *tramway ay* even good ticks tick its lee lethe there is no Lethe no Ay-colored Lethe for you

a hue like Alpha Veta Gamma and so on which no
one knows because no one would teach us Greek
it was an unforgivable mistake on their part it's because of them we cannot sensibly enumerate a single
ship and the running Hermes is like unto a flower but
we scarcely understand this that the other Cape Horn
blow horns but naturally beat drums tra ta ta question is
that a conductor answer no a constrictor why are you
shouting there you feel bad it seemed like that to you I
feel good it's a train coming forgive me now I know precisely it was a train coming but you know I was dozing
and suddenly heard something like someone singing
clickety clak clickety clak clickety clak de dum de dum
netto brutto Italia Italian person Dante person Bruno
person Leonardo artist architect entomologist *if you
want to see flying with four wings step into the moats
of the Milan fortress and you will see black dragonflies*
a ticket to Milan even two for me and Mikheev Medvedev I want dragonflies flying in willows on rivers in moats
uncut along the main railway of the Veta constellation
in the thickets of heather where Tinbergen himself born
in Holland married a colleague and soon it became clear
to them that *ammofila* does not find the way home the
same way *filantus* does and of course you beat a tam-
bourine someone in the train tambour-platform there
tum ta tum ta tum tum there a simply merry song is
being performed on a reed pipe on the Vetochka branch
of the railroad tra ta tra ta ta a cat married a cat married
Tinbergen's cat dancing up and down nightmare witch
she lives with an excavator operator never lets one sleep
at six in the morning sings in the kitchen cooking him
food in pots the fires flame burning boil the pots aboil-
ing have to give her some name if the cat Tinbergen she
will be witch Tinbergen dances in the hall from earliest
morn and doesn't let one sleep sings about the cat and

probably behaves very affectedly. But why "probably?" Haven't you ever seen her dancing. No, it seems to me I have never ever seen her. I have lived in the same communal apartment with her for many years now, but the point is that the witch Tinbergen is not at all the old woman who is registered here and who I see in the mornings and evenings in the kitchen. That old woman is a different one, her surname is Trachtenberg, Sheina Solomonovna Trachtenberg, a Jewess, on a pension, she is a lonely pensioner, and every morning I say to her: good morning, and in the evening: good evening, she replies, she is a very plump woman, she has red hair flecked with gray, curls, she is such a sixty-five year old, we scarcely speak to her, we simply have nothing to talk about, but from time to time, approximately once every two months, she asks to borrow my record player and plays the same record on it every time. She doesn't listen to anything else, she hasn't got any other record. And what is the record? I'll tell that in a minute. Let's suppose I am coming home. From somewhere or other. I should note that I know in advance when Trachtenberg is going to ask for the record players, several days ahead I foresee that soon now, quite soon, she will say: listen, my dear, be nice, how about your record player?   I walk up the stairs and I can feel it: Trachtenberg is already standing there, behind the door, she is in the hall, waiting for me. I enter boldly. Boldly. I enter. Good evening. Boldly. Evening's good, my dear, do me a favor. I get the record player out of the cabinet. A pre-war record player, bought sometime and somewhere. By someone. It has a red case, it's always covered with dust because although I wipe up the dust in the room the way our good and patient mother taught me, my hands never reach the record player. I haven't

wound it up myself for a long time. In the first place I have
no records, and in the second the record player doesn't
work, it's wrecked, a spring broke a long time ago and
the turntable doesn't turn, believe me. Sheina Solomonovna, I say,—the record player doesn't work, you
know that yourself. That's not important, answers
Trachtenberg,—I need only one little record. Oh, just
one, I say. Yesyesyes, smiles Sheina, her teeth are basically gold, she wears horn-rimmed glasses and powders
her face—one little record. She takes the record player,
carries it off to her room and locks the lock. And in
about ten minutes I hear the voice of Yakov Emmanuilovich. But you didn't say who Yakov Emmanuilovich is.
You mean you don't remember him? He was her husband, he died when you and I were about ten, and we
lived with our parents in the room where I now live
alone, or you live alone, in short—one of us does. But
still—who precisely? What's the difference? I am telling
you a very interesting story, and you're starting to pester me again, and I don't pester you after all, I thought we
agreed once and for all that there is no difference between us, or do you want to go *there* again? Excuse me,
in the future I will try not to cause you unpleasantness,
you understand, not everything is right with my memory. And you think mine is all right? Well, excuse me,
please excuse me, I didn't want to distress you. So then,
Yakov died from medicine, he poisoned himself with something. Sheina really tormented him, demanding money,
she seemed to imagine her husband was hiding a few
thousand from her, but he was an ordinary druggist, a
pharmacist, and I'm sure that he didn't have a penny. I
think Sheina's demands for money were a way of pok-
ing fun at him. She was some fifteen years younger than
he and as she said sitting on the benches in the yard

she betrayed him with Building Superintendent Sorokin, who had only one arm, and who later, a year after the death of Yakov, hanged himself in the empty garage. A week before this he had sold the captured automobile which he had brought back from Germany. If you recall, the people on the benches liked to talk about why it was Sorokin needed a car, he couldn't drive it anyway, he wasn't about to hire a chauffeur. But then it all became clear. When Yakov went away on business trips or had all-night shifts on duty in the drugstore, Sorokin would take Sheina into the garage, and it was there, in the car, that she betrayed Yakov. What a blessing, they said on the benches, what a blessing to have one's own car, and it turns out he didn't even want to ride around in it: he'd come to the garage, lock it from inside, turn on the lights, put back the seat—and there you go, have all the fun you like. Well, they said in the yard, it's too bad he's armless. Describe our yard, what did it look like then, such-and-such number of years ago. I would say it was more a junk heap than a yard. Stunted linden trees, two or three garages, and behind the garages—mountains of broken brick and all kinds of rubbish in general. But mainly there were old gas stoves lying around, three or four hundred of them, they had been brought into our of the neighboring buildings right after the war. Because of these stoves there was always a kitcheny odor in the yard. When we opened the ovens, the doors to the ovens, they screeched terribly. And why did we open the doors, why? It strikes me as strange you don't understand why. We opened the doors *in order to* slam them with a bang immediately. But shouldn't we get back to the people who lived in our neighborhood, we knew a lot. No, no, so boring, I'd like to talk a bit about some other things now. You see, in general in our mind something is wrong with time, we don't understand time properly. You haven't forgotten how once many years ago we met our teacher Norvegov at the station? No, I haven't, we met him at the station. He said that an hour earlier he had left the reservoir, where he had been fishing for mosquito grubs. And it is true he had a fishing pole and bucket with him, and I managed to get a glimpse of some sort of creatures swimming in the bucket, but not fish. Our geographer Norvegov had also built a dacha in the region served by this station, only on the other side of the river, and we visited him often. But what else did the teacher tell us that day? Geographer Norvegov told us more or less the following: young man, you have probably noticed what fine weather has been holding in our area for many days in a row now; do you agree that these respected dacha dwellers of ours do not deserve such luxury? Doesn't it strike you, my youthful comrade, that it's time for a storm to break, a tempest? Norvegov looked at the sky, shading his eyes from the sun with his hand. And it will break, my dear fellow, and how it will break—the pieces will fly up every back alley! And not just any old time, today or tomorrow. Bye the bye, have you thought about this seriously, do you believe it?

Pavel Petrovich *was standing in the middle of the platform,* the station clock showed two fifteen, he had on his usual light cap, all covered with little holes, as if eaten by a moth or repeatedly punched by a ticket-checker's punch, but in reality the holes had been put in at the factory so that the buyer's head, in this case Pavel Petrovich's, would not get sweaty during the hot times of the year. And moreover, they thought at the factory, dark holes on a light background—that did mean something, it was worth something, it was better than nothing, that is, better with holes than without them, or so they thought at the factory. All right, but what else did our teacher wear that summer, and generally during the best months of those unforgettable years when we lived at the same station he did, though his dacha was located in the settlement on the other side of the river, and ours was in one of the settlements which were on the same side as the station? It is rather difficult to answer that question, I don't remember precisely what Pavel Petrovich wore. It would be simpler to say what he didn't wear. Norvegov never wore shoes. In the summer at any rate. And that hot day on the platform, on the old wooden platform, he could easily have gotten a splinter in his foot, or both of them at once. That could have happened to anyone, but not to our teacher, he was so small and fragile, and when you saw him running along a dacha path or the school corridor, it seemed to you that his bare feet did not in the least touch the earth, the floor, and when he was standing there in the middle of the wooden platform that day, it seemed he was not standing there at all, but suspended over it, over its fractured planks, over all its burnt matches and butts, thoroughly sucked popsicle sticks, cancelled tickets and dried-up—and therefore invisible—gobs of passenger spit of various qualities. Allow me to interrupt you, it's possible there is something I've understood incorrectly. Do you mean Pavel Petrovich went barefoot even in school? No, apparently I went too far, I meant he went barefoot at the dacha, but perhaps he didn't put on shoes in town either, when he was going to work, and we simply didn't notice it. And maybe we did notice, but it wasn't too

obvious. Yes, somehow not too, in such cases a lot depends on the person himself, and not on the people who
are looking at him, yes, I recall, not too obvious. But
however it was during school terms, you definitely
know that in the summer Norvegov went without shoes.
Precisely. As our father noted one day, lying in the hammock with his newspaper in his hands, why the hell
would Pavel need shoes in hot spells like this! It's only
we official drudges, father went on, who never give our
feet any rest: if not boots then rubbers, if not rubbers
then boots—and that's the kind of torment you go
through all your life. If it's raining outside—then you
have to dry off your shoes, if the sun's shining—that
means be careful they don't crack. And the main thing
is every day in the morning you have to mess around
with shoe polish. But Pavel is a free man, a dreamer, he's
going to die with his feet bare. He's an idler, your Pavel
—our father said to us—that's why he's a barefoot tramp.
All his money's in his dacha probably, up to his neck in
debt, and he keeps on going there—to go fishing, loaf-
ing about on the shore, what kind of dacha-dweller is
he anyway? His house is worse than our shed, but to top
things off he put a windvane on his roof, just think of
it—a windvane! I ask him, the fool: why, I say, why the
windvane, all it does is squeak. And he replies from
there, the roof: why there's a lot of things can happen,
citizen prosecutor, for example, he says, the wind keeps
blowing and blowing in one direction and then suddenly
changes. That's all right for you, he says, I see you read
the newspapers, they write about it there of course;
about the weather, that is, but, you know, I don't sub-
scribe to anything, so that for me a windvane is an absolutely essential item. You know, he says, you learn
from the papers right off if something's not right, but

I'll be using the windvane to get oriented, which is much more precise, more precise than that it's impossible to be—our father told us, lying in his hammock with his newspaper in his hands. Then father climbed out of the hammock, strode off—hands behind his back—amid the pines oozing hot resin and sap from the earth, picked and ate several strawberries from a strawberry bed, looked up at the sky, where at the moment there were no clouds, no planes, no birds, yawned, shook his head and said, with Norvegov in mind: well, he should thank God I'm not his principal, I'd make him dance, he'd learn about the wind from me, the wretched boob, the tramp, the miserable windvane. The poor geographer—our father felt not the slightest respect for him, that's what not wearing shoes gets you. True, around the time we met Norvegov on the platform, to him, i.e., Pavel Petrovich, everything seemed to indicate, it made no difference if our father respected him or not, inasmuch as around this time he, i.e., our instructor, did not exist, he had died in the spring of the year such-and-such, that is, some two years before our meeting with him on that same platform. So as I was saying, with us something is not right about time, let's get it straight. He was sick for a long time, his illness was painful and prolonged, and he knew perfectly well that he would soon die, but he didn't let on. He remained the most cheerful, or to be precise, the only cheerful person in the school, and there was no end to his jokes. He would say that he felt so skinny that he was afraid some chance wind would blow him away. The doctors, laughed Norvegov, forbid me to go closer than half a kilometer to windmills, but the forbidden fruit is sweet: I am drawn to them irresistibly, the ones right by my house, on the wormwood hills, and a time will come when I can no longer resist. In the dacha settlement where I live they call me winddriver and windvane, but tell me, is it so bad to pass for a wind-driver, especially if you're a geographer? Why, a geographer has to be a wind-driver, that's his specialty—don't you think so, my young friends? Don't give in to depression—he shouted fervently, waving his arms,—isn't that right, live at full bicycle speed, get tan and go swimming, catch butterflies and dragonflies, the ones with the most colors, especially those magnificent Blacks and Yellows that are so numerous at my dacha! What else—asked our teacher, slapping his pockets to find matches, and cigarettes and light up,—what else? Know this, my friends, there is no happiness on earth, nothing of the sort, nothing like that at all, but then—Lord!—there is, finally, peace and freedom. The contemporary geographer, like, incidentally, the electrician, and the plumber, and the general, lives only once. So live in the wind, young folk, lots of compliments to the ladies, lots of music, smiles, fishing trips, vacations, knightly tournaments, duels, chess matches, breathing exercises and other nonsense. And if you are ever called a wind-driver, —said Norvegov, rattling the box of matches he had found so loudly it could be heard all over the school,—don't feel offended: that's not such a bad thing. For what do I fear in the face of eternity if today a wind ruffles my hair, freshens my face, puffs the sleeves of my shirt, blows through my pockets and tears at the buttons on my jacket, but tomorrow—destroys the unneeded old buildings, rips out oaks by the roots, stirs and swells the reservoirs and scatters the seeds of my garden all across the earth,—what do I fear, geographer Pavel Norvegov, an honest suntanned man from suburban zone five, a modest pedagogue, but one who knows his business, whose skinny but nonetheless commanding hand turns the hollow globe made of fraudulent papier-mâché from morning to night! Give me time—I'll show you which of us is right, some day I'll give your lazy, squeaky ellipsoid such a whirl that your rivers will back up, you'll forget your false books and newspapers, your own voices, names, and ranks will make you vomit, you will forget how to read and write, you will want to babble and whisper like aspen leaves in August. An angry crosswind will blast away the names of your streets and back alleys and the asinine signs, and you will want the truth. You lousy cockroach tribe! You brainless Panurgian herd, crawling with bedbugs and flies! You will want the great truth. And then I will come. I will come and bring with me the ones you have murdered and humiliated and I will say: there is your truth for you, and retribution against you. From horror and sorrow the obsequious pus which pollutes the blood in your veins will turn into ice. Fear The Sender of Wind, you sovereigns of cities and dachas, cower before the breezes and crosswinds, they engender hurricanes and tornadoes. I tell you this, I, geographer of the fifth suburban zone, the man who turns the vacuous cardboard globe. And saying this, I take eternity as my witness—isn't that right, my youthful assistants, my dear contemporaries and colleagues, isn't that right?

He died in the spring of the year such-and-such in his little house with the windvane. That day we were supposed to take our last exam in a class, his class as it happened, geography. Norvegov promised to come by nine, we gathered in the hall, and waited for the teacher until eleven, but he did not come. The principal of the school, Perillo, said the exam would be postponed until the next day, inasmuch as Norvegov had apparently fallen ill. We decided to visit him, but none of us knew the instructor's city address, so we went to the teachers' room to Assistant Curriculum Director Tinbergen, who secretly lives in our apartment and dances in the entrance hall in the morning, but whom neither you nor I have ever seen, for all one has to do is boldly fling open the door from our room into the hall and you find yourself—fling it open boldly!—in the moat of the Milan fortress and you are watching flying on four wings. The day is extremely sunny, and Leonardo wearing an old wrinkled tunic is standing by an easel with a drawing pen in one hand and a bottle of red India ink in the other, and putting some sort of diagrams on a piece of Whatman paper, sketching leaves of the sedge which has totally overgrown the damp and silty bottom of the moat (the sedge comes up to Leonardo's waist), making sketches of ballistic machines one after the other; and when he gets a little tired he takes a white entomological net and catches black dragonflies in order to study the structure of their retinas properly. The artist looks at you sullenly, he always seems to be dissatisfied with something. You want to leave the moat, return to your room, you are already turning around and attempting to find a door covered with leatherette in the perpendicular wall of the moat, but the master manages to restrain you by the arm, and looking into your eyes he says: homework assignment: describe the jaw of a crocodile, the tongue of a hummingbird, the carillon of the Convent of Novodevichy, describe the bird cherry's stem, Lethe's circumflexion, the tail of any local dog, a night of love, the mirages over hot asphalt, a clear noonday in Berezovo, the face of a flibbertigibbet, the pits of Hell, compare a termite colony with a forest anthill, the dolorous destiny of leaves—with the serenade of a Venetian gondolier, and transform a cicada into a butterfly; turn rain into hail, day—into night, give us this day our daily bread, change a vowel sound into a sibilant, prevent the crash of a train whose engineer is asleep, repeat the thirteenth labor of Hercules, give a passer-by a light, explain youth and old age, sing me a song about how where the bee sucks there suck I, turn your face to the north, to the high courts of Novgorod, and then tell how a yardman finds out if it's snowing outside if the yardman sits in the vestibule all day chatting with the elevator operator and doesn't look out the window, because there is no window, yes, tell precisely how he does this; and moreover, plant the white rose of the winds in your garden; show it to your teacher Pavel, and if he likes it—give teacher Pavel the white rose, pin the flower to his cowboy shirt or his dacha boater, do something nice for the man who is departing into nowhere, delight your old pedagogue—the jovial man, the jester, the driver of winds. O Rosa, the teacher will say, white Rosa Windova, dear girl, sepulchral flower, how I want your untouched body! On one of the nights of a summer embarrassed by its own beauty I await you in the little house with the windvane beyond the blue river, address: dacha locale, zone five, find postman Mikheev, ask for Pavel Norvegov, ring the bicycle bell repeatedly, wait for the rowboat from the misty shore, light up a signal fire, don't be depressed. Lying at the top of the steep sandy slope in a rick of hay, count the stars and weep from happiness and anticipation, remember a childhood which was like a juniper bush covered with fireflies, a Christmas tree trimmed with incredible whimsy, and think of what will come to pass toward morning when the first electric train is going by the station, when the people of the plants and factories awake with their hungover heads, and spitting and cursing the components of their engines and machines, they stride intemperately past the ponds near the station to the station beer-stands—green and blue. Yes, Rosa, yes, teacher Pavel will say, what is going to happen to us that night will be like a flame consuming an icy waste, like a starfall reflected in a fragment of a mirror which has suddenly fallen from its frame in the dark, forewarning its owner of imminent death. It will be like a shepherd's reed pipe, and like music which is yet unwritten. Come to me, Windy Rose, can it be that your old teacher, striding across the valleys of nonexistence and the tablelands of anguish is not dear to you. Come, to ease the trembling in your loins, and to soften my sadnesses. And if your instructor Pavel does say this —Leonardo says to you—inform me about it the very same night, and I will prove to everyone on earth that *in time nothingness is in the past and future and it contains nothing from the present, and in nature it borders on the impossible, from which it follows, pursuant to what we have said, that it has no existence, inasmuch as there would have to be emptiness present where nothing is supposed to be,* but nevertheless—continues the artist, *—with the help of windmills I can produce wind at any time.* And a last assignment for you: this device which looks like a gigantic black dragonfly—see it? it stands on a grassy slope—*try it tomorrow over the lake and be sure to put on a fur strip as a belt so that if you fall you won't drown.* And then you answer the artist: dear Leonardo, I'm afraid I cannot do your interesting problems, except for the problem connected with a yardman's finding out if in fact snow is falling outside on

the street. I can answer this question for any examination committee at any time just as easily as you
can produce wind. But unlike you I will not need a
single windmill. If the yardman sits in the vestibule from
morning to evening and chats with the elevator operator,
and if there are *yok* windows, which in Tatar means
no, the yardman determines if on—or to be more precise, over—the street, or onto the street it is snowing, by
the snowflakes on the hats and collars which hurriedly
enter the vestibule from the street, hastening to meetings with superiors. They, the ones who have snowflakes on their clothing, are usually divided into two
types: well dressed and badly dressed, but it's amusing
that snowflakes fall equally on both the former and the
latter. I noticed this when I worked as yardman in the
Ministry of Agitation. I got all of sixty rubles a month,
but then I made a detailed study of such fine phenomena as snow-fall, leaf-fall, rain-fall, and even hail-showers,
which of course none of the ministers or their helpers
can say of themselves, even though they all got several
times more per month than I. So I make a simple deduc-
tion: if you are a minister you cannot do a proper study
and understand what is happening in the street and in
the sky, because even if you have a window in your
office, you have no time to look out: you have too
many receptions, appointments, and telephone calls.
And if the doorman can easily learn about snow-fall
from the snowflakes on visitors' hats, you, the minister,
cannot, for the visitors leave their outer clothing in the
cloakrooms, and if they do not leave it, by the time
they wait for the elevator and go up the snow flakes
have time to melt. That's why it seems to you, the minister, that it's always summer outside, but this is not so.
Therefore, if you want to be a smart minister, ask the

yardman about the weather, call him on the telephone in the vestibule. When I worked as yardman in the Ministry of Agitation, I spent long periods sitting in the vestibule and chatting with the elevator operator, and the Minister of Agitation, knowing me as an honest, diligent fellow employee, would call me from time to time and ask: is this yardman so-and-so? Yes, I would reply, so-and-so, I've been working for you since such-and-such a year. Well this is Minister of Agitation so-and-so, he would say, I work on the fifth floor, office number three, and third on the left in the corridor, I have a job for you, stop by for a couple of minutes if you're not busy, it's quite urgent, we'll talk about the weather. Oh, by the way, not only did I work in the same ministry as he, we also were, and possibly still are now, dacha neighbors, in the dacha settlement that is, the Minister's dacha is catty-corner from ours. To be on the safe side I used two words here: *were* and *are,* the latter meaning *to be,* present tense. I did so because—although the doctors maintain that I got well long ago—to this day I cannot be precise and make definite judgments about anything that is in the slightest degree connected with the concept of *time.* It would appear to me that we have some sort of misunderstanding and confusion about it, about time, not everything is what it should be. Our calendars are too arbitrary: the numbers that are written there do not signify anything and are not guaranteed by anything, like counterfeit money. For example, why is it customary to think that the second of January comes right after the first, and not the twenty-eighth right away? And in general can days follow each other, that's some sort of poetic nonsense—a line of days. There is no line, the days come whenever one of them feels like it, and sometimes several come all at once. And sometimes a day doesn't come for a long time. Then you live in emptiness, not understanding anything, quite sick. And other people are sick too, but they keep quiet. I would also like to say that every person has his own special calendar of life not resembling anyone else's. Dear Leonardo, if you asked me to make up the calendar of *my* life, I would bring you a sheet of paper with a multitude of dots on it: the whole sheet would be covered with dots, just dots, and every dot would stand for a day. A thousand days—a thousand dots. But don't ask me which day corresponds to this or that dot: I don't know anything about that. And don't ask during what year, month or age of my life I made up my calendar, for I do not know what these words mean, and you yourself, pronouncing them, do not know either, just as you do not know a definition of time the truth of which I would not doubt. Be humble! Neither you nor I nor any of our friends can explain what we mean when we discuss time, conjugate the verb *to be*, and divide life into yesterday, today and tomorrow, as if these words differed from each other in meaning, as if it had not been said: tomorrow is just another name for today, as if it had been granted us to comprehend even a small portion of what happens to us here in the closed space of an explicable grain of sand, as if everything that happens here is, exists,—really, in fact *is, exists.* Dear Leonardo, not long ago (just now, in a short time) I was floating (am floating, will float) down a big river in a rowboat. Before this (after this) I was often (will be) there and am well acquainted with the area. It was (is, will be) very good weather, and the river—quiet and broad, and on shore, on one of the shores, a cuckoo was cuckooing (is cuckooing, will be cuckooing), and when I put down (will put down) the oars to rest, it sang (will sing) to me of how many years of life I have left. But this was (is, will be) stupid on its part because I was quite certain (am certain, will be certain) that I will soon die, if I have not died already. But the cuckoo did not know about that and, one must suppose, my life interested it to a much smaller degree than its life did me. So I put down the oars, and counting what were supposedly my years, asked myself several questions: what is the name of this river drawing me to its delta, who am I, the one being drawn along, how old am I, what is my name, what day is today and what year is it, in essence, and also: the boat, here's the boat, an ordinary boat—but whose? and why precisely a boat? Esteemed master, these were such simple but agonizing questions that I couldn't answer a one and decided that I was having an attack of the same hereditary disease from which my grandmother suffered, my former grandmother. Don't correct me, I intentionally used the word *former* here instead of *deceased,* agree that my choice sounds better, softer and not as hopeless. You see, when grandmother was still with us, sometimes she lost her memory, it usually happened when she looked at something extraordinarily beautiful for a long time. And therefore on the river I thought: it's probably too beautiful around, and so, like grandmother I have lost my memory now and am not in any state to reply to my own commonplace questions. Several days later I went to Doctor Zauze, who was treating me, and consulted him, asking for advice. The doctor told me: my little friend, you should know that you undoubtedly have the same thing your grandmother had. To hell with the countryside, he said, stop going there, look what you've lost there. But doctor, I said, it's beautiful there, beautiful, I want to go there. In that case, he said, taking off or perhaps putting on his glasses, I forbid you to go there. But I didn't obey him. In my opinion he's one of those greedy people who like to be in good places themselves and would like to keep anyone besides themselves from going there. Of course I promised him not to go anywhere outside the city, but I did go as soon as I was let out, and I lived at the dacha the remainder of the summer and even part of autumn until they started making fires for fallen leaves and part of the fallen leaves had floated down our river. During those days it got so beautiful that I could not even go out on the veranda: all I had to do was look at the river and see the many-colored forests on the other side, the Norvegov side, and I'd begin to cry and couldn't do anything with myself. The tears flowed spontaneously, I couldn't say no to them, and inside I was disquieted and feverish (father demanded that mother and I return to the city—and we did), but what had happened on the river, that time in the boat, did not repeat itself—not that summer, or that autumn, or in general ever again after. Obviously I can forget things: an object, a word, a name, a date, but only then, on the river, in the boat, did I forget everything at once. But as I realize now the condition was nevertheless not grandmother's, it was something else, my own, perhaps something not yet studied by doctors. Yes, I could not reply to the questions I had asked myself, but understand this: it did not mean loss of memory at all, that wouldn't cover any of it. Dear Leonardo, it was all far more serious, to wit: I was in one of the phases of disappearance. You see, a man cannot disappear momentarily and totally, first he is transformed into something distinct from himself in form and in essence—for example, into a waltz, a distant, faintly audible evening waltz, that is, he disappears partially, and only later does he disappear totally.

Somewhere in a glade a wind orchestra assumed position. The musicians sat down on the fresh stumps of pine trees, and put their sheet music in front of them not on music-stands but on the grass. The grass is tall and thick and strong, like lake rushes, and it supports the music without difficulty, and the musicians can make out all of the symbols without difficulty. You probably don't know this, but it's possible there is no orchestra in the glade, but you can hear music from beyond the forest and you feel good. You feel like taking off your shoes, socks, standing on tiptoe and dancing to this distant music, staring at the sky, you hope it will never end. Veta, my dear, do you dance? Of course, my sweet, I do so love to dance. Then allow me to ask you for a turn. With pleasure, with pleasure, with pleasure! But then mowers appear in the glade. Their instruments, their twelve-handled scythes, glitter in the sun too, not gold like the musicians', but silver, and the mowers begin to mow. The first mower approaches a trumpeter, and lifting his scythe in time to the playing music, with a quick swish he severs the grassy stems upon which the trumpeter's music rests. The book falls and closes. The trumpeter chokes off in mid-bar and quietly goes away into a bower where there are many cool springs and all kinds of birds are singing. The second mower advances to the French horn player and does the same thing—the music is still playing—that the first did: cuts. The French horn player's book falls. He gets up and goes off after the trumpeter. The third mower strides expansively up to the bassoon: and his book—the music is still playing but it is getting softer—falls too. And then all three musicians, noiselessly, single-file, go to listen to the birds and drink the spring water. Soon—the music is playing *piano*—they are succeeded by the cornet, the percussion section, the second and third trumpets, and also the flutists, and they are all carrying their instruments—each carries his own, the entire orchestra disappears into the bower, and although no one touches his lips to the mouthpieces, the music continues playing. Now *pianissimo*, it lingers in the glade, and the mowers, shamed by this miracle, weep and wipe their wet faces with the sleeves of their red Russian shirts. The mowers cannot work—their hands tremble, and their hearts are like the mournful swamp frogs—but the music continues to play. It lives independently, it is a waltz which only yesterday was one of us: a man disappeared, transposed into sounds, and we will never find out about it. Dear Leonardo, as for the incident with me and the boat, the river, the oars, and the cuckoo, obviously I too disappeared. I turned into a nymphea then, into a white river lily with a long golden-brown stem, or to be more precise put it this way: *I partially* disappeared into a white river lily. That way's better, more precise. I remember well, I was sitting in the boat, the oars at rest. On one of the shores a cuckoo was counting the years of my life. I asked myself several questions and was all ready to answer, but I couldn't and I was amazed. And then something happened to me, there, inside, in my heart and in my head, as if I were turned off. And then I felt that I had disappeared, but at first I decided not to believe it, I didn't want to. And I said to myself: it's not true, this is just an illusion, you are a bit tired, it's very hot today, take the oars and row, row home. And I tried to take the oars, I stretched out my hands toward them, but nothing happened: I saw the grips, but my palms

Nymphea

did not feel them, the wood of the oars flowed through
my fingers, past the phalanges, like sand, like air. No,
on the contrary, I, my former and now no longer exist-
ing palms, let the wood flow through like water. This
was worse than if I had become a ghost, because a ghost
can at least pass through a wall, but I couldn't have,
there would have been nothing to pass through, and
there was nothing left of me. But that's not right either:
something was left. A desire for my former self was left,
and even if I was incapable of remembering who I was
before the disappearance, I felt that then, that is, *before,*
my life had been fuller and more interesting, and I
wanted to become the same unknown, forgotten what's-
his-name again. The waves beat the boat to shore in
a deserted spot. After taking several steps along the
beach I looked back: there was nothing resembling my
tracks on the sand behind. And in spite of this I still did
not want to believe. It could be a lot of things, one, it
could turn out that all this was a dream, two, it's possible that the sand here is extraordinarily firm and I,
weighing a total of only so many kilograms, did not
leave tracks in it because of my lightness, and, three, it
is quite probable that I hadn't even gotten out of the
boat onto shore yet, but was still sitting in it and,
naturally, I could not leave tracks where I had not yet
been. But next, when I looked around and saw what a
beautiful river we have, what wonderful old willows and
flowers grow on this shore and the other, I said to myself: you are a miserable coward, and becoming an
inveterate liar, you were afraid that you had disappeared
and decided to fool yourself, you're inventing absurdi-
ties and so on, it's high time you became honest, like

Pavel, who is also Savl. What happened to you is certainly no dream, that's clear. Further: even if you didn't weigh as much as you do, but a hundred times less, your tracks would still have been left in the sand.   But from this day forth you do not weigh even a gram, for you no longer are, you simply disappeared, and if you want to be convinced of that turn around and look at the boat again: you will see that you are not in the boat either. But no, I replied to my *other* self (although Doctor Zauze tried to prove to me that supposedly no *other* me exists, I am not inclined to trust his totally unfounded assertions), true, I am not in the boat, but then there is a white river lily with golden-brown stem and yellow, faintly aromatic stamens lying in the boat. I picked it an hour ago at the western shores of the island in the backwater where such lilies, and also yellow water-lilies, are so numerous that one doesn't want to touch them, it is better to just sit in the boat and look at them, at each individually or all at once. One can also see there the blue dragonflies called in Latin *simpetrum,* quick and nervous water-striding beetles resembling daddy-longlegs, and in the sedge swim ducks, honest-to-goodness wild ducks. Some mottled species with nacreous shadings. There are gulls there too: they have concealed their nests on the islands, amid the so-called weeping willows, weeping and silvery, and not once did we manage to find a single nest, we cannot even imagine what one of them looks like—the nest of a river gull. But then, we do know how a gull fishes. The bird flies rather high over the water and peers into the depths, where the fish are. The bird sees the fish well, but the fish does not see the bird, the fish sees only gnats and mosquitoes which like to fly right over the water (they drink the sweet sap of the water-lilies), the fish feed on them. From time to time a fish leaps from the water, swallowing one or two mosquitoes, and at that instant the bird, wings folded, falls from on high and catches the fish and bears it in its beak to its nest, the gull's nest. True, the bird occasionally fails to catch the fish, and then the bird again achieves the necessary altitude and continues flying, peering into the water. There it sees the fish and its own reflection. That's another bird, thinks the gull, very similar to me, but different, it lives on the other side of the river and always flies out hunting along with me, it goes fishing too, but that bird's nest is somewhere on the reverse side of the island, right under our nest. It's a good bird, muses the gull. Yes, gulls, dragonflies, water striders and the like—that's what there is on the western shores of the island, in the backwater, where I picked the nymphea which is now lying in the bottom of the boat, withering.

But why did you pluck it, was there some necessity for that, you don't even like to pick flowers—I know— you don't even like to, you only like to stare at them or cautiously touch them with your hand. Of course, I shouldn't have, I didn't want to, believe me, at first I didn't want to, I never wanted to, it seemed to me that if I ever picked it something unpleasant would happen— to me or to you, or to other people, or to our river, for example, it might evaporate. You just uttered a strange word, what did you say, what was that word— *eshakurate?* No, you're imagining things, hearing things, there was no such word, something like that, but not that, I can't remember now. But what was I just talking about in general, could you help me to recapture the thread of my discussion, it's been broken. We were chatting about how one day Trachtenberg unscrewed a handle in the bathroom and hid it somewhere, and when the custodian came he stood in the bathroom for a long time just staring. He was silent for a long time, because none of it made sense. The water was running, making noise, and the bathtub was gradually filling, and then the custodian asked Trachtenberg: where's the faucet handle? And the old woman answered him: I have a record player (that's not true, I'm the only one who has a record player), but no faucet handle. But there's no faucet handle in the bathtub, said the custodian. That's your problem, citizen, I don't answer to you—and she went into her room. And the custodian went up to the door and started knocking, but neither Trachtenberg nor Tinbergen opened to him. I was standing in the entrance hall and thinking, and when the custodian turned to me and asked what to do, I said: knock, and it shall be opened unto you. He started knocking again, and Trachtenberg soon opened to him, and he again expressed his curiosity: where's the handle? I don't know, objected old Tinbergen, ask the young man. And with her bony finger she pointed in my direction. The custodian observed: maybe that kid doesn't have everything upstairs, but it strikes me that he's not so stupid as to unscrew the faucet handle, you're the one who did that, and I'll complain to Building Superintendent Sorokin. Tinbergen burst out laughing in the custodian's face. Ominously. And the custodian went off to lodge his complaint. I just stood there in the entrance hall meditating. Here, on the hat-rack, hung an overcoat and head-gear, here stood two containers used for moving furniture. These things belonged to the neighbors, i.e., Trachtenberg-Tinbergen and her excavator. At least the greasy, eight-pointed cap was his definitely, because the old woman wore only hats. I often stand in the entrance hall examining all of the objects on the hatrack. It seems to me they are benevolent and I feel at home with them, I'm not a bit afraid of them when no one is dressed in them. I also think about the containers, wondering what wood they are made of, how much they cost, and what train, on what branch, brought them to our town.

Dear student so-and-so, I, the author of this book, have a pretty clear picture of that train—a long freight. Its cars, for the most part brown, were covered with scrawls in chalk—letters, ciphers, words, whole sentences. Apparently workers wearing special railway uniforms and caps with tin cockades made their computations, notes, and estimates on some of the cars. Let's suppose the train has been standing on a stub for several days and no one knows when it will start up again or where it will go. And then a commission comes to the stub, examines the seals, bangs hammers on wheels, peeps into the axle-boxes, checking for cracks in the metal and to see if anyone has mixed sand in the oil. The commission squabbles and swears, its monotonous work has long been a bore, and it would take pleasure in going on pension. But how many years is it to pension?—penses the commission. It takes a piece of chalk and writes on anything at hand, usually on one of the boxcars: year of birth—such-and-such, work seniority—such-and-such,

therefore such-and-such a number of years to pension.
Then the next commission comes to work, it is deep in
debt to its colleagues on the first commission, which is
why the second commission doesn't squabble and swear,
but tries to do everything quietly, without even using
hammers. This commission is sad, it too takes chalk
from its pocket (here I should note in parentheses that
the station where this action takes place could never,
even during two world wars, complain about a lack of
chalk. It had been known to have shortages of: sleepers,
handcars, matches, molybdenum ore, semaphores,
wrenches, hoses, crossing barriers, flowers for decorating
the embankments, red banners with the requisite slogans
commemorating events of varying qualities, spare brakes,
siphons and ashpits, steel and slag, bookkeeping records,
warehouse logs, ashes and diamonds, smokestacks,
speed, cartridges and marijuana, levers and alarmclocks,
amusements and firewood, record players and porters,
experienced scriveners, surrounding forests, rhythmical
timetables, drowsy flies, cabbage soup, oatmeal, bread,
and water. But there was always so much chalk at this
station that, as indicated in the telegraph agency's
announcement, it would require such-and-such number
of trains each with such-and-such payload capacity, to
carry away from the station all of the potential chalk.
More accurately, not from the station, but from the
chalk quarries in the area around the station. The station itself was called *Chalk,* and the river—the misty
white river with chalky banks—could have no other
name than the *Chalk.* In short, everything here at the
station and around was made out of this soft white
stone: people worked in chalk quarries and mines, they
received chalky rubles dusted with chalk, they made the

houses and streets out of chalk, they whitewashed with chalk, in school the children were taught to write with chalk, chalk was used for washing hands, cooking pots and teeth were cleaned and scrubbed with chalk, and, finally, when dying, people willed that they be buried in the local cemetery where instead of earth there was chalk and every grave was decorated with a chalk headstone. One would have to think that the settlement of Chalk was singularly clean, all white and neat, and cirrus or cumulus clouds pregnant with chalky rains constantly hung over it, and when the rains fell the settlement got even whiter and cleaner, that is, absolutely white, like a fresh sheet in a good hospital. As for the hospital, it was here too, a good one and big. In it the miners suffered their illnesses and died, sick with a special disease which in conversations among themselves they called "the chalky." Chalk dust settled in the workers' lungs, penetrated their blood, their blood became weak and anemic. The people paled, their pellucid white faces glowed in the murk of the night-shift hours, they glowed against a background of astonishingly clean curtains in the windows of the hospital, they glowed in farewell against the background of pillows on which they would die, and after that the faces glowed only in the photographs of family albums. The snapshot would be pasted on a separate page and someone from the household would carefully draw a box around it with a black pencil. The frame came out solemn, if uneven. However, let us return to the second railroad commission which is getting chalk out of its pocket, and—let us close the parentheses) and writes on the car: so much for Petrov, so much for Ivanov, so much for Sidorov, total—so many chalk rubles. The commission moves along, writing on some of the boxcars and flatcars the word *checked,* but on others—*to be checked,* for it is impossible to check them all at once, and there is after all a third commission: let it check the remaining cars. But besides the commissions there is *noncommission* at the station too, or to put it another way, people who are not members of commissions, they stand outside them, employed at other jobs, or they don't work here at all. Nevertheless, they are among those who cannot resist the desire to take a piece of chalk and write something on the side of a boxcar—wooden and warm from the sun. Here comes a soldier wearing a forage cap, he heads for a boxcar: *two months to demob.* A miner appears, his white hand produces a laconic: *scum.* A D-student from fifth grade, whose life is perhaps harder than all of ours put together: *Maria Stepanna's a bitch.* A woman station laborer in an orange sleeveless jacket, whose duty is to tighten the nuts and clean out the viaducts, throwing the waste onto the rails below, knows how to draw a sea. She draws a wavy line on the car, and truly, a sea is the result, and an old beggar who doesn't know how to sing or play the accordion, and hasn't yet managed to buy a hurdy-gurdy, writes two words: *thank you.* Some drunk and scraggly guy who has accidentally discovered that his girlfriend is being unfaithful, in despair: *Three loved Valya.* Finally the train leaves the stub and rolls along the railways of Russia. It is made up of cars checked by the commissions, of clean words and curse words, fragments of someone's heartaches, memorial inscriptions, business notes, idle graphical exercises, of laughter and curses, howls and tears, blood and chalk, of white on black and brown, of fear of death, of pity for friends and strangers, of wracked nerves, of good impulses and rose-colored glasses, of boorishness, tenderness, dullness and servility. The train rolls along, Sheina Solomonovna Trachtenberg's containers on it, and all Russia comes out onto windswept platforms to look it in the eye and read what has been written—the passing book of their own life, a senseless book, obtuse, boring, created by the hands of incompetent commissions and pitiful, misled people. After a certain number of days the train arrives in our town, at the freight station. The people who work at the railroad post office are worried: they have to inform Sheina Trachtenberg that the containers with her furniture have finally been received. It's raining outside, the sky is full of storm clouds. In the special postal office at the so-called border of the station a one-hundred-watt bulb burns, dispelling the semidarkness and creating comfort. In the post office there are several worried office workers wearing blue uniforms. They worriedly make tea on a hot plate, and worriedly they drink it. It smells of sealing wax, wrapping paper, and twine. The window opens onto the rusty reserve lines, where grass is sprouting up among the sleepers and some kind of small but beautiful flowers are growing. It is quite nice to look at them from the window. The vent in the window is open, therefore certain sounds which are characteristic of a junction station are quite audible: a lineman's horn, the clank of air hoses and buffers, a hissing of pneumatic brakes, the dispatcher's commands, and also various types of whistles. It is nice to hear all this too, especially if you are a professional and can explain the nature of each sound, its meaning and its symbolism. And of course the office workers of the railroad post office are professionals, they have many railway kilometers behind them, in

their time they have all served as heads of postal cars or
worked as conductors of those same cars, a few of them
on international runs even, and as they are wont to say,
they've seen the world and know what's what. And if
one were to show up and ask their supervisor, is it so...

Yes, dear author, that's right: go see him at home, ring
the vibrant bicycle bell at the door—let him hear that
and open. Whom tum tum tum lives here supervisor so-
and-so's here open up we've come to ask and be given an
honest answer. Who is it? Those Who Came. Come tomorrow, today it's too late, my wife and I are sleeping.
Wake up for the time has come to tell the truth. About
whom? about what? About the fellows in your office.
Why at night? At night sounds are easier to hear, the cry
of a baby, the moan of a dying man, the flight of a night-
ingale, the cough of a trolley constrictor: wake up, open
up, and answer. Wait, I'll put on pyjamas. Put them on
they suit you very well very nice check you make them
or buy them? Don't remember, don't know, have to ask
my wife, mama, Those Who Came would like to know
about the pyjamas made or bought and if so where and
how much yes made no bought it was snowing and cold
we were coming back from the movies and I thought
well now my husband isn't going to have warm pyjamas
this winter looked into the department store and you
stayed on the street to buy bananas there was a line for
them and I wasn't in any special hurry looked first at
carpeting and signed up for a meter and a half for a meter seventy-five for three years from now because the factory was closed for repairs and then in the men's section
undergarments I saw those pyjamas right away and some

Chinese shorts with a top sort of shaggy but I just couldn't decide what's better in general I liked the underwear better cheap and a good color one could sleep in them and wear them underneath at work and wear them around home but then we live in a communal apartment with neighbors you know how it is in the hall or in the kitchen you can't go out there but in pyjamas it would be decent and even nice so then I signed up for the pyjamas I return to the street and you're still waiting for the bananas and I say to you give me I say some money I signed up for pyjamas and you say but I don't need them probably some kind of junk no I say not junk at all but a very decent import item with wooden buttons go on look for yourself and in front of you there's some middle-aged woman wearing a plastic raincoat standing in front of you with earrings so plump so gray she turned around and says are you going go don't be afraid I'll be standing here the whole time if anyone says anything I'll say you were behind me and as for the pyjamas you're wrong to argue with your wife I know those pyjamas a very worthwhile buy they'll be last week I bought that kind for the whole family bought father bought brother bought husband and sent some to a brother-in-law in Gomel he's in school studying there so don't think just buy and put an end to it because next time you'll have to look all over town to sign up for the same pyjamas and they'll tell you come in at the end of the month you'll come in at the end of the month and they'll tell you they had them yesterday so don't even stop to think say thanks to your wife and I'll hold the line never fear and then you say well all right let's go in and look we enter the store and I ask how you like them and you shrug and say I don't know the devil only knows not bad only the check is kind of odd

and I think the bottoms are a bit tight you say and
the saleslady hears it a youngish one nice and proposes
what do you mean try them on use the little booth
that's what they're here for not for me I took the pyjamas they were hanging on a wooden hanger we went behind the curtain there three big mirrors when you
started to undress snowflakes or rather not snowflakes
but waterdrops sprinkled right against all the mirrors
and I stuck my head out from behind the curtain and I
shout to the saleslady miss do you have some sort of
cloth and she but what do you need it for and I say have
to wipe the mirror and she but what happened did it get
sprinkled yes a little after all it's snowing outside and
it's so warm here in your store that it all melted then
she got a yellow flannel cloth from under the counter
there she says and asks later well have you tried them on
and I say no still trying it on yet I'll tell you when
everything's ready and then you glance in and give your
advice maybe the pants really are too narrow and tight
I look and you're already wearing the pyjamas and
you're turning around in various directions even squatting once or twice to check the crotch well how are they
I ask and you keep muttering something about the pants
being a bit tight and somehow the check is disturbing
not Russian I should think not I say it's an imported
item and I'll call the saleslady for her advice but just at
that time she has a load of customers she replies in a
minute in a minute but doesn't come and doesn't come
then you say I'll go out to her myself but I don't let you
what's wrong with you there are people around it's embarrassing and you say so what if there are people
haven't they ever seen any pyjamas they all each of
them has ten pairs himself what's so scary about that

you say aren't we people ourselves and you go out of
the booth and ask the girl well how do they fit and she
like they were tailored for you very good even take
them you won't be sorry only one hundred fifty sets
left in that size by tonight there won't be any left
they're going fast then you inquire it seems to me the
pants are a little too tight it just seems like that to you
the girl replies but that style is the most fashionable
now a long jacket and sort of wide but the pants the reverse but if you want you can get them altered let out in
places but now for example in the jacket I would do the
reverse take it in because the jacket really is a trifle wide
in the waist but your wife will do it or take it to a seamstress and she asks me do you have a machine at home
yes only not so good I used to have a Singer foot model
my mother's and when my daughter got married I gave
it to her not sorry of course but still I do regret it a
little but it's essential for my daughter too they have a
little one now occasionally one thing or another has to
be made for him of course let my daughter do it on the
Singer and we'll buy ourselves another one a new completely electric one but it's hard to work on it either it's
a bad one or I'm not used to it the seams it makes are
uneven it'll break the thread but better it than going to
a seamstress the time would be extensive and expensive
so that naturally we'll alter them at home and the girl
says of course you'll alter them at home spend one
evening at it but they'll come out so well that they'll
last more than a year and she asks you and what about
you do you like them you smiled even a little embarrassed I think and normal pyjamas you say what's so
special then the girl says to you and you probably work
on the railroad you and I exchanged glances as if to ask

how did she guess and I ask her the question how did
you find that out I'd be interested to know very simple
she replies your husband has on his head a uniform cap
with a hammer and adjustable wrench on it and my
brother works on trains too he serves the commuter
lines sometimes he comes in the evening and tells all
about his work where what wreck occurred where what
is interesting I even envy him every day something new
but it's always the same thing here nowhere to escape
are you going to take them she says then I ask her to
please wrap up the pyjamas for us and I'll go pay for
them right now and she says first you go pay for them
and then I'll wrap them up right away I went to pay at
the cashier's booth there was a line and you took off the
pyjamas in the dressing booth and I see you're already
taking them to her on a hanger she started to wrap a
ribbon around them even to tie them up not true mama
not true I remember everything it was twine and I
thought like at work we pack packages and retie parcels
we always have whole rolls and skeins of it never ends as
much as you want good twine it was twine there in the
store there at the girl's there where we work ahead of
schedule don't worry stop in drop by check ring the
bicycle bell any time we'll look at the twine we'll read
the Japanese poets Nikolaev Semyon knows them by
heart and reads a lot in general the clever fellow.

A one-hundred-watt bulb burning, the odor of sealing wax,
string and paper. Outside the window—rusty rails, small
flowers, rain, and the sounds of a junction station. Cast
of characters. Supervisor So-and-so, a man who hopes
to be promoted. Semyon Nikolaev, a man with an

intelligent face. Fyodor Muromtsev, a man with an ordinary face. These, and Other Railway Workers are sitting at a common table, drinking tea with rolls. Those Who Came are standing by the door. Boss So-and-so speaks: Nikolaev, Those Who Came have come, they would like to hear some poetry or prose from the Japanese classics. S. Nikolaev, opening a book: quite by chance I happen to have with me Yasunari Kawabata, who writes: "Are there really such cold spells here? You are all heavily bundled up. Yes, sir. We're all wearing winter things already. It's particularly cold at night when the clear weather sets in after a snowfall. It must be below freezing now. Below freezing already? Yes, it's cold. Whatever you touch is cold. There were intense cold spells last year too. Down to twenty-some degrees below freezing. And was there a lot of snow? On the average the snow cover was seven or eight *shaku,* and after intense snowfalls more than one *jo.* It'll probably start to fall soon. Yes, it's just the time for snowfalls, we're waiting. There was snow not long ago, it covered the ground, but then it melted, got down to almost less than a *shaku.* You mean it's melting now? Yes, but you can expect snowfall any time now." F. Muromtsev: now there's a story for you, Semyon Danilovich, isn't it something! S. Nikolaev: it's not a short story, Fyodor, it's an excerpt from a novel. Supervisor So-and-so: Nikolaev, Those Who Came would like some more. S. Nikolaev: if you like, at random then: "The girl was sitting, beating a drum, modestly and sedately. I was watching her back. She seemed very close, in the next room. My heart beat in time with the drum. A drum so enlivens table-talk!— said the forty-year-old woman, also watching the dancer." F. Muromtsev, how about that, eh? S. Nikolaev:

[53]

I'll read some more, here is the verse of the Japanese Zen
poet Dogen. F. Muromtsev: Zen? that's comprehensible,
Semyon Danilovich, but you didn't give his birth and
death dates, please do so if it's not a secret. S. Nikolaev:
forgive me, I'll recall in a moment, yes, they are 1200-
1253. Supervisor So-and-so: only fifty-three years? S.
Nikolaev: but what years they were! F. Muromtsev:
what were they like? S. Nikolaev, rising from his stool:
"Flowers in the spring, a cuckoo in the summer. And in
the autumn—the moon. Cold clean snow in the winter."
(He sits down.) That's all. F. Muromtsev: that's all? S.
Nikolaev: that's all. F. Muromtsev: somehow that's not
much, Semyon Danilovich, eh? A bit too little? Perhaps
there's something else, maybe it got torn off? S. Nikolaev: no, that's all, it's a special form of poem, there is
long poetry, epics for example, and there are shorter
ones, and there are quite short ones, a few lines, or even
one. F. Muromtsev: but why, to what end? S. Nikolaev:
well, how shall I put it—laconism. F. Muromtsev: so
that's it, now I see: if one were to take it comparatively:
rolling stock covers different distances, right? S. Nikolaev: sure, yes it does. F. Muromtsev: and the trains are
different too. There are such long ones that the end
never seems to come as you wait to cross the track, but
there are short ones (he bends down the fingers on his
hand), one, two, three, four, five, yes, five, we'll say,
five cars or flats—that good enough? that's laconism too,
right? S. Nikolaev: basically, yes. F. Muromtsev: so
there, I've got it straight. What did you say: cold clean
snow in the winter? S. Nikolaev: yes, in the winter.
F. Muromtsev: that's very precise, Tsuneo Danilovich, we've always got enough snow in the winter, in
January no less than nine *shaku,* and at the end of the

season it's towards two *jo*. Ts. Nikolaev: maybe not two, one and a half would be more precise. F. Muromatsu: what do you mean one and a half, Tsuneo-san, when it's a solid two everywhere. Ts. Nakamura: how should I put it, it depends on where you look, if on the lee side of a stump, of course, but much less in the open, one and a half. F. Muromatsu: well, what difference does it make, one and a half, Tsuneo-san, why argue? Ts. Nakamura: look, the rain still hasn't stopped. F. Muromatsu: yes, it's raining, not very good weather. Ts. Nakamura: the whole station's wet, nothing but puddles around, and who knows when it'll dry up. F. Muromatsu: it's better not to go outside in slop like that without an umbrella—it'll soak you. Ts. Nakamura: last week at this time the weather was exactly the same, the roof started to leak at my house, it soaked all the *tatami*, and there was no way I could hang them up outside to dry. F. Muromatsu: too bad, Tsuneo-san, this kind of rain is no use to anyone, it's just a bother. True, they say it's very good for the rice, but rain like this brings nothing but unpleasantness to a man, particularly the city man. Ts. Nakamura: my neighbor hasn't been able to get out of bed for a week because of this rain, he's sick, coughing. The doctor said that if it continues to pour much longer he'll have to send my neighbor to the hospital, otherwise he'll never get better. F. Muromatsu: there is nothing worse than rain for a sick person, the air gets humid and the sickness intensifies. Ts. Nakamura: this morning my wife wanted to go to the store barefoot, but I asked her to put on *geta*, after all, you can't buy health at any price, and nothing's easier than getting sick. F. Muromatsu: correct, sir, the rain is cold, one shouldn't think of going out without footwear, on days

like these we should all take care of ourselves. Ts. Nakamura: a little *sake* wouldn't do us any harm would it?
F. Muromatsu: no, but just a tiny bit, one or two cups,
that would enliven the table-talk no less than a drum.
Supervisor So-and-so: Those Who Came are interested in
the fate of certain containers. S. Nikolaev: which ones
exactly? Boss So-and-so: Sheina Trachtenberg's. F.
Muromtsev: Those Who Came, we're worried, have to
write a postcard, they're standing out there in the open,
rain, they'll be soaked through, have to write her, here's
a form, there's the address. Semyon Danilovich, you
write it.

Dear Sheina Solomonovna,—I read, standing in the entrance hall, which at that time seemed almost huge,
because there were no containers yet, —dear Sheina
Solomonovna, we the workers of the railroad post office
herewith inform you that over our entire town, and also
over its surrounding areas, a prolonged pre-autumnal
rain has been observed. It's wet everywhere, the settlement roads are awash, the leaves of the trees are en-
gorged with moisture and yellowed, and the wheels on
the trains, the boxcars and sleepers, have gotten extremely rusty. Days like these are hard on everyone,
especially on us, the men of the railways. And nevertheless we have decided not to get thrown off our good
working rhythm, we are fulfilling our plan, striving to
stick strictly to the usual timetable. And the results are
there for everyone to see: in spite of the depth of some
puddles, which here at the station has reached two or
three *shaku,* in recent time we have dispatched no fewer
letters and parcels than was done in the same period last

year. In conclusion, we hasten to inform you that two containers have arrived at the station in your name, and we request that you make arrangements for their removal from the yard by our office as promptly as possible. Yours truly. Why did you tell me about that, I wouldn't like to think you capable of reading other people's mail, you've disappointed me, tell me the truth, maybe you invented the incident, after all I know how you love to make up different stories, when I'm talking to you I invent a lot too. *There,* in the hospital, Zauze made great fun of us for being such dreamers. Patient so-and-so, he would laugh, honestly speaking, I have never met a person more healthy than you, but your trouble is this: you are an incredible dreamer. And then we answered: in that case you cannot keep us here so long, we demand immediate release from the *here* which is under your supervision. Then he immediately got serious and asked: well, all right, let's suppose I release you tomorrow, what do you intend to do, what will your occupation be, will you go to work somewhere or return to the school? And we replied: to the school? oh no, we'll go to the country, for we have a dacha there, though more accurately, it's not ours as much as our parents', it's unimaginably beautiful there, at one-twenty, awaiting the wind, the sand and the heather, a skiff on the river, spring and summer, reading in the grass, light lunch, skittles, and a deafening multitude of birds. Then comes autumn, the whole countryside vaporous, no, not fog and not smoke, but exquisite sailing gossamer. In the morning there is dew on the pages of the book we left in the garden. Walking to the station for kerosene. But, doctor, we give you our word of honor that we won't drink beer at the green stand by the pond where the dam is. No, doctor, we don't like beer. You know, we've thought about you too, you could probably come for a few days too. We'll set it up with father, and we'll meet you with the special bicycle, the one with the side-car. You know, an old bicycle, and on the side there's a side-car from a small motorcycle. But the side-car probably won't be there: we don't yet know where to get a side-car like that. But we do have the bicycle. It's in the shed along with the kerosene barrel and two empties, sometimes we yell into them. There are boards in there too, and some garden tools and the grand-mother chair, that is, no, forgive us, that's wrong, father always asked us to say it the other way: grandmother's chair. More polite that way, he explained. One day he was sitting in that chair, and we were sitting beside him on the grass reading various books, yes, doctor you're up on things, you know it's hard for us to read the same book for very long, first we read a page from one book and then a page from another. Then one can take a third book and read a page from it too, and only then go back to the first book. It's easier that way, you don't get as tired. So we were sitting on the grass with sundry books, and in one of them there was something which at first we didn't understand at all, because it was quite an ancient book, no one writes in that language any more, and we said: papa, would you please explain something to us, we don't understand what it says here. And then father tore himself away from his paper and asked: well, what have you got there, some more rubbish? And then we read aloud: *And Satan asked God for holy Russia in order to incarnadine it with martyred blood. A good idea, Devil, it pleases us for our world to suffer for Christ's sake.* For some reason we remembered these words, generally we have a bad memory, you know, but if we like something we remember it right away. But father didn't like it. He jumped out of his chair, snatched the book away from us and yelled: where did this come from, where did it come from, the devil take you, what fool gibberish! And we replied: we were taking a ride on the other side of the river yesterday, our teacher lives there, and he inquired what we were doing and what we were reading. We said that you had given us several volumes of a certain contemporary classic. Our teacher laughed and ran to the river. Then he came back, water dripping from his big freckled ears. Pavel Petrovich told us: dear colleague, how glorious it is that the name you uttered not more than a minute ago dissolved, dissipated in the air like road dust, and that those syllables will go unheard by the one whom we call The Sender, how good it is, dear colleague, isn't that right, otherwise what would happen to that remarkable old fellow, in his fury he would undoubtedly fall off his bicycle and then there wouldn't be a stone left of our esteemed settlements when he got through, and by the way, that wouldn't be such a bad thing anyway, because it's high time. As for my moist ears, which you are studying so attentively, they are wet because I washed them in the waters of the reservoir you see before you, in order to cleanse them of the nastiness of the aforementioned name and to meet my forthcoming state of nonbeing with purity of soul, body, thought, language, and ears. My young friend, pupil and comrade, —our teacher said to us,—whether it's the bitter treasury of folk wisdom or sweet adages and dicta, whether it's the dust of the bedamned or the dismay of the beloved, the sacks of bums or Judas's sums, whether it's move-

ment *from* or standing *by,* the lies of the defrauded or
the truths of the defamed, whether war or peace,
whether stages or studios, taints or torments, whether
darkness or light, hatred or pity, in life and beyond it—
whether it's any of these, or anything else, you have to
make good sense of it. There is something to be said
for doing so, not much perhaps, but something. Here
and there, or everywhere, something happens, we
cannot say with certainty what exactly, since so far we
do not know the essence of the phenomenon, or its
name, but, dear pupil and comrade so-and-so, when we
have elucidated and discussed this together, when we
have elucidated the cause and defined the effect, our
time will have come, the time to say our piece—and we
will say it. And if it should happen that you are the first
to make sense of this, inform me immediately, the address you know: standing by the river at the end of day
when those bitten by snakes are dying, ring the bicycle
bell, or better—ring the peasant scythe, saying: the scythe
is lithe in the dew of morn, make hay while the sun shines,
or: along came a spider and sat down beside her, and
where are you now, and so on, until the suntanned
teacher Pavel hears, and doing a dance, comes out of his
house, unties his boat, jumps into it, takes the home-
made oars in his hands, rows across Lethe, gets out on
your side, embraces you, kisses you, says kind and mysterious words, receives, but no, does not read the sent
letter, for he, your teacher, is not among the living,
that's the trouble, that's the rub, not among the living,
but you—you go on living, until you die, rock beer in
barrels and children in carriages, breathe the air of the
pine groves, run through meadows and gather bouquets
—O, flowers! how wondrously beautiful you are, how

wondrously beautiful. Taking leave of this world, I yearned to see a bouquet of dandelions, but my wish was not granted. What did they bring to my house in my final hour, what did they bring? They brought silk and crepe, dressed me in an execrable double-breasted jacket, took away my summer hat, punched all over with a checker's punch, put on some sort of pants, junky—don't argue—junky pants for fifty sweaty rubles, I never wore that kind, they're repulsive, they stick, my body can't breathe or sleep, and the tie—!—they tied a polka-dotted tie around my neck, take it off immediately, open me and at least take off the tie, I'm no bureaucratic rat, I never—understand—I'm not your kind, I'm not your kind—never wore any tie. Preposterous, preposterous wretches, left to live, sick with chlorosis and deader than I, you pooled your funds for the funeral, I know that, and bought all this scaramouche trumpery, but how dare you dress me in the vest and metal-buckled leather shoes of a kind I never wore in my life, oh, you didn't know, you imagined I make five hundred sweaty rubles a month and buy the same useless rags that you do. No, you scalawags, you failed to defame me alive and you'll have no more success when I'm dead. No, I'm not one of yours, and I never made over eighty, and not your kind of rubles, different rubles, pure wind-driver's rubles, unbesmirched by the lies of your disgusting theories and dogmas, beat me as I lie dead if you must, but take this off, give me back my hat, punched all over with a constrictor's punch, give back everything you've confiscated, a dead man is supposed to get his things, give me my cowboy shirt, my sandals in the style of the Roman Empire period when the aqueduct was built, I will put them under my balding head because—to spite you—I am going to go barefoot even in the valleys of nonbeing and my pants, my patched up pants—you have no right, I'm not wearing your crap, turn your trash over to the second-hand shop, give the money back to those who contributed, I don't want a kopek from you, no, I don't want any, and don't tie that tie on me, or I'll spit my blistering poison spit into your worm-eaten mugs, leave geography teacher Pavel Petrovich in peace! Yes, I am shouting and I will go on shouting without sleep, forever—I will shout of the sublime immortality of the sublime teacher Savl, my desire is for you to find me violently repulsive, I will burst into your dreams and your reality like a hooligan bursting into class during a lesson, burst in with bloodied tongue, but implacable. I will shout to you of my unassailable and beautiful poverty, so do not try to cajole me with gifts, I don't need your sweaty rags and your pussy rubles, and stop that music, or I'll drive you mad with my shout, the shout of the most honorable of the dead. Hear my order, my cry: give me dandelions and bring me my clothes! And to hell with your snotty funeral music, ram pikes up the rears of that dipso orchestra.   Malodorous rubbish, mausoleum tumblebugs! Clog the gullets of the requiem lovers, away from my body, or I'll rise up and drive you all away with my damned school pointer, I—Pavel Petrovich, teacher of geography, most prominent turner of the cardboard globe, I am leaving you in order to come, let me go!

Thus spake teacher Pavel, standing on Lethe's bank. From his cleansed ears dripped river water, and the river itself streamed slowly past him and past us along with all its fishes and flat-bottomed boats, with its ancient sailing ships, its reflected clouds, its unseen and future drowners, with the roe of frogs, and duckweed, and tireless water striders, the torn fragments of nets, someone's lost grains of sand and gold bracelets, with empty tin cans and ponderous Monomakh caps, with fuel oil slicks and the almost invisible faces of ferrymen, with bones of contention and pears of despondency, and with little pieces of rubber tubing for caps, without which you can't ride a bicycle, for you can't pump up the tire if you don't put this kind of rubber cap over the valve, and then all is lost, because if you can't use your bicycle it's as if it didn't exist, it virtually disappears, and without a bicycle there's nothing to do at the dacha: you won't be able to go for kerosene, roll down to the pond and back, be at the station to meet Doctor Zauze, who has arrived on the seven-o'clock train: he stands on the platform, turning around, looking in all directions, and you're not there, even though you agreed you would not fail to meet him, and there he stands waiting, and you don't come because you can't find a good valve cover, but the doctor doesn't know about this, although it is beginning to dawn dimly on him: my patient, he conjectures, probably has something wrong with his velocipede, most likely it's the valve cap, the usual thing, those valve caps are really a pain, too bad I didn't think to buy two or three in town, you would have had enough for the whole summer—muses the doctor. Excuse me, please, but what did Pavel Petrovich say to us when giving us the book which so displeased our father? Nothing, the teacher said nothing. Well in my opinion he said: a book. Or even:

here's a book. Or even more: here's a book for you, said the teacher. And what did father say about the book when we reported our conversation with Pavel to him? Father didn't believe a word we said. Why, you mean we weren't telling the truth? No, it was the truth, but you know our father, he doesn't believe anyone, and when I said something about that to him once he replied that the whole world is made up of scoundrels and nothing but scoundrels, and if he were to believe what people said, he'd never have become the town's chief prosecutor, and at best he'd be working as a building superintendent like Sorokin, or a dacha glazier. And then I asked father about the newspapers. What about the newspapers?—he responded. And I said: you're always reading newspapers. Yes, I do, he replied, I read newspapers, and so what. Isn't it true that there's nothing written there?—I asked him. Why do you say that, said father, everything is written there, whatever is needed— is written. And if, I asked, something is written there, then why read it: it's scoundrels that write it. And then father said: what scoundrels? And I replied: those who write. Father asked: write what? And I replied: the newspapers. Father was silent and looked at me, and I looked at him, and I felt a little sorry for him, because I saw how disconcerted he was and how two big flies, like two black tears, crawled across his wide white face, and he couldn't even swat them because he was so disconcerted. Then he said to me softly: get out, out of my sight, you son of a bitch, get out of here. This took place at the dacha. I rolled my bicycle out of the shed, tied my butterfly net to the frame and rode out along the path in our garden. In our garden the first apples were ripening, and it seemed to me I could see a worm curled up in each of them, tirelessly chewing our, that is, father's, fruit. And I thought: autumn will come and there will be nothing left in the garden to pick, nothing but rot. I rode on, and still hadn't reached the end of the garden, but there was no end to it, and when the end appeared, I saw the fence and the gate before me, and mama was standing at the gate. Good day, Mama,—I yelled, you're home from work so early today! My goodness, what work?—she countered, I haven't been working since you started school, almost fourteen years now. Oh, really,—said I, I guess I must have simply forgotten, I've been rushing around the garden too long, all these years probably, and a lot has slipped my mind. You know, there are worms in the baffles, or rather, in the apples, in our garden, we have to think of something, some remedy, otherwise there'll be nothing but garbage left and there'll be nothing to eat, nor even to cook for jam. Mother glanced at my butterfly net and asked: what's wrong, have you quarrelled with father again? I didn't want to upset her, so I answered this way: a little, Mama, we were chatting about Fyodorov, Ivan, the first Russian printer, I expressed the conviction that he—a, bee, see, dee, ee, ef, gee, zee, and so on, but father didn't believe me and advised me to go butterfly hunting, and so I'm going. Good-bye, mama,—I shouted, I'm going to be alone, going for some meadow chanterelles, long live summer, spring and the flowers, great thoughts, the mightiness of passion, and also love, kindness, and beauty! Dingdong, bing-bong, tick-tock, toock-toock, scrip-scrape. Not so long ago I enumerated these sounds, they are my favorite sounds, the sounds of a blithe bicycle flying along a dacha path and the whole settlement already swathed in the gossamer of tiny spiders, even if the real fall was far away. But it made no difference to the spiders, good-bye, mama, don't be sad, we'll meet again. She yelled: come back!—and I looked around: mother was standing at the gate anxiously, and I thought: nothing good will come of it if I go back: mother will undoubtedly begin to weep, make me abandon the bicycle seat, take me by the hand, and we will return to the house through the garden, and mother will start to reconcile father and me, which will take several more years, and life—which in our and neighboring settlements is customarily measured in increments of so-called *time*, days of summer and years of winter—my life will stop and it will stand still like a broken bicycle in a shed which is full of discolored old newspapers, and wooden blocks and rusted pliers lie around. No, you didn't want to be reconciled with our father. That's why when mother shouted after you *come back!*—you didn't go back, although you were somewhat sorry for her, our patient mother. Looking around you saw her big eyes the color of dried grass, tears were slowly coming to life in them and they reflected some tall trees with astonishing white bark, the path along which you were riding, and you yourself with your long skinny arms and thin neck, you, too—in your unstopping motion *away*. To a bystander beaten down by the chimeras of the eminent mathematician N. Rybkin, compiler of many textbooks and anthologies of problems and exercises, a man without imagination, without fancy, you would have seemed at this moment boring bicycle rider blank charting a path from point A to point B, in order to surmount an assigned number of kilometers and then to disappear forever in a cloud of parching roadway dust. But I, initiated into your elevated designs and aspirations, I know that on the aforementioned day, a day marked by uncommonly sunny weather, you were a different kind of bicycle rider, one intransient in time and space. Irreconcilability with surrounding reality, staunchness in the battle against hypocrisy and sanctimoniousness, unbending will, firmness in achieving set goals, exceptional principles and honesty in relation to your comrades—these and many other remarkable qualities set you above the usual type of bicycle rider. You were not only and not so much a bicycle rider as a bicycle-rider-*man,* a velocipede-citizen. Really, I'm somehow embarrassed to have you praising me like this. I'm sure that I don't deserve these eloquent words. It even strikes me that I was wrong that day, I probably should have gone back at my mother's call and calmed her, but I rode on and on with my butterfly net, and it made no difference to me where or how I went, it simply felt good to ride, and as I usually do when no one hinders my thinking, I simply thought about everything I saw.

I recall that I turned my attention to someone's dacha and thought: there's a dacha, two stories high, someone lives there, some family. Part of the family lives there all week, and part only on weekends. Then I saw a small two-wheeled cart, it was standing at the edge of a grove, alongside a hay rick, and I said to myself: there's a cart, various items can be carried in it: earth, gravel, suitcases, pencils from the pencil factory named in honor of Sacco and Vanzetti, raw chalk, the fruits of mango trees, apfelstok, ivory scrimshaw, shingles, collected works, rabbit cages, ballot-boxes and trash cans, fluffy things and the contrary—shot, stolen washbasins, tables of ranks and artifacts from the time of the Paris Commune. And in a moment someone will return and start hauling hay in the cart, it's a very handy cart. I saw a little girl, she was leading a dog on a leash—a simple, ordinary dog—they were headed toward the station. I knew that in a moment the girl would come to the pond, she would swim and wash her ordinary dog, and then a number of years would pass, the girl would become grown-up and start to live a grown-up life: get married, read serious books, hurry and be late to work, buy furniture, talk on the telephone for hours, wash stockings, cook food for herself and others, go visiting and get drunk on wines, envy neighbors and birds, follow the weather reports, wipe away dust, count kopeks, expect a child, go to the dentist, have shoes repaired, please men, look out the window at passing automobiles, go to concerts and museums, laugh when something isn't funny, blush when embarrassed, weep when she feels like weeping, cry out from pain, moan at the touch of her beloved, gradually turn gray, dye lashes and hair, wash hands before supper and feet before bed, pay fines, give receipts for translations received, leaf through magazines, meet old acquaintances on the street, speak at meetings, bury relatives, bang dishes in the kitchen, try smoking, retell the plots of movies, be impertinent to superiors, complain of migraine again, take a train out to the country to collect mushrooms, betray her husband, run from store to store, watch honor guards, love Chopin, pass on idiotic gossip, be afraid of gaining weight, dream of a trip abroad, contemplate suicide, curse out-of-order elevators, save up for a rainy day, sing ballads, expect a child, save old photographs, get promotions at work, scream from terror, shake her head critically, grouse about the incessant rain, regret what has been lost, listen to the latest news on the radio, catch taxis, go to the south, raise children, stand in lines for hours, grow irremediably old, dress in fashion, curse the government, live through inertia, drink medicine, curse her husband, be on a diet, go away and come back, put lipstick on, desire nothing more, visit parents, consider it all over and velveteen (worstedcambricsilkchintzmorocco) very practical, be on the sick-list, lie to friends and relatives, forget about everything on earth, borrow money, live the way everyone lives, and remember the dacha, the pond, and the simple, ordinary dog. I saw a pine singed by lightning: yellow needles. I imagined that stormy July night. At first it was quiet and muggy in the settlement, and everyone was sleeping with open windows. Then a storm cloud appeared secretly, it shrouded the stars and brought with it the wind. The wind gusted—across the entire settlement shutters and doors banged shut, and there was a tinkling of broken glass. Then, in total darkness, the rain began to roar: it soaked the roofs and the gardens, the chaises and mattresses and hammocks, sheets, children's toys, primers—and everything else which had been left out in the yards. People woke up in the dachas. Turned on, and immediately turned off, the lights, walked from room to room, looking out the windows and talking to one another: well look at that storm, well look at it pour. Bolts of lightning flashed, apples ripened and fell to the grass. One bolt of lightning struck right here, no one knew where exactly, but they agreed that it was someplace right in the settlement, and those who didn't have lightning rods on their roofs swore to themselves that tomorrow they would get them. And the lightning struck the pine which lived at the edge of the forest, without setting it on fire, just singeing it, and at that instant the entire forest was lit up, along with the dachas, the station, and the railroad branch. The lightning blinded the moving trains, silvered the rails, whitened the sleepers. And then—oh, I know—then you saw the house in which *that* woman lived, and you left the bicycle by the fence and knocked at the gates: toock-toock, my dear, toock-toock, I've come, your timid, your tender one, open and receive me, open and receive me, I don't ask anything of you, I'll just look at you and go away, don't drive me away, just don't drive me away, my dear, I think about you, I weep and I pray for you.

No, no, I won't tell you anything, you have no right to question me about my personal affairs, you shouldn't have anything to do with that woman, don't persist, you fool, you sick person, I want nothing to do with you, I'll call Doctor Zauze, he can take you *there* again, because I'm sick of you and disgusted with you, who are you, why do you pester me with your questions, stop it, better stop it or I'll do something to you, something bad. Don't pretend that you don't know who I am, if you call me insane then you are just as insane because I am you yourself, but you won't be able to see that woman for two or three months, and when we are released, I'll go to that woman and tell her the whole truth about you, I'll tell her that you're not as old as you claim to be, but only such-and-such an age, and that you're a student in the school for fools not of your own volition but because you weren't accepted at the normal school, you're sick, like me, terribly sick, you're practically an idiot, you can't memorize a single poem, so let that woman throw you over, leave you to stand alone on the dark commuter platform, yes, on a snowy night, when all the lights are broken and all the trains have gone and I'll tell her: the guy who wants you to like him is not worthy of you, and you cannot be with him, because he can never be with you as with a woman, he is deceiving you, he is a crazy snotnose, a bad student in the special school, incapable of learning anything by heart, and you, a serious thirty-year-old woman, you should forget him, abandon him on the snowswept plat-form at night and give preference to me, a real man, an adult male, honest and healthy, for I would like this very much and I have no difficulty memorizing any poem or solving any problem in life. You're lying, that's base, you won't tell her that because there's no distinc-tion between you and me, you are exactly the same, the same kind of stupid and incompetent person and you're in the same class with me, you've simply decided to ex-cuse yourself from me, you love that woman, but I'm in your way, but nothing will come of it for you, I'll go to her myself and tell her the whole truth—about you and about me, I'll confess that I love her and would like to be with her always, a whole lifetime, even though never once have I tried to be with a single woman, but, pro-bably, yes, of course, for her, for this woman, that's not important, for she is so beautiful, so intelligent—no, it doesn't mean anything! and if I don't dare to be with her as with a woman, she will forgive me, after all that's not necessary, not essential, and this is what I'll say about you: soon a person who somewhat resembles me will come to you, he will knock on the door: toock-toock, he will ask you to abandon me alone on the snowswept platform, because I am sick, but please, please, I will say, don't believe him, don't believe any of it, he is counting on being with you himself, but he has no right to do that, because he is much worse than me, you'll realize that right away, as soon as he shows up and starts talking, so don't believe him, don't believe, because he *is not* in this world, he doesn't exist, he has no existence, is not, no him, no, dear, only I, I alone came to you quiet and radiant, kind and pure, that's what I'll say to her, and you, you, who are not, remember: nothing will come of it for you: you love that woman, but you don't know her, don't know where she lives, don't know her name, how will you get to her, you brainless fool, you nullity, you wretched student of the special school! Yes, I do love the woman, I certainly love her, but you are deluded, you are certain that I don't know her, or where she lives, but I do know! Do you understand me? I know everything about her, even her name. You cannot, you should not know that name, only I know her name—I alone in the whole world. You've erred: Veta, her name is Veta, I love the woman whose name is Veta Acatova.

When our dachas are veiled in dusk and the heavenly dipper, tipped over the earth, spills out its dew on enchanting Lethe's banks, I emerge from my father's house and walk quietly through the garden—quietly so as not to awaken you, the strange person who lives beside me. I slink along my old tracks, through the grass and the sand, trying not to step on the glowing fireflies or the sleeping *simpetrum* dragonflies. I go down to the river, and my reflection smiles at me when I untie my father's boat from the gnarled white willow. I smear the oarlocks with thick dark water dipped from the river—and my path is quieter than the flash of stars vanishing into the past, my path lies around the second bend, to the Land of the Lonely Nightjar, bird of the good summer. My path is neither too short nor too long, I will compare it to the path of a tarnished sewing needle stitching a wind-severed cloud. Now I float on, rocked by the waves of phantom ships, now I pass the first bend and the second, and shipping the oars I stare at the shore: it floats to meet me, rushes rustling and a good duck voice quacking. Good evening, Shore of the Lonely Nightjar, it's I, vacationing student so-and-so of the special school, allow me to leave my father's boat by your remarkable cane rushes, allow me to pass along your paths, I would like to visit the woman called Veta. I ascend the high hilly shore and stride in the direction of a high and solid fence behind which one can divine a house with whimsical wooden turrets at the corners, but one can only divine it is there; in fact, on such a dark night among the tight interlacings of acacias and other tall bushes and trees one cannot distinguish either the house itself or the towers. Only on the second story, in the attic, is there a light, clearly and greenly shining to me as I walk, the lamp of Veta Arcadievna, my mysterious woman Veta. I know a place where one can easily climb through the fence, I climb through it and hear her simple ordinary dog running across the high grass of the yard toward me. I get a piece of cut sugar out of my pocket and give it to the shaggy, yellow dog, she wags her tail and laughs, she knows how I love my Veta, and would never bite me. And now I approach the house itself. It is a very large dacha, there are many rooms in it, it was built by Veta's father, a naturalist, an old scientist whose name is world-renowned, who in his youth attempted to prove that the so-called *galls*—swellings on various parts of plants—were nothing but the dwelling places of harmful insect larvae, and that for the most part they, the *galls,* were caused by the bites of various wasps, mosquitoes and elephant beetles which deposit their eggs in these plants. But he, Academician Acatov, was believed by hardly anyone, and one day some men in snowy overcoats came to his house and took the Academician away somewhere for a long time, and somewhere there, where precisely is not known, they beat him in the face and stomach so that Acatov would never again dare to assert all this nonsense. And when they released him it turned out that many years had passed, and he had aged and started seeing and hearing poorly, while the swellings on various parts of plants remained, and all these years, as the men in the snowy overcoats became convinced, the harmful larvae really were living in those swellings, which is why they, the swellings, that is, no, the men, or maybe both the swellings and the men together, decided to release the Academician, and also give him an incentive award so that he could build himself a dacha and quietly, without intrusions, investigate the galls. Acatov did just this: built a dacha, planted flowers on his land, got a dog, kept bees, and studied galls. And right now, the night of my arrival at the Land of the Lonely Nightjar, the

Academician is lost in one of the bedrooms of the mansion, sleeping, unaware that I have come and am standing under the window of your daughter Veta and whispering to her: Veta Veta Veta it is I special school student so-and-so respond I love thee.

CHAPTER TWO

NOW

stories written on the veranda

THE LAST DAY. He was leaving for the army. He realized that the three years would not pass quickly for
him: they would be like three northern winters. And it
didn't matter where they sent him to serve, even to the
south,—no matter what, each of the three years would
become an incredibly long snowy winter. He was thinking this now, as he was going to see her. She didn't love
him. She was too good to love him. He knew this, but
his eighteenth birthday was not long past, and he could
not help thinking of her every minute. He noticed that
he was thinking about her constantly, and rejoiced that
he wanted nothing from her, which meant he really
loved her. This state of affairs had lasted for two years;
he was surprised that he didn't want to think about anything else, and that it didn't bore him. But in general, he
reasoned, he should be done with it. Today he was being
sent off to the army, and tomorrow he would go somewhere far away, for three winters, and there he would
forget everything. He wouldn't write her a single letter:
she wouldn't answer anyway. Now he will go to her and
tell her everything. He had been terribly stupid. In the
evenings he had wandered under her windows till very
late, and when the windows went dark, for some reason
he would keep standing there and standing there, staring
at the dark glass. Then he would go home and smoke in
the kitchen until dawn, flicking the ashes onto the worn
floor. From the window he could see the small night
yard with the summerhouse in it. There was always a
lantern on in the summerhouse, and a board with the

sign "Summer Reading Room" hung under it. At dawn the pigeons went winging. Striding along on the chilly mornings of that call-up autumn, he sensed an odd weightlessness in his body, and in his mind this commingled with the inexplicability of everything that he knew and felt. At times such as these he asked himself many different questions, but usually found answers to none—he would go to the house where she lived. She would emerge from the porch at half past seven and always pass through the yard hurrying, and he would watch her from a plywood summerhouse, which also had a hanging lantern and the same kind of sign—"Summer Reading Room." A stupid sign, he thought, stupid, in the summer no one reads in this summerhouse. Thinking this, he followed the girl at a distance at which she couldn't hear or sense him behind her. Now he was remembering all this, and he realized that today was the last day that he could see the girl, the yard where she lived, and the Summer Reading Room in this yard. He goes up to the second floor and knocks at her door.

THREE SUMMERS IN A ROW. Her father and I—we worked in the same theater. Her father was an actor, and I worked as a stagehand. Once after a performance he took me home with him, treated me to some foreign wine and introduced me to her. The two of them lived on the second floor of a yellow two-story barracks. From the window of their room you could see another identical barracks and a small cemetery with a church in the middle of it. I've forgotten the name of the actor's daughter. But even if I remembered her name now, I wouldn't tell: what business is it of yours. So then, she lived in the yellow barracks at the edge of town and was the daughter of an actor. It's quite possible that you have nothing to do with her. But then you don't have to listen. No one's making anyone do anything. And seriously, as far as that goes you don't have to do anything at all—and I won't say a word to you. Only don't try to find out her name, or I won't tell any of this story at all. We met for three winters and three summers in a row. She would often come and sit through whole performances in the half-empty theater. I watched her, standing behind the holey curtain—my girl always sat in the third row. Her father played bit parts and didn't appear more than three times during the whole show. I knew that she dreamed of her father getting a bigger part at least once. But I guessed that he would not get a good part. Because if an actor hasn't gotten a decent part in twenty years, he won't ever get one. But I didn't tell her that. I didn't tell her that when we were strolling through the city's late evening and very wintery streets after performances, running after trolleys which were screeching around corners, in order to get warm; nor on rainy days when we went to the planetarium and kissed in the empty dark hall beneath the artificial starry sky. I didn't tell her that the first summer, nor the second, nor the third, when her father went away on tour, and on rushed nights we took walks in the small cemetery around the church where lilac, elders and willows grew. I didn't tell her that. Nor did I tell her that she wasn't pretty, and that probably there would be a time when I would not take walks with her. Nor did I tell her about the other girls whom I used to meet or whom I met at this same time on other days. I told her only that I loved her—and I did. But perhaps you think one can love only pretty girls, or you think that when you love one you can't go out with others? Well, I already told you—you don't have to do anything at all in your life, including not walking with a single girl in the world— and I won't say a word to you. But that's not the point. I'm talking about her, not you. She was the one I said I loved. And if I happen to meet her now, she and I will go to the planetarium or to the cemetery which is overgrown with elder, and there, as many years ago, I will tell her about that again. Don't you believe me?

AS ALWAYS ON SUNDAY. And the prosecutor could not stand relatives. I was putting in some window glass for him, and here came a tribe of relations to his dacha, and he walked around the yard all sort of white, with a newspaper under his arm. He was white like the places in the newspaper where nothing is written. And every-one in the dacha settlement and in the village beyond the meadow knew that he couldn't stand relatives or disorder, because wherever there's disorder there's drinking. He always puts it that way. I heard him my-self. I was putting in the glass and that's what he said to his wife then. And his wife is an interesting one too. How many times I put in glass for her, and repaired the stove and fixed up the shed, and never once did she give me refreshments. Money she gives, but when it comes to booze always zero. I'll do any job. I clean out people's outhouses, but never had to for the prosecutor. His wife wouldn't let me. No reason for you to get filthy, she says, I'll do it myself. And it was true. Once in the spring I'm putting in the glass, and she takes the special shovel from the shed and starts carrying shit to around the trees. Later she stopped doing this and asked me to put a lock on the outhouse so it would be locked for the winter, so that neighbors wouldn't carry any of it away free. Otherwise they'll carry it off, she says, and why for free: it's hard to get fertilizer now, she says. Of course, I put in a lock, and later their neighbor, the prosecutor's crony, asked me for the key to the prosecutor's lock. Well, he gave me some refreshments, everything the way it's supposed to be done. So I got him the key, of course. Only later in the manager's office I hear a conversation to the effect that the prosecutor's outhouse had been cleaned out while the prosecutor was away in the city. And what was it to me—I was just putting glass in the manager's office, that's all. There's enough work in this settlement to last me a whole life-time. In the winter all sorts of trash live in the dachas—they knock out glass, wreck the stoves, and all the better for me. As soon as the snow melted away my work started up. And then the prosecutor called me to fix the glass. Our country folks had busted out all his windows over the winter. Even in the attic. And they'd broken in the roof over the veranda besides. That's my job too. When there's time I'll fix the roof. But this particular day I'd been putting in glass since morning. The prosecutor's reading his newspaper while lying in the hammock, drowsing off and waking back up from time to time. At the same time, his wife is digging a huge pit in the middle of the yard. Why, I ask. I'll make channels, she says, from all over the yard to this pit, so that all of the rains will be mine. O.K., I think, dig away, and I'll go on putting in the glass. And the prosecutor, I say, is drowsing off or waking up or getting out of his hammock to go over to the fence and chat with his neighbor and crony. What's going on, Comrade Prosecutor, says the prosecutor's crony, are your windows down to zero? Sure are, the prosecutor replies, in the winter the winds here are probably strong—and the wind knocked them out. By the way, the prosecutor's crony says, I hear someone cleaned out your outhouse recently. Yes, says the prosecutor, they cleaned it out—damned vandalism. Too bad, the prosecutor's crony says, unpleasant. And he himself was the one, the son of a gun, he was the one who cleaned it out. That crony of the prosecutor, he was a funny guy. Comes to the dacha all dressed normal, but soon as he comes right away puts on some sort of nightcap, tricks himself out in all kinds of rags, galoshes on his feet, and a rope for a belt, and the galoshes tied with rope. O.K., I think, tie away, and I'll go ahead and put in the glass. But this evening, you shit-stealer, I'm going to get three rubles off you. And if you don't cough it up, I'll have to report it all to your comrade, the prosecutor. The prosecutor, he can't stand disorder you know. Or relatives. And they happened to show up just in time for supper. The prosecutor—he's gone all white, I say, even stopped reading his newspaper. Walks around his yard stomping on dandelions. He looks like a dandelion himself—round and white like empty newspaper, but he's got plenty of relatives—about nine had arrived for supper. All of them laughing it up, got games going on the grass right away, sent off the prosecutor's son to the store right away. Well, this time we got in with them too. Fine people they were. One was a conductor in the city, one a chauffeur, and two were elevator operators. Also one coach, and also an excavator operator. And he had his daughter with him. Everything worked out well between her and me. And the weather just happened to be dry—as always on Sunday.

THE TUTOR. The physics teacher lived on a sidestreet. When I was a young girl, I went to his place for lessons

twice a week. We studied in a small room in a semibase-
ment where the teacher lived with several relatives, but
I never saw them and don't know anything about them.
Now I'll talk about the teacher himself, and also about
how he and I studied during that stiflingly hot summer,
and what kind of odor there was in the sidestreet. The
sidestreet had a constant and strong odor of fish, because somewhere near was a store called "Fish." The
crosswinds blew the odor through the sidestreet, and the
odor came through the open window to us in the room
where we were looking at obscene postcards. The tutor
had a big collection of these postcards—six or seven albums. He made a special point of frequenting the various train stations in the city and buying whole sets of
such photographs from some people. The teacher was
heavy, but handsome, and he was not too old. When it
was hot he perspired and turned on the table fan, but it
didn't especially help, he perspired anyway. I always
laughed about it. When we got tired of looking at postcards, he would tell me jokes; it was a peaceful, light-
hearted time for the two of us in the room with the fan.
He would also tell me about his women. He would say
that at various times he had had many different women:
big ones, small ones, various ages, but he still had not
decided which, after all, were best—big ones or small
ones. Because, he would say, everything depends on
one's mood. He would tell how he was a machine-gun-
ner in the war, and then, at seventeen, he became a man.
The summer when he was my tutor I reached my seven-
teenth year too. I didn't go on to school, and because of
this I really got it from my parents. I flunked physics
and went into a hospital to become a nurse. The next
year I applied for an institute where you didn't have to
pass physics—and I got in. True, later on they expelled

me, during my second year, because they caught me in the dormitory with a guy. He and I weren't doing anything, we were just sitting and smoking, and he was kissing me, and the door to the room was closed. But when they started knocking we didn't open for a long time, and when we did open up no one believed us. Now I work as a telegraph girl at the station. But that's not important. I haven't seen my tutor for almost ten years. How many times I've run past or ridden the trolley past his street and not once dropped in. I don't know why it happens in life that you just can't do something uncomplicated but important. I've been passing quite close to that building for several years, always thinking about my physics teacher, remembering his funny postcards, the fan, the gnarled wooden cane which he would use to look important, even to go out to the kitchen to check the teakettle. Finally, not long ago, when I was feeling sad, I did drop in. I rang twice, like before. He came out, I said hello, he also said hello, but for some reason he didn't recognize me and didn't even invite me into his room. I asked him to try to remember me, reminded him how we had looked at postcards, told him about the fan, about that summer—he didn't remember anything. He said that at one time he really did have many students, boys and girls, but now he hardly remembered anyone. The years pass, he said, they pass. He had gotten a little old, my physics teacher.

A SICK GIRL. One can spend the nights on the veranda during July—it's not cold. And the big sad moths hardly bother me: they can easily be driven off with cigarette smoke. In this story, which I am writing on a July night on the veranda, the subject will be a sick girl. She is very sick. She lives in the next dacha along with a man whom she considers to be her grandfather. Grandfather drinks heavily, he's a glazier, he puts in glass, he is no more than fifty, and I don't believe he's her grandfather. Once when I was spending the night on the veranda as usual, the sick girl knocked for me. She came through the gate in the fence which separates our small lots. Came through the garden and knocked. I turned on the light and opened the door. Her face and hands were covered with blood—the glazier had beaten her, and she had come to me through the garden for help. I washed her, put iodine on her cuts and gave her some tea. She sat with me on the veranda until morning, and it seemed to me that we had managed to talk about many things. But in fact we were silent almost all night, because she can hardly talk, and her hearing is very poor due to her illness. In the morning, as always, it got light, and I walked the girl home along the garden path. In the country, and in Moscow too, I prefer to live alone, and the paths around my house are barely visible. That morning the grass in the garden was white with dew, and I regretted not putting on my galoshes. We stood by the gate for a moment. She tried to say something to me, but couldn't, and in her misery and sickness she began to weep. The girl turned the latch, which like the whole fence was wet with autumn mist, and ran off to her own house. And the gate was left open. Ever since then we've been good friends. Sometimes she comes to see me and I draw or write her something on Whatman paper. She likes my drawings. She studies them and smiles, and then goes home through the garden. She walks, brushing the apple branches with her head, looking back, smiling at me or laughing. And I notice that after every visit she makes my paths get better and better marked. I think that's all. I've nothing more to tell about the sick girl from next door. No, it's not a long story. Not long at all even. Even the moths on the veranda seem bigger.

IN THE DUNES. It's nice to meet a girl whose mother works on the dredging barges: if someone asks, you say bluntly—she works on the dredging barges. Then everyone envies you. They were deepening the channel; watery sand kasha came up from the bottom through special tubes twenty-four hours a day. This watery mass went onto the shore and gradually sand dunes formed around the cove. Here you could lie out to get a tan even in the windiest weather—if the sun shone at all. I would go to the island on my motorcycle every morning and stand on the highest dune and twirl my faded plaid shirt over my head. As soon as she noticed me from the barge she would get into a big leaky boat that was tied to the barge and quickly row to shore. Here were our dunes, only ours—because it was my girl's mother who had deposited these merry shifting hills. And the summer was like a picture postcard, smelling of river water, willow and the resin of the coniferous forest. The forest was on the other side of the cove, and on the weekends people would relax there with badminton sets. And the Sunday couples would row up and down the cove talking in blue boats. But no one disembarked on our shore, and no one except us tanned themselves on our dunes. We lay on the hot, very hot sand and went swimming or raced each other, and the barge constantly rumbled, and a stout woman wearing blue overalls would walk up and down the deck examining the machinery. I watched her from afar, from the shore, and I always thought that I was really lucky—I had met a girl whose mother lived and worked on that remarkable thing. In August the rains began, and we built a lean-to out of willow branches on the dunes, although, you understand, the rain wasn't the whole point. The lean-to stood right at the water. In the evenings we would light a fire, which reflected in the cove, illuminating various floating pieces of wood. Well, at the very end of the summer we had a quarrel, and I never went to see her again after that. It was devilishly sad that fall, and the leaves rushed through the town as if demented. So, another shot?

DISSERTATION. The professor spent his research leave in the country. He was writing his doctoral dissertation in chemistry: he would make notes from books and fool around with test-tubes, but everything was dominated by an astonishingly warm September. Besides that, the professor loved beer, and before supper he would go into his shed in the depths of the garden. There, in the shed, in the corner, in the coolness, stood the beer barrel. Using a rubber tube the professor would siphon a little beer out into a five-liter receptacle and return to the house, trying not to spill the liquid. A distant relative of his wife made his lunch for him: she had dropped in from somewhere very far away a month ago like a bolt from the blue, or like a relative of his wife, but the professor's wife herself had died long ago, and so far there had not been anyone else. It should be noted that breakfast and supper were made by this same relative of his wife, but usually this happened in the mornings and evenings respectively. In the afternoon the professor would stroll through the dacha settlement or go fishing in the pond beyond the birch grove. There were no fish in the pond, and as a rule the professor failed to catch anything. But this didn't bother him, and so as not to return home empty-handed, he would pick the late field flowers on the edge of the woods and make up some pretty nice bouquets. When he returned to the dacha he silently handed the flowers to the distant relative whose name he could never remember, and kept forgetting to ask. The woman was about forty years old, but she loved signs of attention as much as at twenty, and in the mornings she did calisthenics behind the shed. The professor didn't know about this, but even if the glazier-neighbor, who knew about it perfectly well, having often seen it from behind his fence, even if the glazier had told the professor about it, there is no way he would have believed it, and in any event he wouldn't have gone spying. However, one day at dawn he had an unexpected urge for some beer, and on tiptoe, so as not to make noise, he went to the shed, and while the beer was pouring out through the tube, out of the barrel into the receptacle, the professor was standing at the spider-webbed window and he saw his wife's relative in a scanty bathing suit, flailing her arms, and hopping and squatting on his garden grass. After breakfast the professor did not go to work, he spent his time on some trivia: he got two rusty bicycles out of the attic, fixed them and pumped them up, and then ironed his suit and rode down to the station for some wine. Besides the wine he bought sprats and grapes and he helped his relative make lunch. After lunch the professor talked about what fine weather had been holding for two weeks now, what blue cornflowers were growing in the grove, and what fine rusty bicycles he had gotten out of the attic. That evening they went for a ride. Along the highway. On bicycles. They returned late—with flowers on the handlebars. On the relative's head there was a wreath. The professor had woven the wreath for her himself. This was a surprise for her, because she didn't know that he knew how to weave wreaths and repair bicycles. But then the professor hadn't known that his, in essence, relative was jumping up and down on his garden grass. Every morning. In a scanty swimsuit. Flailing her arms.

THE LOCALE. The railroad passes close by, and the yellow electric trains run past the lake. Some trains go to the city, and others away from the city. But this is a suburban area. And therefore even in the sunniest weather everything here seems unreal. Down the railway line, beyond the right-of-way fences, the city begins with big buildings, and in the other direction, beyond the lake, there is a pine forest. Some call it a park, others a forest. But in fact it is a forest-park. These are the suburbs, and it seems as if one can't see anything distinctive around. At one time this locale was considered a dacha area, but now the dachas have become simply the old wooden houses of the suburbs. The houses smell of kerosene and quiet middle-aged people live in them. A one-track branch of the railroad goes close to the forest-park. The branch leads to a dead-end —trains don't come in here. The rails have rusted, and the sleepers have rotted. There are some brown cars in the dead-end at the edge of the forest-park. Repair workers live in these cars. They have temporary permission to live in the suburban area, and all of them have big families. Every repairman knows that there aren't any fish in the swampy lake nearby, but on their hours off they all go to the shore with fishing poles and try to catch something. One of the workers, who lives in the third car from the forest-park, has a daughter of eighteen. She was born here, in the car, and she likes a young man from the city who comes to the forest-park with his friends fairly often to play soccer on the trash-strewn fields. He's a good lad, he courts the repairman's daughter, and he has already dropped in on them for tea a few times. He likes these little cars at the dead-end too. You know, maybe he'll marry the repairman's daughter soon and start spending even more time here. The wedding will be on a Sunday, dances will be arranged on the lake shore, and all will dance—everyone who lives in the brown cars at the dead-end.

AMID THE WASTELANDS. A door slammed upstairs, on the third floor, and I was left alone. The wind blew in from the wastelands, through the opened door and into the hall, and here on the staircase it was a little warmer than outside in the street. I lit up and went out into the yard where the linen of the inhabitants of this building was drying on lines. Pillowcases, sheets, and blanket-covers were inflated by the wind. I sat down on a bench wet with dew: in front of me loomed an improbably long five-story building: I've never seen such a long building; the shadow from the building ended at my feet. I was illuminated by the helpless September sun. Clouds as flabby as the muscles of old men moved across the sky, and behind my back stretched the infinite suburban wastelands, so infinite that even the ash-heap of the city was lost amid them and only the unpleasant odor reminded one that the city existed. The cigarette which I was smoking quickly ended in the wind, and I didn't have any more, so I decided to go to a store. But I didn't know where a store was. I didn't know anything about this place in general, there were no familiar faces, or familiar streets, I didn't know, and didn't want to know what the woman who had agreed to help us was doing with my fiancee. The woman lived and treated people in this long monotonous building. Passing through the shaded courtyard, I went around the building to the left and came out on the asphalt road. New buildings similar to this one stood all around. Perhaps I was a little afraid of these buildings. But I wanted to smoke and I went to a store, pretending that I had nothing to do with them. And that's the way it was really, I was just a little afraid of them: they looked at my back and eyes from a distance, and there wasn't anyone around. But soon I caught up with a girl. She was carrying two net bags full of groceries, and I decided that she would know where to buy cigarettes. I hailed her and asked. She said she'd show me to the store so I wouldn't get lost. The wind was blowing. The wastelands stretched out behind the buildings. Near the buildings wind-blown bed linen was flapping on lines. Across the wastelands, eating the seeds of grasses, huge flocks of sparrows rustled. The girl seemed very thin, something was wrong with her eyes, but I couldn't figure out what exactly, and then I realized: she was crosseyed. She showed me the way and kept explaining which things were located where in this area, but to me it was quite uninteresting and unncessary. She went into the store with me, waited for me to buy the cigarettes, and said that she wanted to walk me to the station where she worked as a telegraph operator. I don't have to go on the electric, I said, I don't have to. The girl went away. Not far from the store a milk truck was doing business. Middle-aged but talkative women wearing old-fashioned overcoats were standing in line. Each of them had a can and all of them, despite the cold wind, were talking nonstop. One chubby one who had already bought milk walked away from the truck, and I saw her slip and drop the can. The can fell onto the asphalt, the milk spilled out, the old woman fell too, rolling. She had on a black overcoat, she sat there all covered with milk, trying to get up. The line stopped chattering and looked at her. I stood there looking too. I probably would have helped her, but my hands were full: in one there was a cigarette, and in the other a match. I lit up and walked back to the building where they were doing something to my fiancee and which from a distance looked me intently in the eyes.

EARTH WORKS. The coffin hung on the tooth of the scoop, wobbling over the trench, and everything was normal. But then the lid opened and everything fell out into the bottom of the hole. At that point the excavator climbed from his cabin and examined the coffin and saw that there was a little glass window cut in the head of the coffin, and in the coffin lay some plastic boots. And the excavator was very sorry that there was no way to repair those boots, otherwise he would have undertaken the job. But the boots turned out to be very bad ones, and the sole of one of them flopped off as soon as he tried it on. The threads had rotten, and the sole with its plates immediately flopped off, and the top was too tight. So the mechanic-excavator threw the boots away even though he really needed some new footwear badly. But the excavator was more disappointed by something else. The machine operator wanted to look at a skull, because he had never managed to see a real skull in his whole life, never mind touch one with his hands. True, from time to time he touched his own head or his wife's head and imagined what it would be like if you removed the skin from his or his wife's head, and you had a real skull. But to do that you'd have to wait who knows how long yet. And the excavator couldn't stand waiting for anything very long. He loved to do everything that came into his head immediately. So, now, when the machine operator was digging up the coffin, he immediately decided to shake everything out of it and find the skull. He wanted to see what happened to the skull of a man who had died long ago and lay for many years, looking out the coffin window. Yes,—reflected the machine operator, descending into the grave on a ladder,—yes, now I'll have a good skull, otherwise a person can go on living and living and never have anything like it. Of course, I have a bad head, and really it's not so often there's enough free time to palpate it properly. Besides, when you feel your own head, it gives you hardly any pleasure—you need a bare skull, someone else's, without any skin on it, so that you can put it on a stick, or set it wherever you need to. What luck! Now I'll pick through the rags, chuck the bones and take the bare skull—in its natural state. You can't let such moments in life pass you by or else you turn around and someone else is putting your skull on a stick and walking around the street with it, scaring anybody he wants. The machine operator peered under the lid lying on the sand, then crawled out of the trench and peered through the window into the coffin, and then peered not through the window, but simply into the coffin the way people usually look into a coffin when the coffin is hanging on the tooth of a scoop, and the one who is looking is standing on the edge of the grave. But there was no skull in the coffin or under the lid on the sand. Ain't no skull,—said the excavator to himself,—there ain't no skull here, the skull's missing, and maybe there wasn't ever one here—they buried just the torso, eh? But no matter what there

ain't no skull, and I can't put it on a stick and scare anybody I want. It's the other way around, now anybody
can scare me with a skull, a real one, or his own. What
bum luck!—the excavator said to himself.

THE GUARD. Night. Always this cold night. His work
is night. Night is his livelihood and what he hates. In
the day he sleeps and smokes. He never loads the rifle.
What reason is there to load it when it's winter and
there's no one around. No one—winter, fall or spring.
And no one in the actors' houses either. These are the
actors' dachas, and he is the dacha guard. He has never
been in a theater, but once his partner told him that his
son was going to school in the city, and that he went to
the theater. The partner's son: he comes to visit his father on weekends. But no one comes to visit him. He
lives alone and smokes. Before his shift he takes the rifle
to the guard box and then walks along the little streets
of the dacha settlement all night long. Today and yesterday there was a lot of snow. The streets are white.
The trees, especially the pines, are too. They are white.
The moon is dim. The moon can't break through the
clouds. He smokes. He looks from side to side. He
stands at each intersection for a long while. It's very
dark. It will never be light in this settlement in the winter. In the summer it's better. In the evenings the actors
drink wine on their verandas. That is, if summer comes.
But summer never comes, the verandas and their dim
stained glass windows are locked and empty. They
freeze all the way through, they get piled with snow.
And every third evening, after working for two, he takes
his unloaded rifle and walks. Past the windowed dachas.
He walks without paths, without shells, without smokes.
He is going to get something to smoke, to the outskirts

of the settlement where the store is. The store is always empty. The spring on the door is a strong one. An aging woman works there. She is kind, because she gives credit. In the icy cold he doesn't remember her name. Why her, this woman, he wonders. I can get along without her, he thinks, or can I? No, I can't. Without her I wouldn't have anything to smoke. He laughs softly. It's cold, he continues thinking, it's cold. Dark. He sees the woman shut the shutters on her store and head home for bed. There she goes. I'm standing here, he says to himself, I'm smoking, and she's walking past. Do I want to smoke? No. I'm smoking because she's going away. That's all, she's gone. Now alone till morning. A cat runs by. There used to be a lot of them in the settlement. They lived under the porches of the houses. His partner used to shoot his rifle at them. It's cold. No cats. He walks on again, looking at the actors' houses. Snow on top. So it'll be warm. As long as there's no wind. There is a light on one veranda. The actors don't come in the winter, he thinks. Tracks on a plot of ground. A fence broken in one place. Two fence staves lie in the snow, criss-crossed. He has never loaded it, and he's not going to now either. He'll walk up and take a look, see what's up. He approaches. A shot. As if from afar, in the forest. No, much closer. Ah, someone's shooting from the stained glass windows. Hurts a lot, my head hurts. Sure would like a smoke. He falls face down in the snow. He isn't cold any more.

NOW. He came back from the army before his hitch was up, after the hospital. He served in the rocket units, and one night he came under powerful radiation, at night, during a practice alert. He was twenty. On his way home, he sat in the restaurant of the half-empty train for a long time, drinking wine and smoking. The pretty young woman who was traveling in his compartment was not in the least embarrassed about undressing before going to bed, standing in front of the door mirror, and he saw her reflection, and she knew that he saw it and smiled to him. The last night of the trip she invited him into bed with her, below, but he pretended that he was asleep, and she guessed this and laughed softly at him in the darkness of the small and stuffy compartment, and at that moment the train shrieked and flew through the black snow-storm, and the suburban train stops confusedly nodded their dim lights to him as he passed. The first two weeks he sat at home—leafing through books, looking through old photographs, grade school pictures even, trying to decide something for himself and endlessly quarrelling with his father, who had been retired on a big military pension and didn't believe a word he said and considered him a malingerer. The mustering-out pay which the regiment paymaster had issued him came to an end, and he had to look for a job. He wanted to be a driver at the neighboring hospital, but there, in the hospital, they offered him something else. Now, after the army, at the end of the snowy winter, he had become a janitor in the hospital morgue. He was paid seventy rubles a month, and that was enough money for him, because he didn't go out with girls: all he did was drive to the park occasionally, to ride the rollercoaster and watch people he didn't know dancing, through the transparent walls of the dance hall. Once he noticed a girl there whom he had once gone to school with. She had come to the park with some fellow in a sports car, and the janitor, concealed in the murk of large trees, watched them dance. They danced for half an hour, then slammed their car doors and rolled deeper into the park along the little illuminated streets. And a few weeks later, in May, they brought to the morgue a man and a woman who had been crushed in an automobile somewhere outside of town, and he didn't recognize them at first—but finally he did recognize them, though for some reason he just couldn't recall her name, and kept looking at her and thinking about how three or four years ago, even before the army, he had loved this girl and wanted, very much wanted, to be with her constantly, but she did not love him, she was too pretty to love him. And now, thought the janitor, it was all over, over, over, and it was impossible to know what the future would bring...

CHAPTER THREE

SAVL

But Veta does not hear. The night of your arrival in the
Land of the Lonely Nightjar, Veta Arcadievna, a thirty-
year-old teacher in our school, the strict teacher of botany, biology, and anatomy, is in the town's best restaurant dancing and drinking wine with some young, yes,
relatively young, man, a gay, intelligent and generous
fellow. Soon the music will end—the drunken drummers
and fiddlers, pianists and horn-players will quit the
stage. Lights dimmed, the restaurant will count its final
guests, and the relatively young man whom you have
never and will never see in your life, will take your Veta
away to his apartment, and there he will do anything
he wants with her. Stop, I understand, I know, there, in
his apartment, he will kiss her hand and then, right
after that, he will take her home, and in the morning
she'll come here to the dacha, and we can meet, I know:
we'll meet tomorrow. No, that's wrong, you probably
don't understand anything, or you're pretending you
don't, or you're simply a coward, you're afraid to think
about what will happen to your Veta there, in the apartment of the man you will never see, but of course you
would like to have a look at him, or am I wrong? Naturally I would like to make his acquaintance, we could
all go somewhere together, the three of us: Veta, he and
I, to some town park, to the old town park with the
rollercoaster, we would ride it and chat, it would surely
be interesting, I say: interesting, it would be interesting,
the three of us together. But maybe the man is not as intelligent as you say, and then it would not be so interesting, and we would be wasting the evening, it would be
a failure of an evening, that's all, nothing more than

that, but at least Veta would realize that I'm much more interesting than he is, and we would never meet him again, and on the night of my arrival in the Land of the Lonely Nightjar she would always come out at my cry: Veta Veta Veta it is I special school student so-and-so come out I love you just as before. Believe me: she always came out to my cry, and she and I would be together in her garret until morning, and afterwards when it started getting light, cautiously, so as not to awaken Arcady Arcadievich, I would go down to the garden on the outside spiral staircase and go back home. You know, before leaving I usually petted her ordinary dog, and I used to play with it a little so it wouldn't forget me. That's nonsense, our teacher Veta Arcadievna never came out to your call, and you were never in her garret, either during the day or at night. I watch every move you make, you know, that's what Doctor Zauze advised. When they released us from *there,* he advised: if you notice that the one whom you call *he* and who lives and studies together with you is going off somewhere, trying to be unnoticed, or if he simply runs away, follow him, try not to lose sight of him, stay as close to him as possible, find a way to get so close to him as to virtually merge into one with him, your acts becoming his, do it in such a way that a time comes—such a moment will certainly come—that you unite with him in a single whole, a single being with inseparable thoughts and aspirations, habits and tastes. Only in this way, Zauze asserted, will you achieve peace and freedom. And so wherever you went, I followed you, and from time to time I managed to merge with you, your acts becoming mine, but you drove me away as soon as you noticed this, and again I got worried, even terrified. I was afraid of, and in general am afraid of, many things, only I try not to let on, and it strikes me that you are no less afraid than I. For example, you're afraid I'll up and start telling you the truth about what that relatively young man did with your Veta in his apartment the night of your arrival. But I'm going to tell about it anyway, because I don't like you, because you don't want to merge with me, my acts becoming yours, as the doctor advised. I'll also tell you what other young and not-so-young men did to your Veta in their apartments and hotel rooms during those nights when you were sleeping at your father's dacha or in the city or *there,* after the evening injections. But first I have to convince you that you were never in the attic of Acatov's dacha, even though sometimes you did run away to the Land of the Nightjar late at night. You looked at the illuminated windows of the mansion through a crack in the fence and dreamed of entering the park, striding along the path—from the gate to the front porch, I understand you, striding along the path, easily, unselfconsciously, and, striding, to kick two or three of last year's acorns, pick a flower from a flowerbed, sniff it, stand by the gazebo a while—like that, looking all around with a slight squint of deep all-comprehending eyes, then to stand under a tall tree with a starling in it, to listen to the birds—I understand you quite well, I would take great pleasure in doing the same myself, and even more: striding along the path of Acatov's garden (or park—no one knows which it is better to call their lot and everyone calls it whatever occurs to him), I would play with their fine ordinary dog and I would knock at the front door: toock-toock; but now I will confess to you: I, as, incidentally, you too—we are afraid of that big dog. And if we weren't afraid of it, if, let's suppose, it didn't even exist—could we permit ourselves to do all that, is it only because of the dog that we cannot knock at the door?—that's my question to you, I would like to talk about it some more, the theme is one I find terribly absorbing. It strikes me you are dissembling again, is this all really so interesting, you're talking my head off, you don't want me to tell you the whole truth about Veta, about what those young men who you'll never see did to her in their apartments and hotel rooms well why tell me finally why you or why I why we are afraid to talk about that to each other or each to himself in all this there is so much truth why why why yes you know much but you know if I know nothing and you nothing we know nothing about that yet or we no longer know what can you tell me or yourself if neither you nor I ever had any woman we don't know in general what it's like we are just guessing we can guess we just read just heard from others but the others don't really know anything either once we asked Savl Petrovich if he had had women this was at school there at the end of the corridor behind the narrow door where it always smells of smoke and cleanser both in the washroom and the toilet Savl Petrovich was smoking he was sitting on the windowsill it was between classes no after classes I had stayed after class to do the next day's lessons no they made you stay after class to do the next day's lessons in math we're bad students they told mama especially in math it's very hard you get tired it's very bad bad to the point of pain some of the problems for some reason they give too many lessons one has to outline and think they make you do too much Savl Petrovich for some reason they torture us by holding up examples they say that supposedly some of us when we finish school will enter an institute and some of us a few of us part an occasional one of us will become engineers but we don't believe it nothing of the sort will happen for Savl Petrovich you yourself can guess you and the other teachers we will never become any engineers because we are all terrible fools isn't that so isn't this a special school that is not specially for us why do you deceive us with these engineers who needs all that but dear Savl Petrovich even if we did all of a sudden become engineers that's not needed no it shouldn't happen I don't agree to it I would petition to be in the commission I have no desire to be an engineer I will sell flowers and postcards and monkeys-on-a-string on the street or I'll learn shoe-repair, to saw plywood with a fret-saw but I will not agree to work as an engineer until the formation of the very main very biggest commission here one which will straighten out the matter of time isn't that so Savl Petrovich we have a time disorder and is there any sense in working at any serious matter for example belaboring blueprints with blue ballpoints when time is all messed up that's no good at all very strange and stupid you know that yourself of course you and the other teachers.

Savl Petrovich was sitting on the windowsill smoking. The naked bottoms of his feet were resting on the radiator for the steam heat or, as this device is also called, the battery. Beyond the window lay autumn, and if the window had not been covered with a special white paint, we would have been able to see part of the street, along which a moderate northwesterly wind was blowing. Foliage floated in the wind, puddles rippled, passersby, dreaming of turning into birds, precipitantly pushed home in order to prattle with neighbors about the poor weather. In short—it was the usual autumn, the middle of autumn, when the coal has already been brought to the schoolyard and unloaded from trucks, and an old man, our stoker and guard, whom none of us called by name, since none of us knew his name, inasmuch as determining and remembering that name made no sense, because there is no way our stoker could have heard and responded to that name, inasmuch as he was deaf and dumb—and he had already lit the boilers. It got warmer in the school, although as several teachers remarked, shivering and hunching up their shoulders, it was still windy, and—one thinks—Savl Petrovich was right to occasionally go into the bathroom to warm the naked bottoms of his feet. He could have warmed them in the teachers' room, and in class during lessons, but apparently he didn't want to do this too openly, with people around, despite everything he was a bit bashful, mentor Norvegov was. Maybe. He was sitting on the windowsill with his back to the painted-over window, facing the stalls. The naked bottoms of his feet were on the radiator and his knees were pulled high, so that the teacher could rest his chin on them comfortably. And looking at him, sitting that way, from the side, in profile were: a publisher's logo, ex libris, the series book after book, the silhouette of a youth sitting on the grass or the bare ground with a book in his hands, a dark youth against the background of a white dawn, dreamily, a youth, dreaming of becoming an engineer, a youth-engineer if you like, curly-haired, rather curly-haired, book after book, reading book after book against a background, free, ex libris, at the publisher's expense, one after the other all the books in a row, very well-read, he is very well-read, your lad—this to our kind and beloved mother—Vodokachka, teacher of the subjects literature and Russian language written and oral told mama too well-read even, we wouldn't recommend everything all at once, particularly the Western classics, that's distracting, it overloads the imagination, makes one arrogant, lock them up, no more than fifty pages a day for middle elementary school age. The Boy from Urzhum, The Childhood of Tioma, Childhood, A House on the Hill, Vitya Maleev, and now this: life is given to man only once, and you have to live it so as to. And also: to seek and to strive, to find and not to surrender, forward to meet the dawn, comrades in the fight, we'll clear a path with bayonets and shot—the songs of the Russian revolutions and civil wars, hostile whirlwinds, dark eyes, pack up your troubles, all together, heave ho, and then we would recommend music lessons, any instrument, in moderation, therapy, so it won't be awfully hard, beyond this, you know, it's a period of maturation, this age, well, say the *bayan,* or, say the accordion, the violin, the pianoforte, and even more forte than piano, they began: ee-ee-ee barcarolle three quarter flat don't confuse the treble clef with a fiddler's mushroom half-poison boil them ee-ee-ee to the clank of the railroad cars to the station which is on the same branch as ee-ee-ee according to Veta willows are disturbing the sleepy passengers you weep in the train car from love from the unnecessary things in life mama it's raining out do we really have to go out in such slop oh my dear a little music won't do you any harm we did agree after all the maestro will be waiting today it would be awkward it's Sunday, then we'll drop in on grandmother. The station, bushes, noonday, very damp. However, there's winter too: the platform snowcovered, dry snow, crunchy and sparkling. Past the market. No, first the viaduct with the squeaky ice-covered steps. Squeaky, mama. Careful, the way up ee-ee-ee when you see a passing freight below covered all over with chalk graffiti or a clean express with starched-collar curtains try not to look down or you'll get dizzy and fall your arms flailing on your back or face down and the sympathetic passersby who haven't managed to turn into birds will surround your body and someone will raise your head and start slapping your cheeks the poor lad he probably doesn't have any heart it's avitaminiosis anemia a woman in a peasant dress the owner of the baskets holds the accordion and his mama where's his mama he's probably alone taking music lessons look he's got blood on his head of course he's alone God what happened to him nothing now he's now I Veta I'm alone I beg you to forgive me your boy your tender student looked too long at a freight covered all over with chalk graffiti its cars were written on by commissions but after years and after some distances your timid so-and-so will come to you overcoming the storms which pound at man like the spiky fire of silver and he will play on a Barcarolle a wild czardas and God grant he not go out of his mind from the extracurricular passion turning him to ashes toock-toock hell Veta Arcadievna ee-ee-ee here're some chrysanthemums even if they're wilted and faded still what is going to happen will make up totally for everything when will that be? Ten years or so, perhaps. She is forty, she's still young, in the summer she lives at the dacha, swims a lot—and table tennis, ping-pong. And me, and me? Let's count up now. I'm twenty-eight, I finished the special school long ago, and the institute and became an engineer. I have a lot of friends, I am in fine health and saving up money for a car—no, I've already bought one, saved up and bought it, savings bank, savings bank, we'll turn your kopeks into rubles. Yes, that's it precisely, you've been an engineer for a long time and you read book after book, sitting on the grass whole days at a time. Many books. You've gotten very intelligent, and the day is coming when you'll realize that it's impossible to postpone it any longer. You get up from the grass, shake out your trousers—they are beautifully pressed—then you bend down, gather all of the books in a pile and take them to the car. There, in the car, lies a jacket, a good one, a blue one. And you put it on. Then you examine yourself. You are of superior height, much taller than now, approximately so many *shaku* more. Besides that, you're broad in the shoulders, and your face is almost handsome. Precisely *almost*, because some women don't like men who are too handsome, isn't that so? You have a straight nose, languid blue eyes, a stubborn willful chin and strongly compressed lips. As for your forehead, sometimes it is extraordinarily high, as, for example, it is right now, and dark locks of hair cascade down upon it in thick shocks. Your face is smooth, you shave. Having examined yourself, you get behind the wheel, slam the door and you leave the sylvan locale where you have spent so much time reading books. Now you are going straight to her house. But the chrysanthemums! You have to buy them, you have to stop somewhere, buy them at the market. But I don't have a centavo with me, I'll have to ask mother: mama, the thing is that a girl in our class died, no, of course not, not right in class, she died at home, she was sick for a long time, several years, and didn't come to classes at all, none of us students had ever seen her, except in photographs, she was simply on the roll, she had meningitis, like so many people, so then she died, yes, it's terrible, mama, terrible, like so many people have, so then she died and she has to be buried, no, naturally, no, mama, you're right, she has her own parents, no one can make anyone bury other people's children, I was just saying this: she has to be buried, but it's not customary to do that without flowers, it would be awkward, you remember, even Savl Petrovich, whom the teachers and parents' committee disliked so much, even he had a lot of flowers, and now our class has decided to take up a collection for a wreath for this girl, several rubles per person, or more accurately this way: whoever lives with his mama and papa gives ten rubles, and anyone who lives only with his mama or only with his papa, he gives five, so you see I have to give ten, please give me ten and be quick about it the car is waiting for me. What car?—asks mama. And then I will answer: you see, it's happened that I bought a car didn't pay much but even so I had to go into debt. What debt,—mama will wave her arms,—where did you get any money at all! And she'll run to the window to look out in the yard where my car will be standing. You see, I'll answer calmly, while I was sitting on the grass and reading book after book, my circumstances developed in such a way that I was able to finish school and later the institute, forgive me, please, mama, I don't know why but it seemed to me it would be a pleasant surprise for you if I didn't tell you all at once but somehow later, after some time, and now the time has come, and I am informing you: yes, I became an engineer, mama, and my car awaits. Then how much time has passed—mother will say—you mean to tell me you didn't go to your school this morning with a briefcase, and that it wasn't today that I saw you off and ran after you on the stairs almost to the first floor to shove some sandwiches into your overcoat pocket, and you jumped down three steps and yelled that you weren't hungry, but that if I kept forcing these sandwiches on you you would sew your mouth shut with thick thread?—you mean that didn't happen today?—our poor mother will say in amazement. And we, what will we tell our poor mother? We must tell her the following: alas, mama, alas. True, here it is essential to use the half-forgotten word *alas*. Alas, mama, the day when you wanted to put the sandwiches in my overcoat pocket and I refused because I was not altogether well—that day passed long ago, now I've become an engineer, and my car awaits. Then our mother will burst into tears: how the years fly, she'll say, how quickly children grow up, you no sooner turn around than your son is an engineer! But then she'll calm down, sit on a stool, and her green eyes will grow stern, and her wrinkles, especially the two deep vertical wrinkles etched beside her mouth, will become even deeper and she will inquire: why are you deceiving me, you just asked for money for a wreath for a girl who was in your class, and now you're maintaining that you graduated from school and even the institute long ago, do you mean to say you can be a schoolboy and an engineer simultaneously? And besides that, mama will remark sternly, there isn't any car in the yard, if you don't count that truck by the garbage cans, you've made this all up, no car is awaiting you. Dear mama, I don't know if one can be an engineer and a schoolboy together, perhaps some people can't, some are unable, some haven't been given the gift, but I, having chosen freedom, one of its forms, I am free to act as I wish and to be whoever I want either simultaneously or separately, can it be you don't understand this? And if you don't believe me, then ask Savl Petrovich, and although he hasn't been among us for a long time, he will explain everything to you: we have a problem with time—that's what you'll be told by the geographer, the man of the fifth suburban zone. And as for the car—don't get upset, I just fantasized a little, it really isn't there and never will be, but then always, from seven to eight a.m., every day of every year, in full gale or fair weather— the garbage trust's trusty truck will be guarding the garbage cans in our yard, bedbuglike, green as a fly. What about the girl, inquires mama, did the girl really die? I don't know,—you have to answer,—I don't know anything about the girl. Then you must walk quickly to the hall where your coat is hanging on the coat-rack, the jackets and hats of your relatives too—don't be afraid of these things, they're empty, no one is wearing them— and your coat is hanging there. Put it on, put on your cap and fling open the door onto the stairs. Run from the house of your father without looking back, for if thou lookest back thou wilst behold the grief in thy mother's eyes, and you will have a bitter taste as you race across the frozen ground to the second shift at school. As you race to the second shift, you realize you didn't do your homework for today either, but to the hostile question of how this happened, as you stare out the window at the parting day—the town's streetlights aflare, dangling over the street like mute bells with their clappers torn out—answer whichever teacher asks, answer with dignity and don't be embarrassed. Answer: since I consider myself an enthusiastic competitor in the entomology competition announced by our esteemed Academy, I devote my leisure to the collection of rare and semi-rare lepidoptera. Well, so what, the pedagogue will interpose. I dare say, you continue, that my collection will hold considerable scientific interest in the future, which is why, without fear of the materials or time sacrificed, I deem it my duty to supplement it with unique new specimens: so don't ask why I didn't do my homework. Since it's winter what kind of butterflies can you be speaking of, asks the pedagogue with mock surprise, what's wrong—are you crazy? And you respond with unshaken dignity: in the winter one can speak only of winter lepidoptera, those which are called snow butterflies, I catch them in the countryside—in the forest and the field, in the mornings primarily—to the second of the questions you posed my reply is this: the fact of my existence is of no surprise to anyone, otherwise they wouldn't keep me in this damned school along with others who are fools. You're being impertinent, I'll have a talk with your parents. To which the answer should be: you have a right to talk to whomever you like, including my parents, only don't express your doubts about the winter butterflies to anyone, you'll become a laughing-stock and be made to study here with us: there are just as many winter butterflies as summer ones, remember that. Now, put all your folios and folders into your briefcase and slowly, with the tired gait of an aging entomologist, coughing, leave the auditorium.

I know: you're like me—we never liked the school, especially since the day our principal Nikolai Gorimirovich Perillo introduced the slipper system. In case you don't recall, this was the name of the procedure which obliged pupils to bring slippers with them, moreover, you had to carry them not simply in your hands, and not in briefcases, but in specially made cloth bags. Right, in white bags with pullstrings, and on every bag, in india ink, was written the name of the pupil to whom the bag belonged. It was required to write, let's say: *student so-and-so 5 "U" class,* and below that, but in larger letters, it was obligatory to put: *slippers.* And still lower, but even larger: *special school.* Well of course

I remember the time well, it started suddenly one of those days. N. G. Perillo came to our room during class, he came gloomily. He always came gloomily, because, as our father explained, the principal's salary was low and he drank a lot. Perillo lived in a one-story annex which stood in the schoolyard, and if you want I'll describe both the annex and the yard for you. Just describe the yard, I remember the annex. Our red brick school was surrounded by a fence made of the same brick. An asphalt drive led from the gate to the front entrance— there were some trees beside it, and flower beds. Along the facade you could see several sculptures: in the center were two small old chalk men, one wearing a plain cap, the other a military forage cap. The old men stood with their backs to the school and their faces to you, as you race along the drive to the second shift, and each of them had one arm thrust forward—as if they were pointing to something important taking place there, in the stony barrens in front of the school where once a month they made us run cross-country conditioning relays. To the left of the old men a sculpture of a little girl with a small deer was whiling away its time. The girl and the deer were also shiny white, like pure chalk, and they too were looking at the barrens. And to the right of the old men stood a little bugler boy, and he would like to play the bugle, he knew how to play, he could play anything, even an extracurricular czardas, but unfortunately he didn't have a bugle, the bugle had been knocked out of his hands, or more accurately, the white plaster bugle had been broken in transit and the only thing protruding from the boy's lips was the support for the bugle, a piece of rusty wire. Allow me to correct you: as far as I remember, there really was a little white girl standing in the schoolyard, but the girl had a dog, not a deer, she was a chalk girl with an ordinary dog; when we rode our bicycle from point A to point B, this girl with the short dress and the dandelion in her hair was on her way to go swimming; you say that the chalk girl stands (stood) in front of our school and looks (looked) at the barrens where we run (ran) cross-country conditioning relays, but I tell you: she looks at the pond where she'll soon be swimming. You say she's petting a deer, but I tell you the girl is petting her ordinary dog. And you didn't tell the truth about the little white boy: he's standing but he isn't playing the bugle and although some sort of metal is protruding from his mouth, he doesn't know how to play the bugle, I don't know what the metal is, maybe it's the needle he uses to sew his mouth shut so as not to eat his mother's sandwiches wrapped in his father's newspaper. But the main thing is this: I maintain that the little white boy is not standing, but sitting—it is a little dark boy sitting against the background of a white dawn, book after book, on the grass, it is a little boy engineer whose car is waiting, and he is sitting on his base just exactly the way Savl Petrovich sat on the windowsill in the bathroom, warming the bottoms of his feet when we go and enter furiously, carrying in our briefcases entomological notes, plans for the transformation of time, many-colored nets for catching snow butterflies, and the six-foot-long handles of these beautiful devices stick out of the briefcases, catching the corners and the smug portraits of the scholars on the walls. We walk in furiously: dear Savl Petrovich, this terrible school is getting impossible, they give a lot of homework, the teachers are almost all fools, they aren't a bit smarter than us, you know, something's got to be done, there has to be some decisive step—perhaps letters here and there, perhaps boycotts and hunger-strikes, barricades and barracudas, tympani and tambourines, burned rolls and gradebooks, a large-scale auto-da-fé embracing all the special schools of the world, look here in our briefcases we have nets for catching butterflies. We'll break the poles off our own nets, catch all the really stupid people, and put these nets on their heads like dunce caps, and then we'll beat their hateful faces with the poles. We'll arrange a fabulous mass-scale civil execution, and then those who tormented us in our idiotic specschools for so long will have to run conditioning relays themselves—through the stony barrens, and they will have to solve problems about bicycle riders, and we, the former students, liberated from our slavery to ink and chalk, we will get on our dacha bicycles and race along the highways and byways, occasionally greeting in motion girls we know wearing short skirts, girls with ordinary dogs, we will become the suburban bicycle-riders of points A, B, and C, and let those damned fools, damned fools that they are, solve problems about us and for us, the bicycle-riders. We will be bicycle-riders and postmen like Mikheev (Medvedev), or like the one whom you, Savl Petrovich, call The Sender. All of us, the former idiots, will become Senders, and it will be beautiful. Remember, once upon a time you asked us if we believe in this person, and we said that we had no idea what to think about the matter, but now when the incandescent summer has given way to dank autumn, and passersby, heads hidden in their collars, dream of turning into birds, now we hasten to declare to you personally, dear Savl Petrovich, and to all other progressive pedagogues, that we do not doubt the existence of The Sender, as we do not doubt that the future full of bicycle-riders and bicycle-rider-senders, lies ahead. And today, from here, from our disgusting men's toilet with the bespattered windows and the floors which never dry, we shout to the whole wide world: long live the Sender of wind! Furiously.

Meanwhile our thin and barefoot teacher Savl is sitting on the windowsill, looking at us, touched as we boom this greatest of oratorios, and when its final echo reverberates through emptied rooms and corridors which still stink of the classes, when it does this and flies out into the autumn streets, teacher Savl will pull some little scissors from the chest pocket of his shirt, he will cut his toenails, look at the stall doors, all covered with obscene words and decorated with idiotic drawings, and: how much that is vulgar,—he'll say,—How much that is ugly we have in our restroom, O God,—he'll note,—how impoverished our feelings for women are, how cynical we are, we the people of the special school. Is it impossible to select more exalted, profound and tender words instead of these vile and alien ones? O people, teachers and pupils, how fatuous and filthy you are in your ideas and your deeds! But are we the ones to blame for our idiocy and animal lust, are our hands the ones that scribbled on the doors of the stalls? No, no!—he will exclaim,—we are nothing but weak and helpless servants and non-servants of our Principal, Kolya Perillo, and it is he who has inspired us with debauchery and weakmindedness, and it is he who did not instruct us to love tenderly and profoundly, and his hands are the ones which guide ours when we are drawing on the walls here, and he is to blame for our idiocy and our lust. O vile Perillo,—Savl will say,—how loathsome you are! And he will weep. We shall stand there at a loss as to what to say to calm him, our genius of a teacher and man. We shall stand on the tiled floor, shifting from one foot to the other, and the wet filth left by the second shift will ooze underfoot and slowly and quite imperceptibly begin to seep through our canvas slippers, which our poor mother spent such a painfully long time in line to get. One evening, an evening of one of those days: Mama, Perillo came to our classroom gloomily today. He erased everything the teacher had written on the board, erased it with a rag. Attention,—he, the principal, said in the stillness,—from this day forth this special school with all of its chemicals, Faraday lamps, volleyballs, inkwells, blackboards, chalkboards, maps and pirozhki and other fancy-wancies is declared to be the Great Fatherland Mathematician Lobachevsky Model Shockwork Special School, and it goes over to the slipper system. The class got noisier and noisier, and one boy—I don't remember his name, or maybe I simply don't understand it, or maybe I was this boy myself,—this boy began to cry out, for some reason he cried out at great length, like so: a-a-a-a-a-a-a-a! Sorry, mama, I realize there's no need to demonstrate precisely how the boy cried out, especially since father is napping, it's enough to say that a boy cried out, I could say that he shouted very loudly and unexpectedly, and there's no need to demonstrate that he shouted like so: a-a-a-a-a-a-a-a! In doing this he opened his mouth wide and stuck out his tongue, and it seemed to me that he had an exceptionally red tongue, the boy was probably ill, and it was the beginning of an attack,—that's what I thought. I have to note, mama, he really does have a very long red tongue with violet spots and veins, as if the boy drank ink, it's really amazing. It was as if he were sitting at the ear-throat-nose doctor's and the doctor asked him to say his "ah," and the boy opened his mouth and is diligently saying, or rather, shouting: a-a-a-a-a-a-a-a! He shouted for a few minutes, and everyone looked at him, and then he stopped shouting and quite quietly asked, addressing the principal: ah, what does that mean? And at that point everyone remembered that the boy stutters, that sometimes the shift from vowel to consonant comes hard to him, and he gets stuck on the vowel and shouts, because he feels ashamed. And so today he shouted like that: a-a-a-a-a-a-a-a! He wanted to ask the principal: ah, what does that mean,—that's all. And finally he asked and Principal Perillo replied through his teeth: the slipper system is an arrangement whereby every pupil buys slippers and brings them to school in a special sack with pull-strings. Arriving at school, the pupil removes his usual footwear and puts on the slippers he has brought, and the emptied bag is filled with his usual footwear and he hands this to the lady in the cloakroom along with his coat and hat. Am I explaining it comprehensibly?—asked the principal, looking blankly to the ends of the earth. And at this point the boy began shouting horrendously again, this time it was another sound: o-o-o-o-o-o-o! I won't do it any more, mama, I don't know how I could forget that papa is drowsing in his study with the newspaper in his hands, he is obviously tired, he has such a hard job, so many cases, so many doomed fates, poor pop, I won't do it any more, mama, I'll just finish. And at this point the boy shouted: o-o-o-o-o-o-o!—and then he got it out: oh, that's nice. Perillo was ready to leave now, when we, that is, he and I, the other, we stood up and declared: Nikolai Gorimirovich, we are appealing to you personally and in your open and honorable person to the entire administration as a whole with a request to allow us to carry one bag for two people, inasmuch as it would be twice as hard for our mother to sew two bags as one. To which the principal, exchanging glances with the teacher, as if they knew something that no one else knew, as if they knew more than we did, replied: each student of the Great Fatherland Mathematician Lobachevsky Model Shockwork Special School must have his own bag with pull-strings—one bag apiece. And as long as you consider that there are two of you, you must have two bags—no more, no less. If you imagine that there are ten of you, then get ten bags. Curses!— we said loudly and furiously,—it would be better if we didn't exist at all, then you wouldn't pester us with your damned bags and slippers, poor mama, you'll have to sew two bags, sitting up till late at night, whole nights through, at your sewing machine, stitching—tra-ta-ta, tra-ta-ta—through, through the heart, yes it would be better if we turned into a lily forever, into the *nymphea alba,* like that other time, on the river, only forever, to the end of life. Furiously. Principal Perillo took a wadded handkerchief from his inside jacket pocket and carefully wiped the freckled, rubicund bald spot mushed into his skull. He did this to conceal his dismay, he was dismayed, he didn't expect the presence of such infuriated pupils in the school. And he said gloomily: student so-and-so, I didn't imagine that there were people here capable of losing my trust in them to the extent that you have just done. And if you don't want me to expell you from the school and pass your documents along to *that place, there,* sit down at once and write an explanatory note about this lost trust, you must explain everything to me, and particularly your stupid pseudoscientific theory about turning into a lily. Having said this, Perillo turned, clicked his heels militarily—in the school it was said that the principal had served in the same batallion as Kutuzov himself—and exited, slamming the door. Enraged. The whole class looked in our direction, stuck out a red poisonous tongue, aimed slingshots, and giggled, because the whole class, like all the others in the specschool—is stupid and barbarous. The idiots, they are the ones who hang cats on the fire escape, they are the ones who spit in each other's faces during the long recesses and take jam pirozhki away from each other, they are the ones who secretly urinate in each other's pockets and trip each other, they are the ones who twist each other's arms and gang up on weaklings, and they are the idiots who scribbled all over the doors to the stalls.

But why are you so angry with your comrades,—says our patient mother to us,—aren't you like them? If you were different, better than them, we wouldn't send you to study in the specschool. O, you can't imagine what a joy it would be for me and your father! Lord, I would surely become the happiest of mothers. No, mama, no, we are totally different people, and we have nothing in common with those crumbs, we are incomparably superior, better than them in all respects. Naturally, it might seem to the uninitiated that we are the same, and in terms of general academic progress there is no one worse than us, we aren't capable of remembering a single poem all the way, still less a fable, but on the other hand, we do remember things which are more important. Not long ago Vodokachka explained to you that we, your sons, have a so-called selective memory, and that is quite right, mama, this kind of memory allows us to live as we wish, for we remember only what is necessary to us, not what is necessary to those cretins who insolently take it upon themselves to teach us. You know, we don't even recall how many years we have already spent in the specschool, and sometimes we forget the names of school objects, or objects in general, not to mention your formulas and definitions—those we don't know at all. Once, a year or three ago, you found us a tutor in some subject, perhaps mathematics, and as it happens we usually went to his place for lessons, and he got a certain number of rubles for each lesson. He was a sweet and knowledgeable pedagogue, and during approximately the second lesson he informed us: young man,—no, I'm mistaken, he used an odd inverted form of expression: man of youth; man of youth, you are unique, the sum total of your knowledge of this subject is zero. When we came for the third lesson, he left us alone in the apartment and ran to the store for some beer. It was summer, hot, we came from the dacha for lessons, it was unbearable, mama. The tutor said to us: ah, hello, hello, man of youth, I kept waiting and waiting—wiping his hands—it's hot for it's summer, did you bring the money? Give it here, I've been waiting, not a kopek, stay here, I'll hop down for some beer, make yourself at home, do some drawing or something, feed the guppies, the light in the aquarium has burned out, the water is murky, but when the fish swims up to the glass, you can observe and examine it, yes, by the way, take a look at Fishman too, he's on the shelf, it's an exercise book, an excercise book of problems, I recommend number such-and-such, singularly interesting, a bicycle rider is riding along, can you imagine that? He goes from point to point, a most interesting situation, the heat out is impossible, I've been waiting, not a kopek in the whole house, the neighbors are all in the South, absolutely no one to borrow from, in general,

I'm off, make yourself comfortable, do whatever you like, only don't raid the icebox, there's not anything in it anyway—it's empty, and so, for beer, for beer, and again for beer, so it won't be frightfully painful. Absent-mindedly. No, concentrating. Turning around in front of the mirror. When the tutor came back with the beer—thirty bottles, mama—he asked us if we knew how to play chess. We do, we replied. Just that day we had invented a new piece, called the rookinghorse, which could move corner to corner or not go at all, that is, skip a move and stay in place. In this case the player simply says to his partner, the rookinghorse moves, but in reality the rookinghorse stands as if nailed to the ground and looks blankly to all the ends of the earth, like Perillo. The tutor was terribly pleased by the idea of a new piece, and later when we would come to his house he would often sing to the tune of the "Children of Captain Blood": rookinghorse, rookinghorse, smile on. And drink beer, and we never did any work on our subject, we played chess and beat our tutor fairly often. So we don't have a bad memory, mama, it is, rather, selective, and you shouldn't be upset. And at this point the three of us, sitting in the kitchen, heard our father's voice and realized that he was no longer drowsing in his armchair, but moving along the corridor, flopping his houseslippers and rattling the fresh evening newspapers. He was taking a long time, walking tiredly and coughing —that was precisely his voice, it was this in which his voice was expressed. Good evening, papa's wearing pyjamas, don't be concerned that they're old, sometime mama will make or buy you some new ones, and Those Who'll Come will inquire: make them or buy them, make them or buy them, make them or buy them? Your prosecutor-father is very large: when he stands in the kitchen door wearing his checked pyjamas he fills the entire entrance, he stands there and asks: what's going on, why are you shouting here in my house, what's wrong with you, are you crazy? I thought your dumb relatives had come again, a hundred of them at once. What the hell is this, anyway! Can't you keep it down a little, you've let your brat get hopelessly out of hand, things are perfectly clear with him—straight F's. No, papa, that's not the basic thing, you understand, the rookinghorse has slipped into my dreams the way a man's red fist slips into a leather glove, and he has, the poor fellow, a selective memory, the rookinghorse has. What rubbish is this, I don't want to hear your delirium,—father said to me. He sat down on a stool, and it might seem that at any second it would collapse under the weight of this endlessly exhausted body, and he shook a sheaf of newspaper pages to straighten them, and used his fingernail to mark some notice under the heading *advertisements*. Listen,—he addressed mother,—to what it says here: wanted to buy, a winter dacha. What do you think, should we sell our house to this character, he's probably a swindler and rascal, some foreman or collective farm director, and he's got money of course, otherwise he wouldn't bother running an ad. I was just sitting and thinking—continued father,—why the hell do we need that hovel, there's nothing good out there: the pond is filthy, the neighbors are all bums and drunkards, and think what the upkeep alone costs. But the hammock,—said mama,—how glorious it is to lie in the hammock after a hard day, why you know you love to do that. I can hang the hammock up in the city too, on the balcony,—said father,—true, it'll take up the whole balcony, but then not a single relative will turn up there, on the balcony, and that's the main thing,

I'm sick and tired of maintaining a dacha for your relatives, do you understand this or not? Sell it, and everything's here, and no taxes, or glass repairs, or roof repairers and what-not for you, especially since my pension is not sky-high, eh? Whatever you think best,—said mama.

And then I—this time it was precisely me, and not that fellow from the same class who stutters so painfully—then I bellowed at my father: a-a-a-a-a-a-a! I bellowed more loudly than ever before in my life, I wanted him to hear and understand what the cry of his son meant: a-a-a-a-a-a-a-a! wolves on the walls even worse on the walls there are people, people's faces, they're the hospital walls that time when you are dying quietly and terribly a-a-a-a huddled up in the fetal position faces which you have never seen but which you will see years later these are the preludes to death and life for it has been promised to you that you will live in order to be able to sense the reverse movement of time and to study in the specschool and feel infinite love for your teacher Veta Vetka of acacia a fragile woman in tight stockings which susurrate when she walks a girl with a tiny birthmark near her exquisite and provocative mouth, a dacha girl with the eyes of a light-hearted doe a stupid slut for sale from the suburban electric platform over which there is a viaduct and clock and humming wires in the snowy wind snowy wind and higher up a-a-a-a flashing young stars and storms flashing through summers—am I late? excuse me, for God's sake, Veta Arcadievna, I was seeing my mother off, she was going to her relatives for a few days, to another town, but then I suppose you're not interested, to be honest, I don't even know what to do so that things will be interesting for you, well, now,

I thought, let's go for a ride somewhere, let's say to the park or a restaurant, you're probably cold, button up, why are you laughing, did I really say something funny, come on, stop, please, what? you'd like to go to the dacha? but we sold the dacha long ago, we have no dacha, because father retired, let's go to a restaurant, yesterday I got some money, not too much, but some, I work in a certain ministry now, what do you mean, no I'm not an engineer, what? I can't hear, an electric is coming, let's move away from the edge, why did I write you this note? curses, I can't answer like this all at once, we really have to have a little chat, sit down somewhere, let's go to a restaurant all right? what? on the electric? of course, there's no stop here, this is an out-of-town locale, more precisely, a suburban one, I will tell you everything along the way, it's all very important, imagine, there was a time, probably rather a long time ago, I used to come here, onto the snowswept platform, together with my mother, you probably know, don't you, you face in the direction the train's headed, and the cemetery is on the left, my grandmother is buried there—ee-ee-ee-ee-ee—just as they do now, electric trains used to go by, freights, expresses—careful, mama, don't slip—or was that a different platform? they all look so much alike,—the wide white cemetery, but first comes the market, the market, we have to buy sunflower seeds there, the women are wearing peasant kerchiefs, it smells of cows and milk, long tables and stalls, several motorcycles at the entrance, workers in blue aprons are unloading a truckload of boxes, from the crossing with its barrier and striped watchman's box one hears a raucous whistle, two dogs are sitting by the butcher shop, along the fence is a queue for kerosene, a horse which has brought a cistern, and snow is falling onto the horse from the tree under which it is standing, but since the horse is white the snow on its crupper is virtually unnoticeable. Also a water hydrant, and around it iced wet spots, strewn with sand, also—butts thrown into the snowbank, also—an invalid wearing a padded jacket, sellers of dried mushrooms on strings. A wagon wheel leaning against a garbage bin. Mama, will we drop in on grandmother or go straight to the maestro? To grandmother,—replies mother,—first of all to grandmother, she's waiting, we haven't been to see her for a long time, it's simply bad, she might think we've completely forgotten about her, straighten your scarf and put on your gloves, where's your hanky, grandmother will be unhappy about the way you look. Pass the iron gates with their protuberant cast-iron decorations, buy a bouquet of paper flowers—they are sold by a blind crone next to the church, go out into the central walkway, then turn to the right. Keep going until you see the white marble angel in the form of a young woman. The angel stands behind the blue fence surrounding the grave, its fine big wings folded behind its back and its head down: it listens to the train whistles—the line passes a kilometer from here—and mourns for my grandmother. Mama searches for the key to the fence, that is, to the padlock which locks the fence, the wicket gate in the fence. The key is in there somewhere, in mother's nice-smelling purse—along with a compact, perfume bottle, lace hanky, matches (mama doesn't smoke, of course, but she carries matches just in case), national identity card, roll of paper twine, along with a dozen old trolley tickets, lipstick and change for the road. For a long time mama cannot find the key and she gets upset: well where is it, Lord, I know perfectly well that it

was here, you mean we aren't going to get to visit grandmother today, what a shame. But I know that the key
will certainly be found, and I wait calmly—no, not true,
I'm upset too, because I'm afraid of the angel, I'm a
little afraid of the angel, mama, it's so gloomy looking.
Don't say silly things, it's mournful, not gloomy, it's
mourning grandmother. Finally the key is found, and
mama starts trying to open the lock. It doesn't work
right away: wind has blown snow into the keyhole and
the key won't go in, so mama presses the lock into her
palm to warm it, and the snow in the keyhole melts.
If this doesn't help, mama bends over the lock and
breathes on it, as if trying to melt someone's frozen
heart. Finally the lock clicks and opens—a motley winter butterfly, which was resting on an elder branch, is
frightened and flies to the neighboring grave; the angel
just shudders, but doesn't fly away, it stays with grandmother. Mama mournfully opens the gate, walks up to
the angel and looks at it for a long time—the angel is
covered with snow. Mama bends down and gets a fir
whiskbroom from under the bench: we bought it one
day at the market. Mama sweeps the snow from the
bench, then turns around to the angel and brushes the
snow from its wings (one wing is wrecked, broken) and
its head, the angel frowns unhappily. Mama takes a
small shovel—it stands behind the angel's wing—and
cleans the snow from grandmother's mound. *The
mound under which grandmother is.* Then mama sits
down on the bench and takes a handkerchief from her
purse to wipe away her coming tears. I stand alongside,
I don't especially want to sit down, mama, not especially, thanks, no, I'll stand. Well,—says mama to her mother,—well, here we are again, hello my dear, you see,
it's winter again, aren't you cold, maybe I shouldn't

have taken away the snow, it would be warmer, hear that, the train is going by, today's Sunday, mama, there are a lot of people in church, at home—at this point the first tears slip down my mama's cheeks—at home everything is fine, my husband (mama uses my father's name) and I don't quarrel, everyone's healthy, our son (mama uses my name) is in such-and-such a class, he's doing better in school. Not true, mama, not true, I think, I'm doing so poorly in school that if not today then tomorrow Perillo will expell me, I think, and I will start selling paper flowers like that old crone, I think, but I say aloud: grandmother, I try terribly, terribly hard, I'll definitely graduate from the school, please don't worry, and I'll become an engineer, like grandfather. I can't say anything else, because I have a feeling I'm going to burst out crying in a second. I turn away from grandmother and look along the walkway: at the end, by the fence, a little girl is playing with a dog—hello, girl with the ordinary dog, I see you here every time, do you know what I wish to impart to you today, I'm deceiving my former grandmother, somehow it's awkward for me to disappoint her, and I am not telling the truth, none of us imbeciles will ever become engineers, the only thing any of us is capable of is selling postcards or paper flowers like that old crone by the church, and probably not even that: there is certainly no way we will ever learn how to make that kind of flower, so we won't have anything to sell. The girl departs, taking away the dog. I notice that the butterfly, which is now resting three paces from me on the bend of a fresh branch, is spreading its wings, getting ready to fly. I throw open the gate and run, but the butterfly notices me before I manage to cover it with my hat: it disappears among the bushes and crosses. Up to my knees in snow I run after it, mournfully, trying not to look at the photographs of those who are dead; their faces are illuminated by the setting sun, their faces smiling. Dusk descends from the heavenly deeps. The butterfly, after flitting here and there, vanishes utterly, and you remain alone in the middle of the cemetery.

You don't know how to get back to your mourning mother, and you head in the direction of the train whistles which you can hear—towards the line. An engine, blue smoke, a whistle, some kind of clicking inside the mechanism, the blue—no, black, hat of a mechanic, he has his head out the cab window, looking ahead and to the sides, he notices you and smiles—he has a moustache. Raises his arm, apparently to where the controls and signal handle are. You guess that in a second there will be another whistle—the engine will scream, come to its senses, jolt and pull the cars along, begin to emit steam and, increasing speed, blow smoke. Softly, hunched in clumsy constraint from its own inexplicable power, it will roll across the bridge, and vanish—melt away, and never from this day forth will you find consolation for this loss: where can you ever find another—an engine as black as a rook, the moustachioed mechanic—and where will you ever again see these—exactly these, not others—battered little patched-up cars, brown and sad and squeaking. It will vanish—melt away. You will remember the sound of the whistle, the steam, the eternal eyes of the engineer, you will wonder how old he is, where he lives, you will wonder—and forget (vanish—melt away), you will recall someday but be unable to tell anyone else about it—about everything you saw: the engineer and the engine and the train that they both took away over the bridge.

You won't be able to, people won't understand, they'll look at you strangely: what's so unusual about trains. But if they do understand—they'll be amazed. It will vanish—melt away. Crow-engine, engine-crow. Engineer cars rocking on their springs, the cough of couplings and airhoses. A distant route, playing-card houses just outside the right-of-way barriers—government ones and private ones, with frontyard gardens and ordinary apple orchards, in the windows—the lights of the blinking darkness, all around a life unknown and incomprehensible to you, and people whom you will never meet. Vanish—and melt away. Standing in the lengthening dusk—hands in the pockets of your gray spring coat— you wish the train a fast night on the rails, you wish all its stokers, trackmen, and engineers well, you want them to have a good night on the rails where there will be: the somnolent faces of stations, the hum of signal arrows, steam-engines which drink from the T-shaped water hoses of the watertowers, dispatchers' cries and curses, the odor of the car platforms, the odor of burned coal and clean bed linen, the odor of cleanliness, Veta Arcadievna, of clean snow—in essence, the smell of winter, its very beginning, that's what is most important—you understand? My God, student so-and-so, why are you shouting so loudly, it's quite embarrassing, the whole car is looking at us, can't we discuss all this quietly. Then you get up, go to the center of the car, and raising your arm in salutation you say: citizens, suburban passengers, I beg your pardon for talking too loudly, I'm very sorry I behaved badly; in school, in the special school where I once studied, they taught us something quite different, they taught us to speak quietly, no matter what the subject was, I have tried to behave exactly this way all my live. But today I

A School for Fools

am incredibly upset, today is an extraordinary case, today, or rather, for today I arranged a meeting with my
former teacher by writing her an emotional note, and
then my teacher came to the windswept platform in
order to see me after such-and-such a number of years,
and there she sits now, in our electric train car, on that
yellow electric bench, and everything that I am telling
her now and that I will tell her—everything is extraordinarily important, believe me, that's why my voice
sounds a little louder than usual, thank you for your
attention. Excitedly. You want to return to Veta, but
at this point someone puts a hand on your shoulder.
You turn around: before you is a stern woman of more
than forty, almost gray-haired, wearing glasses with thin
gold frames, the woman has green eyes and vertical,
painfully familiar furrows by her mouth. You look
carefully—it is your patient mother. For a solid hour
she has been looking all over the cemetery for you:
where did you go, you repulsive child, why did you
head for the trains again, she thought that something
had happened to you, it was already quite dark. Reply
simply and with dignity: dear mama, I saw a winter
butterfly, I ran after it and so I got lost. Let's go right
now—mother is angry—grandmother is calling you, she
asks to be shown how you learned to play the accordion, play her something mournful, sad— do you hear?
and don't you dare refuse. Grandmother, can you hear
me? I will play you a piece by Brahms called the "Pota-
to," but I'm not sure I've learned it very well. I take
the accordion—the instrument is standing in the snow of
the walkway in its black case. I remove the case and
sit down on the bench. It's evening at the cemetery, but
the white angel—it's right nearby—is quite visible as I sit
with my accordion three quarter. The angel spread its

wings and instilled mournful inspiration in me: ee-ee-ee
—one two three, one two three, in a garden girls were
walking, wa-a-lking, one two three, one two three, don't
cry mama, or I'll stop playing; granny's fine now, you
don't have to get upset, one two three, one two three,
wa-a-lking, she had a selective memory too, grandmother did, wa-a-lking. Remember how the accordion sounds
in the chill cemetery air in the early evening when the
sounds of the railroad come from the direction of the
railroad, when violet trolley sparks cascade off the distant bridge at the very edge of town, corruscating
through the bare elder branches, and when from the
store in the market—you remember this well too—workers use carts to carry away boxes full of bottles? The
bottles clank and ring metallically, the horse stamps its
hooves on the frozen cobblestones, and the workers
shout and laugh—you won't learn anything about those
workers, and they won't learn anything about you either—so, do you remember how your Barcarolle sound-
ed in the chill cemetery air in the early evening? Why
are you asking me about that, it's so unpleasant for me
to remember that time, I am tired of remembering it,
but if you insist, I will reply calmly and with dignity: at
such moments my accordion sounds lonely. May I be permitted to ask the following question, one detail interests
me, I intend to check your, and simultaneously my,
memory: in those years when you or I, when we visited
our grandmother with our mother to play her a new piece
on the accordion or to give a brief plot-summary of
some story we had just read from the series book after
book, —was our teacher Norvegov still alive in those
years or had he already died?

You see, the years which we are now discussing dragged

quietly for rather a long time, they dragged on and on, and in that time our mentor Savl managed both to live and to die. What do you mean, that he lived first, and then died? I don't know, but in any case he died right in the middle of those long dragging years, and it was only at the end of them that we encountered the teacher on the wooden platform of our station, and that some sort of water creatures splashed around in the barrel at Norvegov's. But I don't understand in precisely which end of the years in question our encounter took place—in the earlier or the later. I will explain to you, once in some scholarly journal (I showed our father this article, he leafed through it and immediately threw the entire journal off the balcony, and moreover, when throwing it off, repeatedly shouted the word *Acatovism*) I read the theory of a certain philosopher. There was a preface to it, it said the article was being printed for porpoises of discussion. The philosopher wrote that in his opinion time had a reverse side, that is, that it moved not in the direction we suppose it should move, but in reverse, backwards, because everything which was—all this is just going to be, he said, the real future is the past, and that which we call the future has already passed and will never be repeated, and if we are incapable of remembering the past, if it is concealed from us by the shroud of an imaginary future, it is not our fault, but our misfortune, because all of us have amazingly weak memories, in other words, I thought, reading the article, like you have and I have, like you and I and our grandmother have— selective. And I also thought: but if time is rushing back, that means everything is normal, therefore Savl, who died precisely at the time when I read the article, therefore Savl still *will be,* that is, will come, will return —he is all ahead, as a fecund summer is ahead, full of magnificent water nymphs, a summer of rowboats and bicycles, a summer of butterflies, a collection of which you finally assembled and sent off to our respected Academy in a big box used for some imported eggs. You appended to the parcel the following letter: "Dear Sirs! More than once and more than twice orally (on the telephone) and in writing (by telegraph) I have requested confirmation of the rumors that an academic entomological competition, named after one of the two chalk men standing in the courtyard of our special school, is taking place. Alas, I have received no reply. But since I am a passionate collector and at the same time (which has a backwards flow) one selflessly devoted to science, I consider it my duty to proffer for the exalted perusal of your scholarly council my modest collection of night and day butterflies, among which you will find both summer and winter ones. The latter, apparently, are particularly interesting, inasmuch as— in spite of their numerousness—they are scarcely ever observed in nature or in flight, a fact which yours truly has already made reference to in talks with specialists, among others with Academician A. A. Acatov, who reacted very favorably to the present collection, now composed of more than ten thousand specimens of insects. I request that you inform me of the results of the competition at this address: the railroad, the branch, the station, the dacha, ring a bicycle bell until it is opened unto you." You sealed the envelope, and before putting it on top of the butterflies in their egg box, you wrote on the reverse side of the envelope: with greetings fly, return with reply—across it, from corner to corner on the diagonal, in huge letters. This is what our teacher of Russian language and literature, nicknamed Vodokachka, taught us, even though if you were to look for a person less resembling a watertower both externally and in-

ternally you couldn't find anyone better than our Vodokachka. But the point wasn't in the similarity, but in the
fact that the letters which compose the word itself, or
more accurately, half of the letters (read every other
one, starting with the first)—are her initials, the teacher's: V. D. K. (Valentina Dmitrievna Kaln—that's what
she was called). But two letters are still left over—*ch* and
a—and I've forgotten how they're supposed to be de-
coded. In the minds of our classmates they could mean
anything you like, but no decodification other than the
following was acknowledged: Valentina Dmitrievna
Kaln—the human-arquebus. It's funny, but Kaln didn't
look any more like a human-arquebus than like a watertower, but if anyone were ever to ask you to give her,
Vodokachka, a more precise nickname—although it's incomprehensible why and to whom it could occur to do
such a thing—you would certainly fail to find one. Even
though the teacher didn't look in the least like a watertower—you would say—still in some inexplicable way
she recalls the word itself, the combination of letters of
which it is made up (was made up, will be made up)—V,
O, D, O, K, A, Ch, K, A.

CHAPTER FOUR

SKEERLÝ

Now allow me to clear my throat, look you straight in
the eye and pinpoint one detail from your cover letter.
In it you said something to the effect that Acatov himself had reacted very favorably to our collection, but I
don't recall us ever talking to him on this theme—generally we never did actually meet him, we saw him only
from afar, usually through the crack in his fence, but
how we dreamed of one day walking down Acatov's garden path, knocking on the door to his house, and—when
the old man opened—of saying hello and introducing
ourself: student of your daughter so-and-so, a beginning
entomologist, would like to discuss a few problems with
you and so forth. But not once did we dare to knock on
the door to his house, inasmuch as—or was it for another reason—a big dog lived in the garden. Listen, I don't
like it when you call my collection—*our* collection, no
one gave you any such right, I assembled my collection
alone, and if we should ever merge into one, our acts
identical, this act is not going to have any relation to
butterflies; so there, now about the talk with Acatov:
it's true, I was not deceiving the Academy, I really did
talk to him. One summer, at the dacha, on a Sunday
when father had had us sitting since morning rewriting
the lead articles from newspapers, so that we would
have a better understanding of internal and external *po-
lyticks*. I decided that you would get along fine here
without me. I waited for the moment: you put aside the
pen, turned away to the window and began examining the

structure of the lilac flower—I left the table noiselessly, put on father's cap—it was hanging on a peg in the hall— and took a cane—it belonged to one of our relatives, who had it about five years earlier. On the station platform five years earlier, in the evening. Our mother to the relative: I hope you had a good rest here with us, don't squash the strawberries, wash them, greetings to Elena Mikhailovna and Vanyusha, come together, pay no attention, he's just nervous, works a lot, scads of cases, gets tired, but you know basically he's kind, yes soft and kind deep down, but sometimes he does lose control, so do come, do come, only don't argue with him, wait, where's your cane, oh, how unfortunate, what's to be done. Anxiously. Let's go back, there'll be another electric. The relative: come on, it's not worth it, don't worry, if it were an umbrella it would make sense, it's getting ready to rain, thanks for the berries, I appreciate it and we'll come again for the cane, just think, a cane is rubbish, as they say, happiness doesn't depend on canes, so long, here it comes. However, since that time the relative hasn't come, and the cane was on the veranda until the very day when I took it and set off to the neighboring settlement to visit the naturalist Acatov: toock-toock (the dog runs up and sniffs me, but today I'm not afraid of it), toock-toock. But no one opens the door to the house. And then again: toock-toock. But no one responds. You walk around the house on the thick grass, you peer through the windows to check and see if the house does have the large wall clock with the chimes, which by your reckoning definitely has to be there, so that it can cut dacha time into chunks with its pendulum—but all of the windows were curtained. Fire barrels are dug into the ground at the corners of the house—these are filled with rusty water and some sort of lackadaisical insects live in them. Only one barrel is completely empty, it contains neither water nor insects, and a happy thought occurs to you: to fill it with your shout. Long do you stand there, bent over the dark cylindrical abyss, running over in your selective memory the words which best reverberate in the emptiness of empty chambers. Such words are not numerous, but there are some. For example, if—thrown out of class— you are running through the school corridor when classes are in progress, and deep in your core a desire is born to shout in such a way that your shout will freeze the blood of your mendacious and debauched teachers, so that interrupting their speeches in mid-word they will swallow their tongues and be transformed—to the amusement of the idiot-students—into pillars of chalk, or pillarettes (depending on their height), you can't think up anything more delightful than the cry: bacilli! What do you think, mentor Savl?

Dear student and comrade so-and-so, whether sitting on the windowsill in the restroom, standing at the map in front of the class with a pointer in my hand, playing preference with a few colleagues in the teacher's room or in the boiler-room, I have rarely been witness to the kind of ultramundane terror which your mad cry caused the pedagogues and the students, and even the deaf-mute stoker, for it was said somewhere by someone: deaf man, the time will come and you will hear. Did I not see the capacious shovel with which he tirelessly hurls coal into the insatiable, hellish furnaces during the cold seasons, did I not—I ask—see the capacious shovel fall out of the hands of the miserable old man when the time of your cry came, the time for the deaf to hear, and he, turning to me with his face besooted and horrible in the dancing flecks and reflections of the flame, his ulcerated and unshaven face, he acquired for a moment the gift of speech, and right after you, shaking his hung-over head, he shouted—no, he bellowed the same word: bacilli, bacilli, bacilli. And so vast was his anger, and so powerful his passion, that the fire in the furnaces was extinguished by his bellow. And did I not see the teachers of their special school, who are used to a lot, turn pale and the cards, the playing cards that they were holding in their hands turned into leaves of a forest willow, which has the ability to draw out pus, and they, the pedagogues, moaned in horror. And did I not see the faces of your fellow pupils, which are infinitely obtuse anyway, become even more obtuse from your shout, and all of them opened their mouths—even the most capable of them and those who seemed almost normal, suddenly opened their mouths in an answering, albeit mute, cry, and all the dolts of the specschool howled in a monstrous, deafening chorus, and sick yellow saliva flowed from all these frightened psychopathic mouths. So don't ask me in vain what I think about your fierce and spellbinding shout. O, with what rapturous effort and pain I would shout, if it were my lot to shout even half of your shout! But it isn't my lot, how weak I am, your mentor, before your talent, given from on high. So shout then—most capable of the capable, shout for yourself and for me, and for all of us, deceived, defamed, dishonored and stupefied, for us, the idiots and holy fools, the defectives and schizoids, for the educators and the educatees, for all those to whom it has not been given and whose salivating mouths have already been shut, or will soon be shut, for all those who have been innocently muted, or are being muted, tongues torn out—shout, intoxicated and intoxicating: bacilli, bacilli, bacilli!

In the emptiness of empty chambers there are a few other words which will reverberate fairly well too, but having gone over them in your memory, you realize that not one of the ones known to you suits this situation, for in order to fill the empty Acatov barrel, a uniquely special new word is essential, or several words, inasmuch as the situation strikes you as exceptional. Yes, you say to yourself, here we need a shout of a new type. Some ten minutes pass. There are a lot of grasshoppers in the Acatovs' garden. They hop through the warm amber grass, and each hop is swift and unexpected, like a shot from a specschool slingshot. The fire barrel beckons you with its emptiness: this emptiness, and the stillness abiding in the garden and the house and the barrel, soon became unbearable for you, a person who is energetic, decisive and efficient. That's why you don't want to reflect further on what to shout into the barrel—you shout the first thing that comes into your head: I'm Nymphea, Nymphea!—you shout. And the barrel overflows with your incomparable voice, releasing its surfeit into the beautiful dacha sky, towards the tops of the pines—and the voice rolls over the stuffy dacha mansards and attics which abound in all kinds of junk, over the volleyball courts where no one ever plays, over the hutches containing thousands of fattened rabbits, over garages redolent of gasoline, over verandas with their toy-bestrewn floors and smoking kerosene lamps, over the gardens and heather barrens surrounding the dacha settlements: eya, eya-eya-eya-yayayaya-a-a! Your father, resting in the hammock in his yard, gives a start and awakens: who's shouting there, damn him, mother, I heard your spawn bellowing somewhere on the pond, didn't I tell him to do some work. Father rushes into the house and looks into our room. He sees you sitting at the desk diligently—the diligence is expressed in the way you bend your closely cropped head to the side and contort your back absurdly, as if you had been smashed apart, yes, as if someone had thrown you onto the rocks from a lofty cliff, and then come and smashed you some more, using the adjustable pincers which clamp red hot ingots—writing. But father sees only what he sees, he doesn't know, doesn't guess, that it is only you sitting at the desk, while at this moment the other you is standing beside Acatov's barrel, revelling in your soaring shout. Looking around, you notice by the shed a rather old man in a torn, white robe, like a doctor's. The man has a rope for a belt, there is a cocked hat of yellowed paper on his head and on his feet—look carefully at what he has on his feet, that is, how he is shod—and on his feet— I can't see very well, after all he is relatively far away— on his feet, it seems, he has overshoes. Maybe you're wrong, maybe they're sneakers instead of overshoes? The grass is too high, if it were cut down I could make a more definite statement about his footwear, but this way—you can't make it out, but hold it, now I see: they're galoshes. Well, well, now look at that, I don't think that man has any pants, I don't mean that in general he doesn't have any, but that specifically at this moment he hasn't any, in other words, he's not wearing any pants. Not so unusual, it's summer now, and aren't a robe and galoshes sufficient for summer; wearing pants, if you're going to put on a robe too, would be hot, inasmuch as a robe is practically an overcoat, to some degree it's an overcoat, an overcoat with no lining, or the other way around, a lining with no overcoat, or just a light coat. And if the robe is white, medical, it can also be called a light medical coat, and if the white robe doesn't belong to a physician, but, let's suppose, to a scientist, boldly call this robe a light scholarly duster, or a laboratory jacket. You're explaining it all correctly, but we still don't know whom the robe belongs to, the robe on the man who is wearing the galoshes, or more simply: who is it standing there by the shed so old and quiet—wearing the paper cocked hat and white duster, with galoshes on his bare feet, who is he? You mean you haven't recognized him, it's Acatov himself, who once declared to all the world that strange swellings—the galls —are caused by such-and-such, which was extremely precipitous on his part, even though as you see justice conquered and after such-and-such and such-and-such, which it has long been unacceptable to mention, the academician lives quietly in his dacha, and you, who have turned up here for a talk, are filling his fire barrel with your shout. And the academician, who in his intent wariness resembles a stooped little tree, asks you in a high-pitched and agitated human voice: who are you, I'm afraid of you, are there a lot of you? Be not afraid, sir,—you say, trying to be as suave as possible in your manner and speech,—I am quite alone, absolutely, and if anyone else turns up, don't believe him when he says he is me too, it's not like that at all, and obviously you can guess what the trouble is; when he comes I'll hide in the logpile, and you, you lie to him, lie, I implore you, say you don't know anything, no one was here, he'll look around a bit and then take off, and we shall continue our talk at leisure. But why were you shouting into the barrel like that,—Acatov inquires curiously,—what prompted you? Putting his palm to his ear, he adds: but talk louder, my hearing's not so good. Sir, allow me to approach you through this high grass. Come on, I don't seem to be afraid of you anymore. Hello. Hello. Dear Arcady Arcadievich, the essence of the matter is that I catch butterflies. Ah-a, butterflies, and have you caught many? Snow butterflies or in general?—you answer the question with a question. Snow, naturally,—says the academician. Such-and-such a number,—you say,—I am collecting a collection, at the present time it includes the genera such-and-such and such-and-such. A-ah, how marvelous,—Acatov says in surprise,—but why so loud, I can't stand shouting, collect quietly, for God's sake. His face, wrinkled and tawny, like a pear in compote, goes pale from irritation, However,—he continues,—you'll go on shouting anyway, no matter what happens, I know, it's the fate of your generation, you're young, after all, from the looks of you you're not more than sixteen. Oh no, sir, you are in error, I'm way past twenty, I'm thirty, you see, after all, I have a hat and a cane. So, all right, listen—Acatov interrupts you,—may I consult with you? Animatedly. At your service, sir, I'm all ears. The other day,—the academician looks around and lowers his voice almost to a whisper,—I invented a new invention, follow me, it's in the shed, I've locked up the house and live in the shed now, it's easier, you take up less space. It was an ordinary shed, the sort of which there are many in our dacha locale: the ceiling is the reverse side of the roof, the walls are made of unplaned boards, as is the floor. What did you see inside the shed when you walked in and took off your footwear and left your cane, so as not to track in dirt? A table, a chair, a bed, and a pile of books on the windowsill are what I saw there. And up over all of this, squinting from the white winter sun—wearing a raccoon coat—snowdrifts and snowswept forest in the background—ra-

diant, soaring, reigning supreme—is your incomparable
Veta, teacher of biology, botany, anatomy—and on her
amazing face, which was overwhelming, like a stifling
noose, there was nothing which would remember you or
which spoke to you one-to-one, O, Nymphea, her face
was the face for anyone who ever looked upon it, and it
was promised to many—but can it be that in that terrible, irreversible multitude, indistinguishable in the
darkness of hotel rooms and apartments, can it be that
there was a place for you among them too, you, the de-
ficient dolt from the special school, you who, in a fren-
zy of tenderness and ecstasy, turned into the flower
which you yourself had picked, can it be that you, who
desired it infinitely more times than any of the others,
that you too were among them?! Lord sir what an astonishing photograph she is like alive here that is no I'm
mistaken a stylistic mistake I wanted to say like real like
during class beautiful and inaccessible who took that
when why I don't know anything some scoundrel with a
camera who is he what is his relation to her here or else-
where a legion of questions. Now then, I invented a certain invention: you see, an ordinary stick, eh? it would
seem. Yes yes it would seem sir it would seem I come
here fairly often in the winter too but I come alone
without any of your photographers I don't have any acquaintances with cameras, she should it would seem
have informed me that such and such and so and so and
such and such and so and so and she was going to the
Land of the Nightjar by car with a certain engineer a degree candidate an art historian a director a book-keeper
dammit she got photographed against a snowdrift background at the dacha she could have said something like
we didn't even drop in so as not to have to clear the
snow from the paths we walked for half an hour and re-

turned to town after all I would have believed it. But
that is a most profound misapprehension, observe,
youth, I move it from one vertical position to another
vertical position, or to put it another way—I turn it upside down, and now what is revealed to our astonished
gaze? I am howling sir howling for I have been betrayed
I Nymphea 'tis I bald weak flatfooted with a high forehead like on a real cretin and a face old from doubts
look I am absolutely awful my nose is all covered with
disgusting blackheads and my lips puffed forward and
flattened as if I were born of a duck and it makes no difference that once upon a time in the flower of my crucial age I learned to play on a mother-of-pearl three
quarters Barcarolle that didn't help me nevertheless it is
excruciatingly painful. We see an ordinary nail, hammered into the top of our stick, it was hammered in
head first, and its pointed end is staring at us like a
deadly steel stinger,—but have no fear, youth, I will not
aim it in your direction, I will not cause you any piercing wound, but I will direct it at any paper which pollutes my dacha lawn, and I will stab it with my unique
invention, and when they, the papers, are collected in
sufficient quantity on the tip, I will remove them from
the nail, as a *bogatyr* removes the enemies he has run
through from his lance, and I will cast them into the
abyss of the garbage pit which is in the corner of my
garden—and that is my invention, which allows me, an
old man, not to abandon the ranks of unbending war-
riors: because of my ailments I cannot bend down and
pick up a piece of paper, but thanks to an ordinary stick
with a nail I fight for cleanliness without bending; so
then, inasmuch as you seem to me an uncommonly decent person, I will allow myself to ask you advice, to
wit: is there, in your view, any sense in taking out a pa-

tent and patenting this stick?

Restraining the indignant birdlike shriek which is surg-
ing in your tonsillitic throat between unremoved glands:
dear Arcady Arcadievich, I have the greatest respect
for your invention, however, at the moment I need
your advice—and even more than you need mine,
yours is a question of ambition, while mine—excuse me,
I am talking like in a novel and so I feel somehow embarrassed and ridiculous—my question to you is one of
an entire life. Hold it, hold it, I'm starting to be afraid
of your presence again, do you really intend to ask me a-
bout something important, let me sit down, do you really
need something from an aging, half-blind dacha resident,
and after all, who are you to be asking me questions,
and stop shouting in my beautiful barrel too. I won't do
it any more, sir, I'm prepared to explain everything, I
live in the neighborhood, at my parents' dacha, and it's
so beautiful around here that an unpleasant thing happened to me once, but about that later, the main thing
is that I hate a certain woman, a Jewess, Sheina Tinbergen, she is a witch, she works as the assistant principal in
our school, she sings about the cat, well you probably
learned the song when you were a little boy: tra-ta-ta,
tra-ta-tat, Cat was looking for Tomcat, wants to wed Cat
Catovich,—oh, by the way, remember what the cat's
name was, sir? A moment, youth,—Acatov rubs his pulsating blue temples, straining his memory,—the tomcat's
name was Trifon Petrovich. Right, however, that's not
the thing that interests me either, to the devil with Trifon Petrovich, he's a common excavator, let's talk about
Sheina herself instead. Imagine her, the lame crone,
moving through the vast empty hall dancing (every oth-

er light is off, the second shift has run home, and only I
have been left after school to do the next day's lessons),
and as I stand at the end of the hall or go forward to
meet her, holding a polite bow of the head at the ready,
I get even more nauseated than in my sleep after injections. No, she never did me any harm, and I talk to her
only about the record player; and although it hasn't
worked for a hundred years and there is no way it
should play, when Sheina takes it into her room and
turns it on, it plays like new. More precisely, it doesn't
play, but talks: the old lady spins a record of her late
husband's voice, he hanged himself because she was be-
traying him with Sorokin in the garage, or no, Sorokin
hanged himself, and her husband, Yakov, he poisoned
himself. I see,—responds Acatov,—but what sort of text
is recorded there, on the record? Ah-a, there now, that's
just it, the main thing—there, on the record, the late Yakov reads *Skeerlý*. Forgive me, youth, I've never heard
of that before. A nightmarish thing, sir, I won't even repeat...but, briefly it goes like this: you see, *Skeerlý*—is
the name of a fairytale, a horrific children's fairytale
about a bear, I can't exactly...basically, in the woods
there lives a bear, it would seem nothing out of the ordinary, it would seem! But the trouble is that this bear
is an invalid, a cripple, he's minus one leg, but how all
this happened is a mystery, all that's known is that the
leg is gone, a hind leg I think, and in its place the bear
has a wooden prosthetic device. He, the bear, cut it out
of the trunk of a linden tree with an ax, and when the
bear walks through the woods the screech of the prosthetic device is distantly audible, it screeches as in the
name of the fairytale: *skeerlý, skeerlý*. Yakov does a
good imitation of the sound, he had a screechy voice, he
worked as a pharmacist. Another character in the fairy-

tale is a little girl, who is apparently made of chalk, she's
afraid of the bear and never leaves home, but one day—
the devil knows how this happened—the bear pounces
on her anyway and carries her off in a special—wicker, I
think—basket to his lair and he does something with her
there, exactly what is unknown, it's not explained in the
fairytale, it ends with that, it's terrible, sir, one doesn't
know what to think. When I recall *Skeerlý*—even though
I try not to remember it, it's better not to remember—it
occurs to me that the girl might not be a girl, but a certain woman acquaintance of mine, with whom I have
close relations, you understand, of course, you and I are
no longer children, and it occurs to me that the bear is
not a bear either, but some man I don't know, a man,
and I can almost see him doing something there in a hotel room with my acquaintance, and the accursed *skeerlý* resounds repeatedly, and I get sick with hate for the
sound, and I suppose that I would kill that man if I
knew who he was. Thinking about the *Skeerlý* fairytale is painful for me, sir, but since I rarely do my homework, they often keep me after school to do the lessons
for the next day and the day before, and after I'm left
alone in the classroom, I usually go out to take a walk in
the hall, and when I go out I encounter Tinbergen there,
and when I see her drawing nigh, with a crippled but also sort of merry, dancing gait, and I hear the melancholy—like the call of the lonely nightjar—squeak of her
prosthetic device, then, spare me, sir,—I cannot help
thinking of the fairytale *Skeerlý,* because the sound is
exactly the same as the one in the hotel, and she herself,
the graybearded witch with the sleepy face of an old
woman who has died but then been forced to awaken
and live, she, in the crepuscular light of the deserted hall
with its shimmering parquet floor, she herself is the

Skeerlý, the embodiment of all that is saddest in this story of the little girl, although to this day I can't figure out what was going on, and why it was all like this, and not some other way.

Yes, youth, yes, I have no difficulty understanding you. Thoughtfully. Something similar happened to me once, something of the sort happened in my youth, of course I don't remember what it was specifically, but to one degree or another everything was like your case. But— Acatov suddenly asks—what school are you in, I can't make sense of this, after all you are already past twenty, you are thirty, what school? The special, sir. Ah, so that's it,—says the academician (you both leave the shed and you look back at her photograph for the last time), —and what is the specialty of your school? By the way, if it is difficult or awkward for you, or if it's a secret,— don't answer, I'm not forcing you, there is scarcely any need for your answer, as there isn't for any question, we're talking quite casually, after all this is not an examination at Oxford, understand me properly, I was simply curious, I asked just to ask, so to speak, as part of the delirium, any of us has a right to pose any question and anyone has a right not to answer any question, but, unfortunately, here—here and there, everywhere, there are still a lot of people who haven't assimilated this truth, *they* made me answer every question they asked, *they*, in the snow-covered...But I'm not *them*,—continues Acatov, whipping shut his white scientific duster, open and shut—and don't answer me if you don't feel like it, we'll sit silently instead, look around, listen to the song of summer, etc., no, no, don't answer, I don't want to know anything about you, as it is you've come to seem so *sympatico* to me, that cane and hat go with your face astonishingly well, only the hat is a trifle large, you probably bought it to grow into. Yes, precisely, to grow into; but I would like to answer, there is nothing awkward about it at all: the school where I study specializes in mental defectives, it's a school for fools, all of us who study there are abnormal, each in his own way. Just a moment, I've heard something about just such an institution, someone of my acquaintance works there, but who exactly? Perhaps you mean Veta Arcadievna, she works in our school, handling such-and-such and such-and-such. Well, of course! Veta, Veta, Veta, coquetta and curvetta,—Acatov sang, without any melody, absent-mindedly snapping his fingers. What a wondrous song, sir! Rubbish, youth, a family jingle, a trifle from earlier years, innocent of meaning or melody, forget it, I fear it will debauch you. Never, never,—anxiously. What? I said I'll never forget it, I really like it, I can't do anything; yes, there is a certain difference in age between us, but, how can I define this best, formulate it—there's more which unites us than disunites us, you ask what it is I'm talking about, but in my opinion I am expressing myself with utmost clarity, Arcady Arcadievich. The common factor to which I just alluded is an attraction to all that you and I as men of science call living nature, everything that grows and flies, flowers and swims—in fact this is the purpose of my visit to you—not only butterflies, although I (my word of honor) have been catching them since childhood and won't ever stop catching them until my right arm dries up and drops off, like the arm of the artist Repin, and I came to you not in order to shout into the barrel, although I am inclined to see exalted meaning in this occupation, and I will never give up shouting into barrels and with my shout I will fill the

emptiness of empty chambers until I have filled them
full, so it won't be excruciatingly painful, however, I am
digressing again, to be brief: I love your daughter, sir,
and am prepared to do anything for her happiness.
Moreover, I intend to marry Veta Arcadievna as soon as
circumstances allow. Triumphantly, with dignity and a
slight bow.

Poor Acatov, this was so unexpected, I'm afraid
you upset the old man a bit, surely you should have prepared him better for this kind of conversation, for
example, you could have written two or three warning
letters, informed him of your arrival in advance, called
him or something like that, I'm afraid that you behaved
tactlessly, and moreover, it's dishonorable to do what
you did: you had no right to ask for Veta Arcadievna's
hand alone, without me, I will never forget her either
and in some inexplicable way everything that grows and
flies joins me to her too, we too, she and I, also have in
common everything that grows and flies, you know
that, but naturally you didn't tell Acatov anything
about me, about the one who is much better and more
deserving than you, and for that I hate you and I'm going to tell you how a certain person, indistinguishable in
the obscurity of a hotel corridor, leads our Veta to his
room, and there: there. No wait I'm not guilty at all
you were staring at the lilac petal you were rewriting the
article I left my father's house by chance I didn't dream
I would succeed nothing might have worked out I only
wanted to see Acatov about the butterflies I would certainly have told him everything about you and your vast
superhuman feeling which I you know this yourself
which I so respect I would have told him that it wasn't

just me alone but that there are two of us and I did tell him about that in the beginning I would have said sir yes I love your daughter but there is a person who being incomparably more deserving and better than me loves her a hundred times more fervently, and although I am grateful to you for a positive resolution of the question, it is obvious that this other person should be invited too, undoubtedly he will appeal to you even more, if you want I'll call him, he's here, not far, in the neighboring settlement, he had intended to come, but was somewhat busy, he has some work, some urgent copying (what is he, a copyist? no, no, of course not, it's just that there are people, or more accurately, one person, who makes him copy things out of newpapers, he has to do that, otherwise it wouldn't be very easy for him to live in that house), and besides that, he got to staring at the lilac petals, and I decided not to distract him, let me call him,—I would have said to the academician, if the resolution of the question had turned out to be positive. Do you mean Acatov refused you? Only you better tell me the whole truth, don't lie, or I'll hate you and complain to our mentor Savl: dead or alive, he never put up with sneakiness or bias. I swear to you by the name which flames in our hearts that from this day forth I, student of the special school so-and-so, nicknamed Nymphea Alba, a man of exalted aspirations and ideals, fighter for eternal human joy, hater of callousness, egotism and sadness, no matter where manifested, I, heir to the finest traditions and utterances of our pedagogue Savl, I swear to you that my lips will never be besmirched by a single word of falsehood, and I will be pure as a drop of dew born on the banks of our enchanting Lethe in the early morn—born and flying to moisten the brow of our little chalk girl Veta, who is sleeping in the garden so many years in the future. O, speak on! how I love thy utterances, full of power and eloquence, inspiration and passion, bravery and intellect, speak, hurrying and swallowing the words, we still have to discuss many other problems, and there is so little time, probably no more than a second, if I understand correctly the meaning of the aforementioned word.

Then Acatov (no, no, I myself figured that he would laugh, make fun of my hat, or rather father's, and of the fact that I'm not very handsome, more than that, ugly, and despite this I was asking for the hand of such an incomparable woman) simply looked at me, lowered his head and stood there pondering something, most likely our conversation, my confession. If up to my last words he had looked like a stooped little tree, during this time —right before my very eyes—he came to look like a stooped little tree which has dried up and ceased to feel even the touch of the grass and the wind: Acatov was pondering. Meanwhile I was reading the newpaper headlines on his cocked hat and examining his wide, loose scientist's duster—out of which, like a clapper from a bell, hung Acatov's thin and veiny legs, the legs of a thinker and an ambitious person. I liked his duster, and I thought that I would have worn the same kind with pleasure, if I had an opportunity to buy one. I would have worn it everywhere: in the garden, in the orchard, at school and at home, in the shade of the trees across the river, and in the long distance postal *diligence* when out the window one could see rain and villages floating past, covered with straw, ruffled up like wet hens, and when my soul is wounded by human sufferings. But until—until I become an engineer—I don't have duster, I

wear ordinary pants with cuffs, made out of hand-me-
downs from my prosecutor father, with a four-but-
toned, double-breasted jacket and shoes with metallic
buckles—in school and at home. Sir, why are you silent,
can I have offended you somehow, or do you doubt the
sincerity of my words and feelings for Veta Arcadievna?
Believe me, I would never lie to you, a man, the father
of the woman I adore, don't doubt that, please, and
don't be silent, otherwise I will turn and leave, to fill
with my shout the emptiness of our dacha settlements—
a shout about your refusal. O no, youth, don't leave, I
will be lonely, you know, I have no hesitation about
accepting your every word on faith, and if Veta agrees I
will have no objection. Have a chat with her, talk to her,
after all you haven't opened up to her yet, I guess she
doesn't suspect a thing yet, and what can we decide
without her agreement, you understand? We can't decide anything. Thoughtfully with difficulty selecting
words selecting words seeking them with his eyes be-
forehand in the dry grass where somehow dissatisfied
grasshoppers are hopping and every one is wearing a
green dress coat conductors selecting words in the grass.
Sir, I will not conceal the fact that indeed I have not yet
had a talk with Veta Arcadievna, there simply hasn't
been time; although we meet fairly often, our talks usually touch on other things, we speak mostly about matters
of science, we have a lot in common, that's as it should
be: two young biologists, two natural scientists, two
scholars, who *sew promise*. But aside from that—on both
sides—something quite special is maturing—has matured
already—the communality of interests is being supple-
mented by another communality. I understand you perfectly, youth, when I was your age something similar
happened to me, to me and a certain woman, we were

naive, good-looking and we lost our heads. Dear Arcady Arcadievich, I intend to make one other simultaneous confession to you. You see, I'm not absolutely sure that Veta Arcadievna likes me as a man, it's possible that the communality of which I spoke is, from your daughter's point of view, based only on philanthropy, what I mean is that she loves me only as a human being, I don't insist this is so I'm just hypothesizing out of a fear of seeming ridiculous, I wouldn't want to find myself in an awkward position. But inasmuch as you are Veta Arcadievna's father and you know her tastes and character far better than I, I make so bold as to ask you: in your opinion am I handsome enough that Veta Arcadievna will like me as a man too, somehow I'm vaguely worried that I'll seem somehow uninteresting to her. Look, examine me carefully, is this so in reality, or am I just imagining it. Are my features so ugly that even the most elevated of all feelings attainable by man would not improve my face and my build? But for God's sake don't lie, I beg of you. What nonsense,—answers Acatov,—you're quite normal, quite, I imagine there are a lot of young women who would agree to go through life arm and arm with you—and who would never regret it. The one thing I would advise you as a scientist is to use your handkerchief more often. Purely arbitrary I know, but how it ennobles, distinguishes, and lifts a personality over the muck of circumstances and your contemporaries. True, at your age I didn't know this either, but then I did know a lot of other things, I was getting ready to defend my first dissertation and marry the woman who subsequently became Veta's mother. By that time I was already working, I had worked a lot and had earned a lot —and you? Yes, by the way, how do you propose to arrange your family life, on what basis, are you aware of the kind of responsibility which lies on you as the head of the family? that's very important. Sir, I could hardly help anticipating that you would ask such a question, and I was ready for it long before I came to visit you. I understand perfectly well what you mean, I know everything already, because I read a lot. I found out a few things even before the conversation with our geographer Norvegov, but after we met him in the restroom one day and had a frank discussion about everything, almost everything became comprehensible to me. Moreover, Savl Petrovich gave me a book to read, and when I read it I understood every last thing. What is it that you understood?—asks Acatov,—share it with me.

Savl Petrovich is sitting on the windowsill with his back to the painted glass, and his face to the stalls; the bare bottoms of his feet rest on the radiator, and his knees are pulled up so that it's easy for the teacher to rest his chin on them. Ex libris, book after book. Staring at the stall doors, all scribbled with hooligan words: how much that is vulgar, how much that is ugly we have in our restroom, how impoverished our feelings for woman are, how cynical we are, we the people of the special school. We don't know how to love tenderly and powerfully, no —we don't know how. But dear Savl Petrovich,—standing before him wearing white canvas slippers, on the malodorous tile, I object—in spite of not even knowing what to think or how to calm you, the best teacher in the world, I consider it essential to remind you of the following: after all, don't you, you yourself, you personally—don't you love one of my fellow classmates powerfully and tenderly, the chalk girl Rosa. O Rosa

Windova,—you said to her one day,—dear girl, sepulchral flower, how I desire your untouched body! And you also whispered: on one of the nights of a summer embarrassed by its own beauty I await you in the little house with the windvane beyond the blue river. And also: what happens to us that night will be like a flame consuming an icy waste, like a starfall reflected in a fragment of a mirror which has suddenly fallen from its frame forewarning its owner of imminent death, it will be like a shepherd's reed pipe and like music which is yet unwritten. Come to me, Rosa Windova, isn't your old teacher, striding across the valleys of nonexistence and the tablelands of anguish dear to you. And also: come, to ease the trembling in your loins, and to soften my sadness. But, my dear fellow, I did say or perhaps only will say those or similar words to her, but since when have words ever meant anything? Only don't think that I was being hypocritical (will be hypocritical), that's not characteristic of me, I am incapable of that, but there are times when—and some day you will be convinced of this yourself—times when a man lies, without suspecting it. He is sure he's telling the truth, and sure that he's doing what he promised. This happens most often in childhood, but then in adolescence too, and then in one's youth and old age. This is what happens to man when he is in a state of passion, for passion is like unto madness. Thanks, I didn't know that, I'll mull it over, I had only a suspicion of that—of that and a lot of other things. You understand, I'm worried by a certain circumstance, and today, here, after classes, when it's damp and windy outside and the second shift of future engineers has gone home, finishing off the smushed sandwiches from their briefcases (the sandwiches have to be eaten, in order not to disappoint their

patient mothers), I intend to impart to you, Savl Petrovich, certain information which, probably, will strike
you as improbable, it might make you disillusioned with
me. I have long intended to ask your advice, but I kept
putting off the conversation every day: too many quiz-
zes, much too much tiresome homework, and even if I
don't do it, the awareness that I should depresses me.
It's exhausting, Savl Petrovich. But now the time has
come when I want to and can inform you. Dear teacher!
in forest cottages lost in the fields, in long distance postal *diligences*, at bonfires the smoke of which creates
coziness, on the banks of Lake Erie or—I don't remember
precisely—Baskunchak, on the ships of the Vigel class,
on the roofs of European omnibuses and in the Geneva
Bureau of Tourist Information and Better Family Living, in the thicket of heather and religious sects, in parks
and gardens where there are no places to sit on the
benches, behind a stein of beer in the mountain inn *At
the Cat*, on the front lines of the first and second world
wars, tearing across the green Yukon ice on dogsleds,
wracked by gold fever, and in other places—here and
there, dear teacher, I have pondered what woman is, and
how to behave if the time ever came to act, I pondered
the nature of convention, and the peculiarities of the
fleshly in humans. I have thought about what love is,
and passion, and eternity, what it means to give in to desire and what it means not to give in to it, what lust and
carnality are; I have reflected on the details of copula-
tion, dreaming of it, for from books and other sources I
knew that it gave pleasure. But the trouble is that in
none of these places, or anywhere else, did I once in my
whole life happen to *be with,* or to put it more vulgar-
ly,—*sleep with* a woman. I simply don't know what it's
like, I would probably be able to, but I can't imagine

how to begin all that, or, mainly, with whom. Obviously some woman is necessary, and it would be best if she were someone you've known for a long time, who would prompt you in case something went wrong, in case something didn't work out right away; you need a very kind woman, I've hear it's best if she's a widow, yes, for some reason they say a widow, but I don't know a single widow, except Tinbergen, but after all she's the assistant principal, and she has Trifon Petrovich (but only I have the record player), and I don't know any other women— only Veta Arcadievna, but I wouldn't want to with her, for I love her and intend to marry her, those are different things, I absolutely never think—I force myself not to—about her as a woman, I realize that she is too beautiful, too upstanding, to permit herself anything with me before the wedding—isn't that so? True, I also know some girls from class, but if I started courting one of them, for example, the girl who died not long ago from meningitis and for whose wreath we took up a collection, I'm afraid Veta Arcadievna wouldn't like it very much, that sort of thing gets noticed immediately: in a small collective, in view of one's fellow students and the teachers—it would be obvious in no time, Veta would realize that I intended to betray her, and she would have a perfectly reasonable grievance, and then our marriage might be upset, all hopes would collapse, and we have nurtured them so long! A few times, Savl Petrovich, I have tried to strike up the acquaintance of women on the streets, but apparently I don't know the approach, I'm not elegant, my clothes are ugly. In short, nothing came of it, they shooed me away, but I won't conceal that one day I almost managed to strike up an acquaintance with an interesting young woman, and although I can't describe her, inasmuch as I don't remember her face or her voice or her walk, I will go so far as to assert that she was extraordinarily beautiful, like most women.

Where did I meet her? Probably in the movies or the park, or, most likely, in the post office. The woman was sitting there behind the window and cancelling envelopes and postcards. It was the All-Union Pan-Universal Day for the Defense of the Nightjar. That morning I had promised myself I would spend the whole day collecting stamps. True, I didn't have a single stamp at home, but I did find a matchbox label with a picture of a bird which all of us should defend on it. I realized that this was the nightjar, and set off for the post office so they would cancel it for me, and I took an immediate liking to the woman sitting there behind the window. You told our teacher that you can't describe the woman; in that case at least describe the day on which your encounter occurred, tell a story about what it was like outside, and what the weather was like, if, naturally, this doesn't put you out any. No, no, there's nothing particularly complicated about that, and I'd be happy to meet your request. That morning the clouds were scudding across the sky more swiftly than usual, and I saw white cotton batting faces appearing and dissolving in each other. They were floating and colliding with each other, their color mutating from gold to lilac. Many of those whom we call passers-by, smiling and squinting from the diffused but still powerful sunlight, were observing the shifting clouds just as I was, and like me they sensed the approach of the future, heralds of which were these *untutored* clouds. Don't correct me, I'm not mistaken. When I go to school or the post office for them to cancel the matchbox label with the picture of the nightjar it is easy for me to find, both in my surroundings and in my memory, things, phenomena—and I enjoy thinking about them—which it would be impossible either to give as homework or to memorize. No one is capable of memorizing: the sound of rain, the aroma of night violets, premonition of nonexistence, the flight of the bumblebee, Brownian motion and many other things. All of this can be studied, but *memorized*—never. In the same category are rainclouds and stormclouds bursting with turbulence and future tempests. Besides the cloudy sky that morning, there was the street, cars with people in them were going by, and it was really hot. I could hear the uncut grass growing on the lawns, baby carriages screeching in the courtyards, the clanging of garbage can tops, elevator doors slamming in the entranceways, and in the schoolyard the first shift students were running invigorating wind sprints headlong: the wind bore me the beating of their hearts. I heard from somewhere very far, perhaps from the other side of town, a blind man wearing dark glasses the lenses of which reflected the dusty foliage of the weeping acacias and the scudding clouds and the smoke creeping from the brick stack of the offset printing factory, ask people walking by to help him across the street, but no one had time and no one stopped. I heard two old men in a kitchen— the window onto the sidestreet was open—chatting (the subject was the New Orleans fire of 1882), cooking meat and cabbage soup: it was the day when the pensions were paid; I heard the bubbling in their pot, and the bookkeeper counting out cubic centimeters of expended gas. I heard, in the other apartments of this and neighboring buildings, the pounding of printing and sewing machines, the darning of socks, and magazine files being leafed through, I heard people blowing noses and laughing, shaving and singing, closing their eyelids or, from lack of anything to do, drumming their fingers on tautly stretched glass, imitating the sound of slanting rainfall. I heard the silence of deep apartments whose owners had gone to work and would return only towards evening, or who wouldn't return because they had gone into eternity; I heard the rhythmical rocking of pendula in wall clocks and the tick of various brands of watches. I heard the kisses and whispers and close breathing of men and women unknown to me—you will never understand anything about them—doing *skeerlý*, and I envied them, and dreamed of meeting a woman who would allow me to do the same with her. I was walking along the street reading, in order, the signs and advertisements on the buildings, although I long since knew them by heart, I had memorized every word on the street. Left side. REPAIR OF CHILDREN'S CONSTRICTORS. In the show-window—a poster boy dreaming of becoming an engineer, he is holding a large model of a glider in his hand. POLAR REGION FURS. In the show-window a white bear, a skin with open maw. MOVIE-LEAFFALL-THEATER. The day will come and we will come here together: Veta and I; which row do you prefer?—I'll ask Veta,—the third or the eighteenth? I don't know,—she'll say,—it makes no difference, pick any. But then add: but I do like to be close, take the tenth or seventh, if it's not too expensive. And I say reproachfully: What silliness, my dear, money is no object, I'm ready to give everything if only it makes you feel good and comfortable. BICYCLE RENTAL. After the movie we have to rent two bicycles. The girl who rents the bicycles is blond and smiley, with an engagement ring on her right hand, seeing us, she laughs: finally some customers, it's odd, a warm spell like this but no one wants to go riding, it's simply odd. Nothing odd about it,—I say cheerfully,—with weather like this the whole town's gone out to the country, after all today's Sunday, everyone's been out at the dachas since early morning, and everyone there has his own shed with his own bicycle in it, we intend to go to the dacha now too, on your bicycles, straight along the highway, at our own speed: it's probably stuffy on the electric in spite of the ice cream. Look out,—warns the girl,—be careful, there's a lot of traffic on the highway, stay close to the shoulder, obey the signs, don't exceed the speed limit, pass only on the left, caution—pedestrian crossing, the traffic is regulated by radar and helicopters. Of course, we'll be careful, we have no reason to lose our heads, especially now, a week after the wedding, we had been hoping for so long. Ah, so that's it,—the girl will smile,—so this is your honeymoon trip. Yes, we've decided to take a little ride. That's what I thought when you came in—newlyweds: you suit each other awfully well, congratulations, it really pleases me, I got married myself not so long ago, my husband is a motorcycle racer, he has a great motorcycle, we ride really fast. I like races too,—Veta says, holding up her end of the conversation,—and I would like my husband to be a motorcyclist too, but unfortunately he's an engineer, and we don't have a motorcycle, we only have a car. Yes,—I reiterate,—unfortunately only a car, and it's a used one, but in principle I could buy a motorcycle too. Of course, do buy one,—smiles the girl,—buy one and my husband will teach you how to ride, it doesn't strike me as too complicated, the main thing is to release the clutch in time and regulate the radiator. And then Veta will propose: you know what, why don't you and your husband drop in on us next week come on the motorcycle, our dacha is located right on the water, the second clearing to the left, it'll be a lot of fun, we'll have dinner, drink some tea. Thanks,—the girl will reply,—we'll definitely come, I'm going to have some leave time starting day after tomorrow, only tell me what kind of cake you like: crow's feet or holiday, I'll bring one for tea. Better holiday, yes, and if it's not too much trouble, pick up a kilogram or two of truffles at the same time, I'll pay you back right away. Oh, come, what do you mean money! FISH-FISH-FISH. WILD-BULLFINCH-GAME STORE. Aquariums with tritons and green parrots on perches. REGIONALHISTORYMUSEUM. Show some curiosity, study your region, it's a useful thing to do. ASP—Agency for Secret Portage. GLOVES. And I read the word "glove" as "love" on the store. FLOWERS. BOOKS. A book is the best present, all that is best in me I owe to books, book after book, love books, they refine and ennoble one's taste, you look into a book and it's clear as mud, a book is man's best friend, it decorates any interior, exterior, fox terrier, a riddle: a hundred jackets but none with buttons—what's that? the answer: a book. From the encyclopedia: the *Bookmaking in Russia* article: bookprinting in Russia began under   Ivan Fyodorov, popularly known as the first-printer, he wore a long library duster and a round cap knitted from pure wool. And then the ship's cook Ilya gave him a book: take this and read it. And through the cover of meagre needles, moistening the pale moss, the hail capered and bounced like pellets of silver. Then also: I approached the appointed place—all was darkness and whirlwind. When the smoke cleared there was no one on the square, but along the river bank strode Burago, the engineer, his socks flapping in the wind. I'm saying only one thing, general, I'm saying only one thing, general: what's this, Masha, have you been gathering mushrooms? I often sent back doom with nothing more than a signal cannon. At the beginning of July, at a particularly hot time, toward evening, a certain young man. And you—say, eh, you-u-u! Are there any white ones? There are. Tsoptsop, tsaida-braida, eenie meenie miney moe. Shine, shine, stars in the sky, freeze, freeze tail of a wolf! Right side. BOATS-UMBRELLAS-CANES, all in the same store, so you can buy everything without messing around. FASHION SHOP, building on the left. SALAMI. Some get salami, and now some like it hot on a bun! HABERDASHERY-KNITTED GOODS. PARK OF REST the fence stretches for twenty and a half parsecs. And only after it ends—POST OFFICE. Hello, may I put a cancellation on my stamp, or more accurately, may I have it put on for me, or even better: what do I have to do so that with your help I can get a cancellation put on my stamp, cancelling it. Give it here, show me, what kind of stamp is this, boy, it's a matchbox. I know, I simply didn't think it would make any difference to you, there's a nightjar depicted here too, look. She glanced at it and smiled: you have to steam off the label. All right, fine, I'll steam it, I don't live far, it strikes me I'll be able to persuade mama to let me put the teakettle on (mama, may I warm up the teakettle? you want some tea? since when do you drink tea before school, how can you drink tea when it's time for supper. The point is mama, that it's necessary to use steam to unstick the label. Steam? Steam that's what they said at the post office. O, Lord, you've made up something again, what post office, who said, why, what label, you'll steam off your face!), but I'm not positive— couldn't that be done here in the post office, one day I

happened to see (the window was open) you drinking tea in the room where the parcels and tube mailers
are, you were drinking from an electric teakettle, there
were several women and one man wearing an overcoat,
you were laughing. Yes, true,—she said,—we do have
one, come here, boy.

And you followed her down a long corridor hung with
naked lightbulbs and it smelled of a real post office:
sealing wax, stickum, paper, twine, inks, stearin, casein,
overripened pears, honey, squeaky boots, crème-brûlée,
cheap comfort, vobla, bamboo shoots, rat droppings,
the tears of the senior clerk. There was a medium-sized
chamber at the end of the corridor, as if crowning it:
thus a river is crowned by the lake into which it empties. In this chamber were racks of parcels and tube
mailers, addressed there and here, the window was
barred, and on a table in the center of the room was the
argent glow of an electric teakettle with a striped cord
ending in a plug. The woman stuck the plug into a sock-
et, she sat down on a chair and you sat on another—and
you both started waiting for it to boil. I know you well:
by nature you are fitful, you don't have enough perse-
verance either at home or school, you're still too young,
and therefore you can't abide another person's silence,
prolonged pauses in a conversation, they make you ill at
ease, not yourself, in a word, you cannot endure passivi-
ty, inaction, or silence. Right now, if you were the one
in this post office room you would fill it with your
shout just the way you fill the empty school auditori-
ums, rest rooms, and hallways during your leisure time.
But you're not alone here, and although the indescrib-
able howl that is being generated in the depths of your
being is splitting you apart, and is ready to burst out at

any instant, splitting and cracking you like an early April bud and turning you completely into your own shout —I Nymphea Nymphea Nymphea, eya-eya-eya, ya-ya-ya, a-a-a,—you cannot, you have no right to frighten this nice young woman. For if you do shout, she will drive you away and won't put the cancellation on the nightjar, don't you shout here no matter what, in the post office, otherwise you won't have the collection of which you have dreamed for so long, a collection consisting of a single cancelled stamp. Or label. Control yourself, distract yourself, think about something else, something mysterious, or start a conversation which doesn't oblige you to anything with this woman, all the more so that, as I understand it, you liked her right away. All right, but how does one begin, with what words, I've suddenly forgotten how one is supposed to begin conversations which do not oblige one to anything. Very simple, ask her if you can ask her a question. Thanks, thanks, right away. Can I ask you a question? Of course, boy, of course. Well, what now, what do I say next? Now ask her about postal pigeons or about her work, find out how things are with her in general. Yes, that's it: I would like to find out from you how things are here with you in the poached office, no, I mean the post office, the postal posterior postnatal postscript post mortem. What's that, the post office? All right, boy, all right, but why does that interest you? You, no doubt, have postal pigeons, right? No, why? But then where would postal pigeons live if not here on your posts? No, we don't have any, we have postmen. In that case you know postman Mikheev or Medvedev, he looks like Pavlov and he rides a bicycle too, but don't expect to see him out that window, he doesn't ride here, not in town, he works in the country, in the dacha settlement, he has a beard—so

you've never been introduced to him? No, boy. Too
bad, if you had you and I could enjoy chatting about
him and you wouldn't be bored with me. Well I'm not
bored as it is,—answers the woman. Now that's great, so
you do sort of like me, I have some business with you,
if I'm not mistaken: it occurred to me to strike up a
friendship with you, and even more than that, my name
is such-and-such, what's yours? What a funny one,—said
the woman,—so funny. Don't laugh, I'll tell you the
whole truth the way it really is, you see, my fate is decided: I'm getting married, very soon, maybe yesterday
or last year. But the woman who is to become my wife—
she is extremely moral, you know what I mean? and
there is no way she will agree to the wedding. But I need
it very much, it's essential, otherwise my inhuman shout
will drain out like blood. Doctor Zauze calls this condition a posterior nerve core fit, therefore I have decided
to ask you to help me, to do me a certain favor, a kindness, it would be extremely kind of you, after all, you
are a woman, I imagine you'd like to shout from your
postal nerve core too, so why shouldn't we gratify our
velleities together, don't I appeal to you at all, I've tried
so hard to make you like me! You can't imagine how
I'm going to miss you after we've unstuck the label and
you do the cancellation and I go back, to the house of
my father: I will find no consolation anywhere. Or maybe you already have someone with whom you gratify
your velleities? My God, what business is it of yours,—
says the woman,—you've got a lot of nerve. In that
event I am ready right now to prove that I am superior
to him in all respects, even though you've already admit-
ted as much. Isn't it clear that my intellect is the quin-
tessence of suppleness and logic, is it not a fact that if
there is only one future engineering genius in the whole

world—I'm the one. And I am the one who will tell you
a story right now, yes, something that'll bowl you over.
Here. Let me present to you, in my own words, the
composition which our Vodokachka passed last week. I
will begin at the very beginning. *My Morning. A composition.*

The whistle of the shunting train sings "cuckoo" at
dawn: a shepherd's pipe, a flute, a cornet-à-piston, a
child's crying, doodelee-dey. I wake up, sit on the edge
of the bed, examine my bare feet, and then look out the
window. I see a bridge, it is totally empty, it is illuminated by green mercury lights, and the lampposts have
the necks of swans. I see only the roadway part of the
bridge, but all I have to do is walk out on the balcony
and the whole bridge will open up before me, its entire
gantry—the spine of a frightened cat. I live with my mama and papa, but sometimes it happens that I live alone,
and my neighbor, old Trachtenberg—or more likely Tinbergen, lived with us in our old apartment, or she is going to live at the new one. I don't know what the other
parts of the bridge are called. Under the bridge is the
railroad line, or to put it better, several tracks, several
transport tracks, a certain number of identical tracks of
identical gauge. In the mornings the witch Tinbergen
dances—danced, will dance—in the hall, humming the
song about Trifon Petrovich, the tomcat and the excavator. She dances on the red mahogany containers, on
their upper surfaces, near the ceiling, and beside them
too. I have never seen it, but I've heard. Near the ceiling.
Across them—hither and thither—goes the "cuckoo"
shaking on all the switches. Tra-ta-ta. She beats out the
rhythm with maracas. She pushes and pulls the brown

boxcars. I hate the shaggy crone. Wrapped in rags, long hooklike nails protruding, furrowing her face with the wretched wrinkles of centuries, club-footed, she frightens me and my patient mother in the daytime and at night. And at dawn—she starts singing—and then I wake up. I love that whistle. Doodelee-dey?—it asks. And after waiting a moment, it answers itself: da-da-da, doodeley-dey. She was the one who poisoned Yakov, the poor man, man and pharmacist, man and druggist, and she's the one who works in our school as curriculum director of the studies section, a section of the studies section of respect section of arsenic. Thus, in drawing conclusions about my morning one may say that it begins with the cuckoo cry, the sound of the railroad, the loop railroad. If one were to look at the map of our town, where the river and the streets and the highway are shown, it appears that the loop road is strangling the town, like a steel noose, and if, after begging permission of the constrictor, you were to get on a train going past our home, in one day this freight train will make a full circle and return to the same place, the place where you boarded it. The trains which go past our home move along a closed—and therefore infinite—curve around our town, which is why it is virtually impossible to leave our town. There are only two trains which work on the loop line: one goes clockwise, the other counterclockwise. In this relation it is as if they mutually destroy each other, and at the same time destroy movement and time. So goes my morning. Tinbergen gradually stops stomping through the young bamboo groves, and her song, vigorous, self-satisfied and merciless as old age itself, dies away in the distance, beyond the coral lagoons and only the booming and drumming and tambourining of the cars which surge across the bridge destroys—and that rarely—the quiet of our apartment. It vanishes—melts away.

A beautiful, beautiful, beautiful composition,—Savl says. We hear his resonant, mist-covered pedagogical voice, the voice of the region's leading geographer, the voice of a farsighted guide, fighter for purity, truth and filled-up spaces, the voice of the intercessor for all of the insulted and bloodied. We are here again, in the cleaned men's rest-room, where often it is so cold and lonely that steam streams from our blue student lips—symptom of breathing, phantom of life, a fair indication that we still exist, or that we have gone to eternity, but, like Savl, we will return in order to perform or complete the great deeds begun on earth, to wit: receipt of all and sundry academic prizes, a large-scale auto-da-fé involving all special schools, the acquisition of a used automobile, marriage to the teacher Vetka, the thrashing of all the world's idiots with the poles of butterfly nets, the improvement of selective memory, the smashing of the skulls of chalk old men and women like Tinbergen, the capture of unique winter butterflies, the cutting of the stout threads in all sewn-shut mouths, the establishment of a new kind of newspaper—papers in which not a single word would be written, the abolition of windsprints, and also the free distribution of bicycles and dachas at all points from A to Z; moreover—the resurrection of mentor Savl accompanied by his reinstatement in work in his special field. A beautiful composition,—he says, sitting on the windowsill, warming the bottoms of his feet on the steam heating radiator,—how late we discover our students, what a pity that I didn't discern your literary talent earlier, I would have persuaded Perillo to excuse you from literature classes, and you could have done whatever you liked in the leisure that resulted—you understand me? anything you like. Thus you could have tirelessly collected stamps with pictures of the nightjar and other flying birds. You could have rowed and swum, run and jumped, played red rover and mumbledy-peg, gotten tempered like steel, written poetry, drawn on the asphalt, played paper-rock-scissors, muttering the charming and incomparable: scissors cut paper, paper covers rock, rock breaks scissors—no don't talk and are you coming to the ball? Or sitting in the forest on a tree toppled by a storm, quickly and in an undertone, having in mind no one and nothing, repeat to yourself the time-tested tongue-twister: higgledy-piggledy, three Japs went willikers—Yak, Yak-Tsidrak, Yak-Tsidrak-Tsidroni; higgledy-piggledy, three more Japs went willikers—Tsipa, Tsipa-Dripa, Tsipa-Dripa-Limponponi; they married each other: Yak to Tsip, Yak-Tsidrak to Tsipa-Dripa, Tak-Tsidrak-Tsidroni to Tsipa-Dripa-Limponponi. O, there are so many things there are to do on earth, my youthful comrade, things which one could do instead of the stupid, stupid writing done in the literature classes! With regret for what is impossible and lost. With sadness. With the face of a man who never was is or will be. But, student so-and-so, I'm afraid you won't escape those lessons, suffering terrible pain you will have to memorize bits and pieces of the works which in our contry are called literature. You will read our prostrate and mendacious monsters of the pen with revulsion and sometimes you will find it impossible to go on, but once you have passed through the forge of this unhappiness, you will be hardened, you will rise over your own ashes like the phoenix, you will understand—you will understand everything. But, dear teacher,—we object,—didn't the composition which we retold to the woman at the post in our own words convince you that even as it is we have long understood that there's absolutely no need for us to pass through any kind of literary forge? Unquestionably,—answers our mentor,—I realized it from your first words, it's true you don't need a forge. I was speaking of the necessity of a forge—which for you is apparently a false necessity —only so as to somehow console you as you ponder the impossibility of being excused from classes in the afore-mentioned subject. Would you believe it, it wasn't so long ago I could have easily persuaded Perillo to offer you voluntary attendance of all classes in general, you no doubt know the kind of authority your humble ser-vant enjoyed in teachers' circles—in the school and in the ministry of people's edufaketion. But since some-thing happened to me—what precisely I still don't com-pletely understand, I have been deprived of everything: flowers, food, tobacco—did you notice I've stopped smoking?—women, my railway pass (the constrictor as-sures me that my paper expired long ago, but there is no way I can buy a new one, inasmuch as they also de-prived me of my salary), amusements, and, the main thing—authority. I simply can't imagine how this can be: no one listens to me—neither the teachers at peda-gogical meetings, nor the parents at the PTO meeting, nor the students in class. They don't even cite me as they used to. Everything is happening as if I, Norvegov, no longer existed, as if I had died. And here Savl Petro-vich filled the restroom with a soft flickering laughter. Yes, I am laughing,—said he,—but through tears. Dear student and great friend Nymphea, something has defi-nitely happened to me. Formerly, not so long ago, I knew precisely what it was, but now it seems to have slipped my mind. To use your terminology, my memory had become selective, and I'm particularly happy we've met here, at point M, inasmuch as I am counting on your help. Help me, help me remember what happened. I've asked people about it, but no one could—or did they want to?—explain anything to me. Some simply didn't know the truth, some knew but concealed it: they quibbled and lied, and some simply laughed in my face. But as far as I know, you will never lie about anything, you are incapable of lying.

He fell silent, his voice no longer filled the emptiness of space, and the sounds of the evening city became more distinct. Someone large, polyped, and infinitely long, like the prehistoric dinosaur which later turned into the snake, was walking past the school outside, slipping on the bare ice, whistling a Schubert serenade, coughing and cussing, asking questions and answering them for himself, striking matches, losing hats, hankies, and handbags, squeezing in his pocket a recently purchased exerciser, looking at a watch from time to time, eyes running over the pages of the evening papers, making conclusions, looking at a pedometer, losing and finding the way, analyzing the system of house numbers, reading signs and billboards, dreaming of acquiring new plots of land and of ever-increasing profits, recalling the deeds of days gone by, suffusing the surrounding air with the odor of cologne and crocodile purses, playing on a harmonica, stupidly and nastily sniggering, envying the fame of the dacha postman Mikheev, desiring untried possession and knowing nothing about us, mentor and students, chatting here in the melancholy confines of M. This someone, polyped, like a prehistoric dinosaur, and as unending as medieval torture, kept walking and walking, knowing neither weariness nor peace, and still couldn't get all the way past, because it could never get all the way past. Against the background of its movement, against the background of this unceasing, susurrating striding, we listened to the trolley whistles, the squeal of brakes, the hissing created by the slippage of the trolleybus contact antennae along the electric wires. Then came hollow blows, caused by the quick impact of a wood mass on the galvanized mass of ordinary tin: probably one of the special-schoolers, who didn't want to return to the home of his father, was methodically pounding a stick on the water pipes, attempting to play a nocturne on the flute of the pipes—as a sign of protest against everything. The sounds which were generated inside the building, however, were the following. In the cellar worked deaf-mute stoker so-and-so—his shovel scraping against the coal, the boiler doors screeching. An old lady was washing the floor in the hall: the brush with the wet rag wrapped around it would plunge rhythmically into the bucket, choke, slosh onto the floor and noiselessly moisten a new section of dry surface—the swimming of a rubious steed, the waltz of a man with a cold, *skeerlý* in a filled bathtub. Along another hall, a floor higher, walked the curriculum director Sheina Solomonovna Trachtenberg, her prosthetic device was thumping and squeaking. It was empty and quiet on the third floor, and on the fourth, in the so-called auditorium, a rehearsal of the combined choreographic ensemble of the town's special schools was going wild: fifty idiots were getting ready for some new concerts. Now they were rehearsing the dance ballad "Boyars, Here We Are": they were singing and yelling, stomping and whistling, snorting and grunting. Some were singing: Boyars, she's a dummy, young folks, she's a dummy. Others were promising: But we'll teach her, Boyars, but we'll teach her, young folks. The tympani banged with metallic disdain, slowly unwinding, the oboes crawled along, a bass drum with a goat's face drawn on the side was thumping, a sharpwinged pockmarked piano was in a convulsive fit of hysterics—skipping notes, hitting wrong notes, and swallowing its own keys. Then an ominous pause came to the fourth floor, and within a second, if we understand this word correctly, all of them, the dancers and the singers in chorus, intoned, bawled the Hymn of Enlightened Humanity, at the initial chords of which anyone who possesses ears must put aside whatever he is doing, stand up, and tremorously attend. We barely recognized the song. Passing through all the barriers, it did reach point M, but the bannisters, the steps and the stairwells, the sharp corners at the turnings, distorted and disfigured its inflexible members, and it reached us bloodied, snowswept, in the torn and filthy dress of a girl whom someone forced to do everything they wanted. But amid the voices performing this cantata, among the voices which meant nothing and were worth nothing, among the voices mingling in that senseless, meaningless, voiceless noisy clot of sound, among voices doomed to oblivion, among the incredibly commonplace and off-key voices, there was one voice which came to us as the embodiment of purity, strength and triumphant mortal grief. We heard it in all its undistorted clarity: it was like unto the flight of a wounded bird, it was a dazzling snowy color, the voice sang white, white was the voice, buoyant the voice, buoyant and melting, melted the voice. Piercing through everything, despising everything, it would rise and then fall, in order to rise. The voice was naked, stubborn, and filled with the loud pulsating blood of the singing girl. And there were no other voices there, in the auditorium, only her voice was there. And—do you hear it?—Savl Petrovich said in a whisper, a whisper enchanted and ecstatic,—do you hear that, or is it my imagination? Yes-yes-yes, Savl Petrovich, we hear Rosa Windova singing, the dear girl, sepulchral flower, the best contralto among the defectives of all the schools. And from this day forth, if—to the question: what are you doing here, here in the restroom?—if you reply to us: I am resting after classes, or: I am warming the bottoms of my feet,—we will not believe you, you splendid, but sly, pedagogue. Because now we understand it all. Like an ordinary schoolboy with a crush, you are waiting for the rehearsal to end, and she will descend from the auditorium along with the other damaged and still-born children—she, the one with whom you have arranged a rendezvous on the back stairs in the right wing where there isn't a single unbroken lightbulb left—and it's dark, so dark, and smells of dust, where the discarded gym mats are piled in a heap on the landing between the second and third floors. They are ripped, sawdust is spilling out of them, and there, precisely there, this is what happens: come, come, how I want your untouched body. Ecstatic whisper. Only careful, someone might hear—the Chechens wander all around. Or to be more precise: watch out for widow Tinbergen. All night long, sleeplessly and tirelessly, she wanders from floor to floor of the sealed, sagely silent school for fools. Starting at midnight the only thing you will hear in the building is footsteps—ee-ee-ee, one-two-three, one-two-three. Humming, muttering witchlike chants, waltzing or tap dancing, she moves through the halls and the classrooms and the stairways, hanging down in the stairwells, turning into a buzzing dung fly, pivoting on the steps, clacking her castanets. Only she, Tinbergen, and only the clock with the gilded pendulum

in Perillo's office: one-two-three—at night the entire
school is the lonely night pendulum, cutting the darkness into even, softly-dark slices, into five hundred, into
five thousand, into fifty, according to the number of
students and teachers: for you, for me, for you, for me.
You'll get your share in the morning, at dawn. In the
frosty morning, which smells of a wet rag and chalk,
when handing in your shoes in bags and putting on your
slippers—along with your claim check—you'll get yours.
So take it easy there on the mats.

Therefore, says our teacher Savl to us, I am listening to
you attentively, the truth and only the truth. You are
obliged to open my eyes to verity, let me recover my
sight, raise my lids. A huge nose, like a Roman legion
soldier, flat, gravely compressed lips. His whole face is
coarse-cut, and perhaps coarse-chopped, from white
marble with rose veins, a face with merciless wrinkles—
the consequence of a sober evaluation of the earth and
the men on it. The grim look of a Roman legion soldier
marching in the front ranks of an unbending legion. Armor, a white cloak trimmed with the fur of the purple
Italianate wolf. His helmet studded with evening dew,
brass and gold clasps here and there—misted over, but
flashes from the near and far fires flaming along the Ap-
pian Way nevertheless make the armor and the helmet
and the clasps glitter. All that is happening here is
spectral, grandiose and terrible, because it has no future.
Dear Savl Petrovich, obeying your unforgettable com-
mandments—they pound at our hearts like the ashes of
Klaus—we have in fact attained one of the highest of
human qualities, we have learned how never to lie about
anything. We note this without false modesty, for in the

conversation here with you, our teacher, you become our conscience and our happy youth,—it would be
out of place. But, mentor, no matter how elevated the
principles by which we guide ourselves in relation to
other people, they, the principles, will in no way take
the place of our repulsive memory: as before it is selective, and it's very unlikely we shall be able to shed light
and raise your heavy lids for you. We scarcely remember
what happened to you either, after all, a lot of time has
passed—or will pass—since. True, answers Savl, quite a
bit, true, quite a bit, not unlikely, more truly, a lot. But
nevertheless, do try, strain your amazing, albeit repulsive memory. Help your teacher, who is suffering in his
ignorance! A drop of dew dripped from the washbasin
faucet and dropped into the rusty, thousand-year-old
basin in order, following the dark slimy sewer pipes, and
by-passing the sediment tanks and prize-winning modern
filters, to slip quietly into the grief of the river Lethe as
someone's serene soul; Lethe, moving backwards, bears
out your boat and you, transformed into a white flower,
onto a white sandbar; for an instant the drop will cling
to the mandolin-shaped blade of your paddle and again
drop triumphantly into Lethe—it will vanish—it will
melt away—and in a second, if you properly understand
the meaning of the word, it will gleam immortally in the
inlet of a just-built Roman aqueduct. Leaf-fall September, such-and-such a date, of such-and-such a year B.C.,
Genoa, the Palace of Doges. A birchbark pictograph
rolled into a tube. Beloved Senator and Legion Soldier
Savl, we hasten to inform you that we, your grateful
students, have finally remembered some details of the
event which happened to you sooner or later, the one
which so disturbed you. We have managed to strain our
memory and now, it would seem we can guess precisely

what happened, and we are prepared to raise your
clanked-shut lids for you. We hasten to inform you that
Principal N.G. Perillo, incited to do this malicious deed
by S. S. Trachtenberg-Tinbergen, relieved you of your
position at your own request. That's impossible,—objects
Norvegov,—I did nothing that could...why? for what? on
what grounds? I don't remember anything, tell me.
Anxiously.

CHAPTER FIVE

TESTAMENT

It was one of the days of that enchanting month when early in the evening Saturn, soon to descend below the horizon, can be seen in the Western part of the sky in the constellation Taurus, and during the second part of the night bright Jupiter stands out in the constellation Capricorn, and toward morning, markedly lower and to the left, in the constellation Aquarius, Mars appears. But above all it is when the racemosa in our school's lilac garden blossoms dizzyingly: and we, the fools of several generations, are the ones who planted it, much to the envy of all the smart people who pass by in the street. Esteemed Savl Petrovich, allow us to note here that we, the prisoners of the special school, slaves of the Perillo slipper system, deprived of all rights to a normal human voice and therefore forced to explode in an inarticulate uterine shout, we, pitiful gnats entangled in the stiff spider nets of the class schedule, nevertheless, in our own way, in our stupid way, we love it, our hateful special, with all its gardens, teachers and cloakrooms. And if someone were to propose to us that we transfer to a normal one, an ordinary school for normal people, and inform us that we had gotten better and become normal,—no, no, we don't want to, don't force us out!— we would weep, and wipe away the tears with our cursed slipper sacks. Yes, we love it, because we are used to it, and if we ever, after spending several so-called years in each class, if we ever graduate from it with its graffiti-covered black and brown desks, we will be terribly dismayed. For in leaving it, we would lose everything—everything that we had. We would be left alone, and lonely, life would toss us to its corners, through the crowds of the smart ones who are striving to attain power, to attain women, cars, engineer's diplomas, but we—utter fools that we are—we don't need anything of the sort, we have but one wish: to sit in class, look out the window at the wind-torn clouds, paying no attention to the teachers, except for Norvegov, and await the white-white bell, which is like an armful of racemosa during that dizzying month when you, Savl Petrovich, geographer of the highest level, quickly—if not to say *headlong* —enter our class for the last lesson in your life. Barefoot. Warm spell. Warm wind. When the door is flung open—the windows, the frames of the windows—open out. Warmth wafts in. Pots of geraniums are strewn across the floor, smashed to smithereens. Glistening rain worms wriggle in the clods of black earth. Savl Petrovich, and you—you laugh. You laugh, as you stand on the threshold. You wink at us, recognizing every one of us, to the last man. Hello, Savl Petrovich on a warm Thursday in May, wearing a sport shirt with sleeves rolled up, pants with wide cuffs, a summer hat with a multitude of holes poked in it by a conductor's punch. Hello, devils, sit down, come on, nuts to these absurd ceremonies, because it's spring. By the way, have you noticed how the whole man is invigorated when caught up in the fresh breath of spring, eh? All right, I'll find some way to tell you about it. But right now we shall begin the lesson. My bosom friends, today according to the plan we have a discussion of mountain systems, Cordilleras or Himalayas or something. But who needs all that, who needs it, I ask you, when across our entire beloved earth run automatic machines whose wheels splash the taut water of puddles, thus spattering all of our sweet little girl-friends wearing their short little skirts in the streets. Poor babies! The drops fly right up into their most secret spots even, way above the knees—do you understand what I'm trying to say? Merrily, hitching up his sail-cloth pants and doing a little dance by the map of both hemispheres, which suggest gigantic blue glasses without rims. Student so-and-so, do me a favor, enumerate some women's names for us, the way I taught you, in alphabetical order. One of us students—now, from the distance, I can't see exactly who—gets up and speaks in a rapid semi-whisper: Agnes, Agrippina, Barbara, Christina, Galina... Yes,—you repeat with the smile of a person who is touched,—Leocadia, Valeria, Yulia, thank you, sit down. My faithful friends, how happy I am to attest my respect for you today, a spring day. Spring: it's not like your winter, when my yard is isolated, blanketed by the sad snow, the sleighbell rang out. Now there's a story. On the Island, on a night crossing, I took three bottles of cliquot and toward morning of the next day I was approaching the desired goal. All was darkness and whirlwind. No, on the contrary, today we will devote our efforts to a desert incarnadined with the blood of seals. Student so-and-so, I behold something terrible: of the three windows which give onto the open sky, only two are open, so open the third one too! Thanks. Today I will tell you a story which I found in a bottle of cliquot on the bank of the dacha river Lethe. I have called this story *The Carpenter in the Desert.*

My bosom friends, in the desert there lived a carpenter, a great master of his craft. When the occasion arose he could build a home, a dome, a carousel, a swing, knock together a mailing crate or any other kind. But the desert, in the words of the carpenter himself, was empty: no nails, no boards. *Esteemed legionnaire Savl, we are obliged to put the following fact to you immediately: no sooner did you utter the words no nails no boards, than it seemed to get dark and gloomy for an instant in the St. Laurence Mars Flame Orebearer University, where you are giving your regular lecture, it seemed to us that someone's shadow—a bird or a pterodactyl or a heli-plane—fell across the podium, replacing the sun. But then immediately went away.* Some people,—you continued, as if having noticed nothing,—will say: that's not true, there is no place where there isn't at least a board or two and a dozen nails, and if one looks around carefully, one can find material anywhere for a whole dacha with a veranda like all of us have, as long as the desire to do something useful hasn't disappeared, as long as one has faith in success. But I, angry, will reply: the carpenter really did manage to find one board, and then a second. Besides that, he had had one nail in his pocket since times of yore, the master was saving it just in case, a lot can happen in a carpenter's life, many are the uses to which a carpenter can put a nail, for example, scratching a line, marking drill holes, and so on. But I should add: in spite of the fact that the carpenter had not lost his desire to do something useful, and he believed in success to the end, the master could not find more than the two ten-millimeter boards. He had walked and ridden the whole desert over on his small zebra, studied every shifting dune and each gully overgrown with scrawny halogetons, he had even ridden along the sea shore, but—the devil take it!—the desert gave him no material. *Mentor Savl, we're afraid, it seems the shadow was just here again—just a second ago.* One day, exhaust-

ed by his quest and the sun, the carpenter said to himself: all right, you have nothing to build a home, carousel
or crate with, but you do have two boards and one good
nail—so you at least have to make something out of this
small quantity of materials, after all a master cannot sit
on his hands. Having said this, the carpenter placed one
of the boards across the other, got the nail out of his
pocket, and took a hammer from his tool box, and he
used the hammer to pound the nail into the point where
the boards intersected, thus firmly joining them: the result was a cross. The carpenter took it to the summit of
the highest sand dune, set it up vertically there, pounding it into the sand, and he rode away on his small zebra,
in order to admire his cross from a distance. The cross
was visible from almost any distance, and the carpenter
was so happy about this that from joy he turned into a
bird. *Very, very scared, dear Savl, the shadow again
loomed across your podium, loomed and dissolved,
loomed and dissolved, dissolved, the shadow of a bird,
that bird, or not a bird.* It was a huge black bird with a
straight white beak which emitted abrupt cawing sounds.
*Savl Petrovich, could it be the nightjar? The cry of the
nightjar, the cry of the nightjar, protect the nightjar in
its habitat, by the reeds and the hedges, hunters and
huntsmen, grasses and shepherds, watchmen and signal-
men, tra-ta-ta, tra-ta, ee-ee-ee-ee.* The bird flew up and
perched on the horizontal bar of the cross, sitting there
and watching the movement of the sands. And some
people came. They asked the bird: what's the name of
the thing you're sitting on? The carpenter replied: it's a
cross. They said: we've got a man with us here that we'd
like to execute, could we crucify him on your cross,
we'd pay a lot. And they showed the bird some grains of
rye. *Beloved Senator and Legionnaire Savl, look, for all*

our sakes, look out the window, it seems to us that someone is sitting there, on the fire escape railing, perhaps the nightjar, perhaps he's the one that's casting a shadow on your podium? And they showed the bird several grains of rye. Yes, said the carpenter, I'm agreed, I'm happy that you like my cross. The people went away and after a time returned, leading on a rope behind them some skinny and bearded person, to all appearances a beggar. *O, Mentor, you don't hear the mute and anxious outcry of our class, alas! Again: look back in fear! There, outside the window, on the fire escape.* They went up to the summit of the sand dune, stripped the rags off the man and asked the black bird if he had nails and a hammer. The carpenter replied: I have a hammer, but not a single nail. We'll give you nails, said they, and soon they brought many—big ones and bright ones. Now you must help us, said the people, we're going to hold this man, and you pin his hands and his feet to the cross, here are three nails for you. *Attention, Captain Savl, off the starboard bow—a shadow, order a broadside, your spyglass is fogged over, ulalum is nigh.* The carpenter replied: I think it's going to be bad for this man, it'll be painful for him. However that may be, objected the people, he deserves punishment, and you are obliged to help us, we have paid you, and will pay more. And they showed the bird a handful of wheat grains. *Woe unto you, Savl!* Then the carpenter decided to be crafty. He says to them: can't you see that I'm an ordinary black bird, how can I pound in nails? Don't pretend, said the people, we know perfectly well who you are. You are a carpenter after all, and a carpenter must pound nails, that's the work of his life. Yes, replied the carpenter again. But I am a master craftsman, not an executioner. If you have to execute a person, crucify him yourself, that's not for my hands. Stupid carpenter, they laughed, we know that in your miserable desert you haven't got a single board or one nail left, therefore you cannot work and you cannot work and you are suffering. A little more time—and you will die of inactivity. If, however, you agree to help us crucify the man, we will bring you much choice building lumber on camels, and you will craft yourself a home with a veranda, like all of us have, a swing, a boat—everything you want. Agree to it, you won't be sorry. *How sorry you will be, mentor, that you need not our mute advice—look out the window, look!* The bird thought for a long time, then flew down from the cross and turned into a carpenter. Hand me the nails and hammer,—agreed the carpenter,—I'll help you. And he quickly pinned the hands and feet of the condemned man to his cross, while they, the others, held the wretch. The next day they brought the carpenter the promised goods, and he worked a great deal and with pleasure, paying no attention to the large black birds which flew in with the blue dawn and pecked at the crucified man all day, and only that evening flew away. Once the crucified man called the carpenter. The carpenter mounted the sand dune and asked what the man needed. He said: I'm dying, and I want to tell you about myself. Who are you?—asked the carpenter. I lived in a desert and was a carpenter,—the crucified man replied with difficulty,—I had a small zebra, but almost no boards or nails. Some people came and promised to give me the needed material if I helped them crucify a carpenter. At first I refused, but then I agreed, for they offered to give me a whole handful of wheat grains. Why did you need grain,—the carpenter said in surprise as he stood on the sand dune,—can it be that you know how to turn into a bird too? *Why don't you look out the*

window, mentor, why? Why did you use the word *too,*
—replied the crucified carpenter,—O foolish man, do
you really not yet realize that there is no difference between you and me, that you and I—are one and the
same carpenter, don't you realize that on the cross which
you have created in the name of your sublime carpenter's craft, you have crucified yourself, and when they
were pinning you down, you pounded in the nails yourself. After saying this, to himself, the carpenter died.

Finally, our good mentor, finally, having heard our dis-
aster warnings, finally you are looking around. But it's
too late, teacher: the shadow which starting with a certain moment—*no nails, no boards*—has been disturbing
our minds, is no longer sitting on the fire escape railing
and is not looming over the podium—and it is not a shadow, and not a nightjar, and not the shadow of the nightjar. It is the directress Tinbergen, hanging down on the
other side of the window, which is wide open to the sky.
Clad in rags bought secondhand from a train-station
gypsy, in an old crone's knitted cap, from under which
closely cropped Medusa serpents protrude, flecked with
platinum gray, she hangs there outside the window, as if
dangling from a rope, but in fact she is hanging there
without the help of outside forces or objects, simply using her witch's powers, hanging like a portrait of herself—filling the window frame, covering the entire opening, hanging there because she wants to hang there,
hovering. And without coming into the classroom,
without even stepping on the windowsill, she will scream
at you, incomparable Savl Petrovich, tactlessly and un-
pedagogically paying no attention to us, frozen and
chalky from agitation, she will scream, baring those rotten

metallic teeth of hers: sedition! sedition! sedition! And then disappear, Mentor Savl—are you crying, you, with a rag and piece of chalk in your hand, you, standing there at the board, which in English is called *blackboard?* They were eavesdropping on us, eavesdropping, now they'll fire you on their own, only on what basis? We'll write a petition! My God,—this is you talking now, Norvegov,—do you really imagine I'm afraid of losing my job? I'll manage, I'll get by somehow, I don't have long to go. But, my friends, it's very painful to part with you, the future and past ones, with Those Who Came, and who will go away, bearing with them the great right to judge, without being judged. Dear Mentor, if you believe that we, who have appeared in order to judge, will ever forget your steps dying away in the hall and then on the stairs, you are in error—we will not forget. Almost soundless, your bare feet have left an imprint in our brain and frozen there forever, as if you had imprinted them in asphalt softened by the sun, walking across it to the triumphal ceremonial march of the Julian calendar. It is a bitter thing for me to recall this story, sir, I would like to have a moment of silence together with you in our garden. If I may I'll sit down there in that wicker chair, so as not to tromp pointlessly on the grass, wait a moment, I'll continue soon. When I return.

As you walk onto the bridge, notice the railings: they are cold and slippery. And the stars are flying. The stars. The trolleys are cold, yellow, unearthly. The electric trains below will request permission to pass the slow freights. Descend the stairway to the platform, buy a ticket to some station, where there is a station snackbar, cold wooden benches, snow. There are several drunks at the tables in the snackbar, drinking non-stop, reciting poetry to each other. This is going to be a cold, numbing winter, and during the second half of the December day this station snackbar will be the same way. It will be under demolition by the concertinas and poetry inside. People will be singing wildly and hoarsely. *Drink your tea, sir, it'll get cold.* About the weather. Mainly, about dusk. In the winter in the dusk, when you are little. Dusk is coming. It's impossible to live, and impossible to walk away from the window. Tomorrow's lessons are not in any of the known subjects. A fairytale. Outside it's dusk, snow the color of blue ashes or the wing of some sort of pigeon. Homework isn't done. Dreamy emptiness of the heart, of sunny linkages. The melancholy of all man. You are little. But you know, you already know. Mama said: that'll pass too, childhood will pass, like an orange trolley rattling across the bridge, showering cold fiery sparks which barely exist. A tie, watch, and briefcase. Like father's. But there'll be a girl, sleeping on the sand by the river—just an ordinary girl wearing a clean, tight, white swimswuit. Very pretty. Almost pretty. Almost unpretty, dreaming of field flowers. In a sleeveless blouse. On the hot sand. It'll get cold when dusk sets in. When it's evening. A steamer happens by: the whistle causes her simple eyelashes to quiver—she looks up. But you still don't know if—if she's the one. All covered with lights, the steamer leaves its cozy foam to the care of the night. But it's not yet night. An incoming surge of violet waves. By the shore, deep, there are springs. This water can be drunk, by leaning over. The lips of the dear, tender girl. The rumble of the steamer, the plash, the flickering lights recede. On the other shore, chatting with a chum, someone lights a fire to make tea. They laugh. One can hear their matches striking; Who you are, I don't know. The mosquitoes spend the night in the tops of the pines, in their crowns. The very middle of July. Later they'll descend to the water. It smells of grass. Very warm. This is happiness, but you still don't know about it. So far you don't know. The bird is a corncrake. The night ebbs and flows, solicitously turning the millstones of the heavenly mill. What is that river called. The river is called. And the night is called. What will you dream? Nothing. You'll dream of the corncrake, the nightjar. But you don't know yet. Almost unpretty. But incomparable, because she's the first. A wet salty cheek, silence invisible in the night. My dear, how impossible you are to make out in the distance. Yes, you'll find out, you'll find out. The song of years, the melody of life. All the rest is un-you, all the others—are alien. Who are you yourself? You don't know. You'll only find out later, stringing the beads of memory. Consisting of them. You will be all memory. The dearest, most evil and eternal. Pain trying for a whole lifetime to get out of the sunny entanglement. But what about the girl? Don't rattle the page, don't rustle it. She's sleeping. Morning. *I stood in the wind lonely and abandoned, like a church. You came and said that golden birds do exist.* Morning. Dew disappearing underfoot. A brittle willow. The sound of a bucket borne to the river, the soundlessness of a bucket borne away from the river. The dust of silver dew. The day taking on a face. Day in its flesh. Love day more than night, folks. Smile, try not to move, this is going to be a photograph. The only one which will survive after everything that is going to happen. But so far you don't know. Later—such-and-such a number of years in a row —comes life. What's it called? It's called *life*. Warm sidewalks. Or the other way around—one's swept by snow.

It's called *the town*. You rush out of a doorway wearing
high clacking heels. You have a nice figure, it's early in
the morning, you're surrounded by perfume and the
nimbus of a Parisian hat. Clacking. Children and birds
begin to sing. Around seven. Saturday. I see you. You I
see. Clacking all over the courtyard, all over the boule-
vard with its unblossomed lilacs. But they will blossom.
Mama said. Nothing else. Only this. Though there is
more. But now you know. You can write letters. Or
simply shout, going insane from your dream. But that'll
pass too. No, mama, no, that will remain. Wearing heels.
Is she the one? She. The one? She. The one? She. Tra-
ta-ta: right through. The whole town smells of that perfume. And it's too late to speak, consumed.   But one
can write letters. Saying *farewell* at the end every time.
My love and my joy, if I die from illness, madness or
sadness, if before the time allotted me by fate is up, I
can't get enough of looking at you, enough joy in the di-
lapidated mills on the emerald wormwood hills, if 1
don't drink my fill of the transparent water from your
immortal hands, if I don't make it to the end, if I don't
tell everything that I wanted to tell about you, about
myself, if one day I die without saying farewell—forgive
me. Most of all, I would like to say—and to say it before
a very long separation—to say what you have long known
yourself, of course, or what you are just surmising. We
all make surmises about it. I want to say that there was
already a time when we were acquainted on this earth,
you no doubt remember. The river is called. And
now we've come again, we've returned in order to meet
again. We are Those Who Came. Now you know. Her
name is Veta. Veta.

Lad, what's wrong? Are you asleep? Hey! No, how could that be, I just retreated into myself for a bit, but now I've returned... Don't worry, Doctor Zauze calls it dissolving in the environment—it happens fairly often. A man dissolves as if he had been put in a bathtub full of sulphuric acid. One of my comrades—we are in the same class together—says that he got a whole barrel of acid somewhere, but maybe he's lying, I don't know. In any case, he intends to dissolve parents in it. No, not all parents in general, just his own. I don't think he likes his parents. So what, sir, I imagine they are harvesting the fruits which they themselves sowed, and it is not for you and us to decide who is right here. Yes, lad, yes, not for you and me. Shaking his head, clicking his tongue, buttoning and immediately unbuttoning the buttons on his duster. Stooped and wooden and dry. But let's return to the sheep, sir. One day during that same remarkable month a rumor spread through the specschool that you, Savl Petrovich, had been fired as if by magic. Then we sat down and wrote a petition. It was laconic and severe in style; it said: To the School Principal, N. G. Perillo. A Petition. In connection with pedagogue-geographer P. P. Norvegov being fired at his own request, but in fact not—we demand the immediate surrender of the guilty parties by prison transfer convoy. And the signatures: respectfully, student so-and-so and student so-and-so. The two of us made our appearance together, pounding and knocking, slamming every door in the world. We made our appearance, furiously, and Perillo was sitting in his armchair relaxing and gloomy, in spite of the fact that it was still the morning of his middle years, a hale and hearty morning full of hopes and *planctons* for the future. In Perillo's office the clock with the gilded pendulum was rhythmically cutting nonexistent time into units. Well, what have you written?—said our director. You and I—we started searching for the petition in our pockets but couldn't find anything for a long time, and then you—precisely you, and not me—got a crumpled sheet of paper out from somewhere behind your back and put it on the glass before the Principal. But it was not the petition—I immediately realized it wasn't the petition, because we wrote the petition on a different kind of paper, on beautiful crested paper with watermarks and several special seals, on petition paper. But the sheet which lay on Perillo's glass now—glass reflecting the safe, the barred window, the chaotic foliage of the trees outside, the street going about its affairs, the sky— was ordinary lined notebook paper, and what you had written on the sheet—and it most certainly was you who wrote it—was not a petition but that old note explaining lost faith, about which I managed to forget a hundred years ago, I would never have written it if it hadn't been for you. That is, I hasten to underline that you wrote it, and that I never had anything to do with it. Woe unto us, Savl, we were betrayed by a third party, all was lost: the petition vanished, and it was beyond our strength to recreate the text, we had already forgotten it all. We recall only that during this whole time Nikolai Gorimiro- vich's face—after he started to read the explanatory note —became somehow different. Of course, it continued to be gloomy, inasmuch as it could not not be gloomy, but it also became something else. There was a nuance. A shade. Or like this: it was as if a slight wind had blown across the Principal's face. The wind did not take any- thing away, it only added something new. A sort of spe- cial dust. We probably wouldn't be mistaken in saying: Perillo's face became gloomy and special. Correct, now this was a special face. But what was Perillo reading,—

Savl asks with interest,—what did you do there, my friends? I don't know, ask *him*, he was the one who wrote it, *the other*. I'll tell you right away. Here's what was there. As your humble correspondent has already informed the Italian artist Leonardo, I was sitting in the boat, not holding onto the oars. A cuckoo was counting my years on one of the banks. I had asked myself questions, several questions, and was already prepared to answer, but I could not. I was surprised, and then something happened inside me—in my heart and in my head. As if I had been turned off. And at that instant I felt that I had vanished, but at first I decided not to believe it. Didn't want to. And I said to myself: it's not true, it just seems like it, you're a little tired, it's very hot today. Get busy, and row, row home, to Syracuse, enumerate the Taurian ships. And I tried to grasp the oars, and stretched my hands out to them. But it didn't work. I saw the handles, but couldn't feel them with my palms. The wood of the oars flowed through my fingers like sand, like air, like immobile, nonexistent time. Or vice versa: I, my former palms, were flowed round by the wood, as if by water. The boat was washing to shore in a deserted spot. I walked a certain number of steps along the beach and looked back: there was nothing resembling my tracks left in the sand, and in the boat lay a white water lily, called by the Romans Nymphea Alba, that is, white lily. And then I realized that I had turned into it and no longer belonged to myself, or the school, or you personally, Nikolai Gorimirovich,—to no one on earth. From this time forth I belong to the dacha river Lethe, which streams against its own current at its own desire. And—long live The Sender of Wind! As for the two slipper sacks, ask my mother, she knows everything. She'll say: that'll pass too. She knows.

Mama, mama, help me, I'm sitting here in Perillo's office, and he's calling *there,* for Doctor Zauze. I don't want to, believe me. Please come, I promise to do everything you want, I give my word. I'll wipe my feet at the door and wash the dishes, don't give me away. Better yet, I'll start going to the maestro again. With pleasure. You see, in the course of these few seconds, I've rethought a lot of things, I've come to realize that in essence I love all music inordinately, especially the accordion three-quarter. Ee-ee-ee, one-two-three, one-two-three, ee-one, ee-two, ee-three. On the Barcarolle. Come on, we'll go visit grandmother again, we'll talk, and from there—straight to the maestro, he lives quite close, you remember. And I give my word that I'll never again spy on you. Believe me, it makes no difference to me what you do there with him, there, in the tower, on the second floor. Go ahead—and I—I will be memorizing the czardas. And when you come back down the skeerlying stairs, I'll play it for you. Sextets or even scales. And please, don't worry. What business is it of mine! We've all been grown-ups for a long time—you and maestro and me. Isn't it reasonable for me to understand. And could I ever carry tales? Never, mama, never. Come on and tell me, when did I ever tell papa anything—even once. No. Go ahead and do it, do it, and I'll be memorizing the czardas. Imagine it, how it'll be when we go again. Sunday, morning, and papa is shaving in the bathroom. I am cleaning my shoes, and you are making our breakfast. An omelette, fritters, coffee with cream. Papa is in a splendid mood, yesterday he had a difficult meeting, he said that he was devilishly tired, but then everybody got what they deserved. That's why as he shaves, he is humming his favorite Neapolitan song: After a bit of a trip, a hole in

her hip, in a Neapolitan port, Gianetta sent the rigging;
before weighing anchor, all sailors went ashore, whirla-
gigging. Well, what's happening, are you going for your
lesson?—he asks after breakfast, though he knows better
than us that yes we are going for the lesson. Yes, papa,
yes, music. How is he, your one-eyed fellow, I haven't
seen him for a long time, is he minstrelizing as usual,
composing all sorts of hibbeldy-dibbeldy? Of course,
papa, what else has he to do, after all he's a handicapped
veteran, he has loads of free time. Oh I know these
veterans,—papa smirks,—these veterans ought to be load-
ing barges, not sawing on fiddles, if it were up to me
they'd do some sawing to a different tune, the no-
count Mozarts. But,—you remark, mama,—he doesn't
play the violin, his main instrument is the horn. All
the more,—says papa,—if it were up to me, he'd blow
the horn where one's supposed to. It'd be better,—continues papa, wiping up the remains of the fried eggs with
a piece of bread,—it'd be better if he washed his socks
more often. What have socks got to do with this,—you
answer, mama,—we're talking about music; naturally,
everyone has his weaknesses, the man is a bachelor, he
has to do everything all by himself. There you are,—says
papa,—you go ahead and wash his socks for him if you
feel sorry for him, just think of it—we've found a genius
so great that he's incapable of washing his socks! Finally
we go out. Well, get going,—papa sends us off, standing
on the threshold,—get going. He is wearing his favorite
and only pyjamas and has a bundle of newspapers under
his arm. His big face—it is virtually wrinkleless—gleams
and shines from the recent shave. I will do some reading,—he says,—careful with that accordion, don't scratch
the case. The electric is full of people—everyone going
somewhere off to their dachas. There's absolutely no

place to sit, but as soon as we appear, everyone looks around at us and they say to each other: let the mother with the boy through, don't get in their way, sit the mother and the boy with the accordion down, seat them, let them sit down, they have an accordion. We sit down and look out the window. If the trip to my lesson happens to take place on a winter day, outside we see horses hitched to sleighs, we see snow and various tracks in the snow. But if it happens in the autumn everything outside is different: the horses are hitched to carts or simply wandering through the meadows by themselves. Mama, I'm sure the constrictor is going to come in a moment. How do you know? That's not for sure. You'll see, just wait. Tickets,—says the constrictor, coming in. Mama opens her purse, she searches for our tickets, but can't find them for a long time. Upset, she pours out all of the small things which there are in the handbag onto her knees, and the entire car looks on as she does so. The car examines the things: two or three handkerchiefs, a bottle of perfume, lipstick, a note-book, a dried cornflower in memory of something that happened long ago, a case for glasses, or, as mama calls it—an eyecase, keys to the apartment, a pincushion, a spool of thread, matches, a compact and the key to *grandmother*. Finally mama finds the tickets and holds them out to the approaching constrictor, a fat man wearing a special black greatcoat. He turns the tickets in his hands, languidly checks their color, languidly closes one eye, and he punches it with a punch, which looks like: sugar tongs, a barber's hair-clippers, a dyna-mometer, tiny tongs, tooth-pulling tongs, a "beetle" flashlight. Noticing the accordion, the fatty languidly winks at me and asks: a Barcarolle? Yes,—I say,—a Barracuda, three quarters. We're on the way to his lesson,—adds mama, upset. The whole car is listening, slightly rising from the yellow lacquered benches, trying not to let a word slip by. The teacher is waiting for us,— continues mama,—we are a little late, didn't make the nine o'clock, but we'll make up the lost time on the way from the station. We'll walk a little faster than usual, my son has a very talented pedagogue he's a composer true he's not quite well the front you know but very talented and he lives completely alone in an old house with a tower you yourself understand it's not too comfy at his place and sometimes it's a mess but what does that matter if we are talking about the fate of my son you see the teachers advised that we give our son a musical education at least an elementary one he doesn't have a bad ear and then we found this teacher we have a friend and he recommended him to us we are very grateful they were together at the front our friend and the teacher have been friends for many years now by the way if you have a son and he has an ear if you'd like I could give you the address an honest man and a remarkable musician a specialist in his craft one can only bow down to him he doesn't charge much if it had to be earlier for you an agreement could be reached and he'd come to your house it's not hard for him all the more that for you too it would be cheaper here I'll write down your address. No need,—languidly says the constrictor,—nuts to all that music and a Barcarolle alone costs who knows what. Wrong, wrong, mama answers after all the accordion can be bought in a second-hand store and it's not in the least expensive there and can one think about money if one is talking about the fate of one's son in the final analysis you could get a loan here I'll have a talk with your wife we women always understand each other better yet my husband and I could loan you the money if not the whole amount then at least part of it you could gradually repay us we would trust you you can after all. No need,—answers the constrictor,—I'd be glad to borrow from you, but I don't want to bother with all that music, why the teacher alone costs who knows how much, and besides that I don't have a son anyway, no son, no daughter, no, so excuse me, thanks. Languidly. The constrictor walks away, the people in the car sit down in their places and present their tickets. When we exit from the train and descend from the platform I look back: I see the whole car staring after us. Going along minding our own business, we are reflected in the eyes and glass of the train as it gathers speed: my medium-height mother in the brown spring jacket with the collar of a sick steppe fox, mama in a scaly, hard-looking hat, made from no one knows what, and wearing shoes; and I—skinny and tall, in a dark duster with six buttons, made out of my prosecutor father's greatcoat, in an awful wine cap, shoes with clips and galoshes. We fly further and further from the station, dissolving in a world of suburban objects, noises and colors, with each movement penetrating further and further into the sand, the bark of the trees, we mingle with the sunrays, we become optical illusions, inventions, children's amusement, a play of light and shadow. We burst into the voices of the birds and people, we attain the immortality of the non-existent. The maestro's house stands on the edge of some annexes, calling to mind a ship made of matchboxes and blocks. You see the maestro from afar: he is standing in the center of a glassed-in veranda, in front of a music stand, practicing on a smallish flute which on some other days seems to be a telescope; moreover, he is wearing a black eye bandage, like a pirate captain. The garden is filled with black wind-twisted trees, and across the lake, touched by the elegant melody, boats float glassily in the Sunday sky's cold and harsh luminescence. Good day, maestro, here we are, we've come again, to learn. We have missed music so much, and you and your garden. The doors of the veranda are flung open, the captain moves unhurryingly to meet us. Mama, look at your face! Can the wind from the lake have changed it so? Now, right now. Mama, I can't keep up with you. Now. Now we step across the threshold of the house and are submerged in its peculiar architecture, absorbed in its halls and stairways and floors. Here we go in. One. Two. Three.

Excuse me, sir, I seem to have digressed rather far from the essence of our conversation. What I wish to say is that Savl Petrovich is sitting on the windowsill with his back to the window as before. The naked bottoms of his feet rest on the radiator, and the teacher, smiling, is talking to us: yes, I remember quite well that Perillo wanted to fire me on request. But after thinking it over he gave me a probationary period—two weeks, and so as not to get kicked out of work I decided to show myself at my best. I decided to try very very hard. I decided not to be late to school, I decided to buy and wear some sandals, I swore to conduct the lessons strictly according to the plan. I would have given away half of the dacha summer to someone, if only I could remain with you, my friends. But then the very thing that I keep asking you about happened. I don't remember—you understand? I don't remember what took place during my probationary period, apparently right at the start. All that I know is that it happened on the eve of the regularly scheduled examination. Student so-and-so, do me a favor, help me. Every day my memory is getting worse and worse, getting dull, like table silver which lies un-used in the buffet. So breathe on this silver and wipe it with a flannel cloth. Savl Petrovich, we reply, standing on the Dutch tile—or whatever else these tiles are called —Savl Petrovich, we know, now we know, we remember, only don't worry. But I'm not worried, Lord, just tell me, please, tell me. Anxiously. Savl Petrovich, this might be extremely unpleasant news for you. Come on,—the teacher urges us,—I'm all ears. Well, you see, the thing is that you yourself wanted to know what happened, you informed us about it yourself at the time. Yes, yes, of course, that's what I'm saying: my memory is like unto silver. So listen. That day we were supposed to take the last examination in some class, your class in fact, geogra-phy. It was set for nine o'clock, we gathered in the class-room and waited for you till twelve, but you never came. Clicking his heels at the corners, Perillo appeared and said that the examination was being postponed until the next day. Some of us surmised that you were sick, and we decided to visit you. We went off to the teachers' commons room, and Tinbergen gave us your city ad-dress. We set off. The door was opened by some woman, extraordinarily pale and gray. To be frank, we have never met such a chalky woman. She spoke barely audibly, through her teeth, and she was dressed in a nondescript duster the color of a sheet, without buttons and without sleeves. Most likely it was not even a duster, but a sack, sewn from two sheets, in which only one hole had been cut—for the head—you understand? The woman said she was your relative, and asked what message there was. We replied that that wasn't necessary, and inquired where we might find you, Savl Petrovich, how, we said, can we see you. And the woman says: he doesn't live here now, he lives outside of town, at his dacha, because it's spring. And she offered to give us the address, but, thank God, we know your dacha, and we decided to set off immediately. Wait,—interrupts Savl,—by that time I really had moved to the dacha already, but you went to the wrong apartment, because there couldn't have been any such woman in my apartment, all the less a relative, I have no relatives, even male ones, my apartment is always empty from spring to fall, you mixed up the address. Possibly, Savl Petrovich,—we say,—but for some reason the woman did know you, after all, she wanted to explain how to get to your dacha. Strange,—replies Savl pensively,—what was the apartment number, do you remember? Such-and-such, Savl Petrovich. Such-and-such?—the teacher asks again. Yes, such-and-such. I'm very concerned,—says Savl—I don't understand any of this. I'm very concerned. Where could the woman have come from? Well, did you happen to notice if there, by the door, on the stairwell landing—was there a sled there? There was, Savl Petrovich, a child's sled, yellow, with a strap made from a wick for a kerosene lamp. Right, so, right, but, my God, what woman? And why gray-haired, why in a duster? I don't know any such women, I'm very concerned, but—continue. Crushed. And so we set out to your dacha. The morning was already ending, but despite that, the nightingales, countering the trains, went on singing harmoniously all along the railroad, in the bushes outside the right-of-way fences. We stood on the connecting platform eating ice cream and listening to them—they were louder than anything in the world. We don't imagine, Savl Petrovich, that you have forgotten how to get from the station to your dacha, and we won't describe the road. We must only remark that there was still melted cold water in the roadside ditches, and the young leaves of the plantain were hurriedly drinking it, in order to survive and live. One may also make reference to the fact that the first people had already appeared in the garden plots: they were burning trash fires, digging in the earth, pounding hammers, and warding off the first bees. Everything in our settlement that day was precisely the same as on the corresponding day last year and all the past years, and our dacha stood drowning in the joyous six-petalled lilacs. But there were now some different dacha folk in our garden, not us, inasmuch as by this time we had sold our dacha. Or maybe hadn't yet bought it. Here nothing can be asserted with confidence, in this given case everything depends on time, or vice versa—nothing depends on time, we could be mixing up everything, it may seem to us that that day was then, but in actuality it falls in a completely different period. It's really terrible when things keep getting combined without any system. That's right, that's right, now we aren't even in a position to maintain with certainty if we had, our family had, any dacha, or if we had and do have it, or if we just will have it. A certain scientist—I read this in a scientific journal—says: if you are in the city and at a given moment you think that you have a dacha in the country, this doesn't mean that it is there in fact. And vice versa: lying in a hammock at the dacha, you cannot seriously believe that the city, where you intend to go after supper, does in fact exist in space. Both the dacha, and the city, between which you race all summer,—writes the scientist,—are only fruits of your somewhat disordered imagination. The scientist writes: if you want to know the truth, then here it is: you have *nothing* here—no family, no work, no time, no space, nor you yourself, you have made this all up. Agreed,—we hear Savl's voice,—as far as I can recall, I've never doubted that. And here we said: Savl Petrovich, but nevertheless something *is*, this is just as obvious as the fact that the river has a name. But what, what specifically, teacher? And he answers: my dears, you might not believe me, your goatish, retired drummer, cynic and troublemaker, wind-driver and windvane, but believe the other person in me—the indigent citizen and poet who came in order to enlighten, to cast a spark into hearts and minds, so that people would be enflamed with hatred and a zeal for freedom. Now I shout with all my blood, the way one shouts of vengeance to come: there is nothing in the world, there is nothing in the world, there is nothing in the world—except The Wind! And The Sender,—we asked. And The Sender too,—replied the teacher. Water rumbled in the bowels of the unpainted radiators, outside strode the inexorable, indestructible polyped street, our stoker and guard rushed from one open boiler to another in the basement, with a shovel in his hand, muttering, and on the fourth floor the quadrille of fools boomed like cannon, shaking the foundations of the entire establishment.

So, our dacha stood drowning in the six-petalled lilac. But other people were bustling around in our garden now, not us, or, possibly, it was us nevertheless, but rushing past ourselves towards Savl's we didn't recognize ourselves. We went down to the end of the street, turned left, and then—as often happens—right, and found ourselves on the edge of an oats field, beyond which, as you know, the waters of the dacha Lethe stream and the Land of the Nightjar begin. On the road which bisects the oats field we ran into the postman Mikheev, or Medvedev. He was slowly riding his bicycle, and although there was no wind, the postman's beard was swept back in the wind, and from it—clump after clump—clumps of hair were flying as if it were not a beard but a cloud doomed by a storm. We said hello. But sullen—or just sad?—he didn't recognize us and didn't answer, and he rolled along in the direction of the water-tower. We looked after him and: have you seen Norvegov? not turning around, the embodiment of the postmanbicyclist, a monolith, a slave pinned dead to his saddle, Mikheev shouted hoarsely as a raven one word: *there*. And his hand, separating from the handlebar, made a gesture which subsequently was immortalized in a multitude of ancient ikons and frescoes: it was the hand witnessing goodness and the hand which gives, the inciting hand and the calming hand, the arm bent at the elbow and wrist—palm turned up to the flawlessly shining sky, the entire gesture serene and restrained. And this hand pointed *there*, in the direction of the river. O friends,—interrupts Norvegov,—I am glad that you ran into our esteemed postman on the way to see me, that's considered a good omen in our parts. But I'm getting anxious again, I want to go back to the conversation about that woman, I expect some new details from you. Tell me whom or what you could compare her to, give me a metaphor, a simile, otherwise I am unable to imagine her very distinctly. Dear retiree, we could compare her to the cry of a night bird embodied in human form, and also to the bloom of a withering chrysanthemum, and also to the ashes of burned-out love, yes, to ashes, to the breath of the breathless, to a phantom, moreover: the woman who opened unto us was grandmother's chalk angel, the one with the broken wing, the one—well, you probably know. So that's it,—responds Savl,—I am beginning to suspect the worst, I am in despair, but that cannot be, after all here I am chatting with you normally, I can hear your every word, I feel, I perceive, I see, and nevertheless it's as if, as it were, as follows from your descriptions... no, I still have the right not to believe it, not to acknowledge it, to say—no, isn't that right? Decisively. With disheveled gray hair. Gesticulating. Savl Petrovich, where the oats field ends—Lethe begins almost immediately. Its bank is rather high and precipitous, it consists for the most part of sand. Pine trees jut up on the very summit of the precipice, on a grassy flat. The other bank and the entire river are quite visible—upstream and downstream from this square. The river's color is a deep blue; it pushes its clean waters along solicitously, leisurely. As for its width, about that it would be best to ask those rare birds which. They fly out and do not return. Approaching the precipice we immediately saw your house—as always, it stood on the other bank, surrounded by foliage, with flowers swaying and teeming dragonflies. There were swifts and swallows too. And you, Savl Petrovich, you yourself were sitting by the water, with several fishing lines in, rods resting on special slingshot-like sticks. There were bites now and then, and the little bells attached to the saplings would tinkle and awaken you from noonday dreaming. You would awaken, hook and drag out the next grouse, or rather, gudgeon. No, no,—remarks the geographer,—I never once managed to catch a single fish, there simply aren't any fish in our Lethe, it was the tritons biting. I must say that they are not a bit inferior to crucian or perch, even better. Dried, they recall the taste of vobla, quite nice with beer. Sometimes I would sell them at the station: take a whole bucket and sell them, there, beside the beer stand. It used to be they'd dry out right before your eyes as you were carrying them, right there in the bucket, if it was hot, of course. And then we approached the precipice, saw you, sitting on the opposite sand, and when we said hello: hi, Savl Petrovich! are they biting? How do you do,—you replied from the other bank—not much today, it's burning hot. We fell silent for a bit, one could hear Lethe flowing backwards. Then you asked: and you, my friends, why aren't you in class, why are you out strolling? No, no, Savl Petrovich, we have come for you. Did something happen in school? No, no, nothing, or rather, the following—it so happened that you didn't come for the examination today, mountain systems, rivers and other things—geography. Now how about that,—you replied,—but I can't today, don't feel so very well. What do you have, tonsils? Worse, boys, much worse. Savl Petrovich, wouldn't you like to come over to our side, you have a boat, but we don't have anything here, although our boat is here, the oars are locked in the shed, we have a present for you, we brought a cake. Dig in yourselves, friends,—you said,—I have no appetite at all, and besides I don't like sweets, thanks, don't be shy. All right,—said we,—we'll eat it right now. We untied the box, cut the cake into two equal parts with a penknife and started eating. A motorized barge went past, linen hanging on ropes on the deck, and an ordinary little girl swinging on the swing on deck. We waved the cake box-top to her, but the girl didn't notice because she was looking up at the sky. We quickly ate the cake and asked: Savl Petrovich, what should we tell Tinbergen and Perillo about when you'll *be*? I don't understand, can't hear,—you replied,—let the barge get past. We waited for the barge to get by, and said again: what should we tell Trachtenberg about when you'll *be*? Don't know how things will work out here, boys, the point is that obviously I won't come at all, say that as of this

Tuesday I'm not working there any more, I'm quitting. But what is this, Savl Petrovich, we're very sorry, we'll miss you, this is unexpected. Don't grieve,—you smiled, —there are plenty of qualified pedagogues in the special without me. But from time to time I'll fly in, look in, we'll see each other, chat a bit, the devil take it. Savl Petrovich, but would it be possible for us, the whole class, to visit you on the other side next week? Come ahead, I wait joyously, only warn the others: no snacks are needed, complete loss of appetite. But what is your sickness, Savl Petrovich? It's not a sickness, friends it's not a sickness,—you said, standing up and rolling down the pants rolled up around your knees,—the thing is that I *died*, you said,—yes, still and all, I did die, dammit, I died. Of course, our medicine is crap, but in these cases it's always precise, no mistakes, the diagnosis is a real diagnosis: *died*,—you said,—it's damn maddening. Irritatedly. Just as I thought,—says Savl. Sitting on the windowsill, warming the naked bottoms of his feet on the radiator,—when you mentioned the woman who opened the door, I immediately had a kind of bad premonition. Well it's clear, now I remember everything, she was a certain acquaintance of mine, or more likely even a relative. So what happened next, student so-and-so? We went back to town, went to school and told everyone what had happened to us, or rather, you. Immediately everyone was somehow aggrieved, the faces of many went dead and they cried, especially the little girls, especially Rosa.... O Rosa!—says Savl,—poor Rosa Windova. And then came the funeral, Savl Petrovich. You were buried on Thursday, you lay in the auditorium, a great many people came to pay their last respects: all the students, all the teachers, and almost all the parents. You see, they loved you awfully much, especially us, the

specialschoolers. You know what's interesting: a huge
globe was placed at the head of your coffin, the biggest
one in the school, and those who served in the guard of
honor took turns rotating it—it was beautiful and solemn.
Our wind orchestra played the whole time, five or six
fellows, there were two horns, and the rest were drums,
big ones and little ones, can you imagine that? Speeches
were made, Perillo wept and swore that he would get
the Ministry of People's Edufaketion to get the school
renamed in honor of Norvegov, and Rosa—you know?—
Rosa read some astonishing and beautiful poetry to us,
she said she hadn't slept all night and wrote it. Really?
But I somehow vaguely.... can you remember at least a
line or two? Just a second, a second, it seems, roughly
like this:

> I slumbered yesterday to the sound of seven winds,
> So sepulchral and cold, to the sound of seven winds.
> And Savl Petrovich died to the sound of seven
>   winds.
> I cannot sleep at home now to the sound of seven
>   winds.
> A dog continues howling to the sound of seven
>   winds.
> And someone's walking very close, through snow
>   and winds,
> Walking toward my voice, and he whispers some-
>   thing to me,
> And straining to reply, I called to him by name—
> He came unto my gloomy tomb,
> And suddenly he knew me.

O Rosa,—says Savl in agony, my poor little girl, my tender one, I knew you, I recognized you, I thank you.

Student so-and-so, I beg of you, take care of her for me,
for our ancient friendship, Rosa is very sick. And please
remind her not to forget, to visit me, she knows the way
and the address. I still live in the same place, on the opposite bank, where the windmill is. Tell me, is she doing
as superbly as before? Yes, yes, nothing but A's. And at
this point we heard a rumbling, howling, screeching on
the fourth floor, and then down the whole front stairs—
from top to bottom—this meant that the rehearsal was
over and rushing down, emptying out of the auditorium
and towards the street. The fools of the choreographic
ensemble careened to the cloakrooms in an instant, the
entire idiotic mass, spitting in each other's faces, halloo-
ing, grimacing, distorting their bodies, tripping each other, grunting and giggling. When we again turned our
faces towards Savl Petrovich, he was no longer with us—
the windowsill was empty. And outside the window
strode the inexorable polyped street.

What a sad story, lad, how well I understand your feelings, the feelings of a student who has lost his favorite
teacher. Something similar happened, by the way, in my
own life. Would you believe it, I didn't become an Academician overnight, I had to lose more than a dozen
teachers first. But still,—continues Acatov,—you promised to tell me about some book, your pedagogue apparently gave it to you that time. That slipped my mind
totally, sir. He gave me that book during another meeting, either earlier or later, but with your permission, I'll
tell you now. Savl Petrovich was sitting there again, on
the windowsill, warming his feet. We had entered pensively: dear mentor, you probably know that the feelings
which we have for our teacher of biobotany Veta

Arcadievna are not void of sense and basis. Apparently our wedding is not on the far side of the mountain, with your permission to say so, systems. But we are utterly naive about certain delicate matters. Couldn't you, simply speaking, tell us how one has to do that, after all you had women. Women?—asks Savl again,—yes, as far as I can remember, I did have women, but there's a catch here. You understand, I can't explain anything sensibly, I no longer know myself precisely how that goes. As soon as it's over, you immediately forget everything. I don't remember a single woman of all those I had. That is, I remember only the names, faces, and clothes they were wearing, their individual utterances, smiles, tears, their anger, but on the subject you are asking about, I will say nothing—I don't remember, I don't remember. For all of that is structured rather on feelings than on sensations, and in any event certainly not on common sense. And feelings—well, they are somehow transitory. And I'll make just one remark here: every time *it* is precisely the same as it was the previous time, but simultaneously it is totally different and new. But no time is like the first time, the only time with the first woman. But I won't say a word in general about the first time, because there's absolutely nothing to compare it to, and we still haven't invented a single word that one can say about it and not be saying nothing. Ecstatically. With the smile of one who is dreaming about the impossible. But here's a book for you,—continued Norvegov, pulling a book from inside his bosom—I have it merely by chance, it's not mine, someone gave it to me for a couple of days, so you take it, read it, maybe you'll find something there for yourself. Thanks,—we said, and went to read, reading. Sir, that was a fine translated brochure by a certain German professor, it was about the family and marriage, and as soon as I opened it everything immediately became clear to me. I read only one page, opened at random, approximately page such-and-such—and then immediately returned the book to Savl, inasmuch as I understood everything. And what precisely, lad? I understood precisely how my life with Veta Arcadievna would go, what its bases would be. It was all written there. I memorized the whole page. This is what was printed there: "He (that is, I, sir) was away for several days. He missed her, and she (that is, Veta Arcadievna) him. Should they (that is, we) conceal this from each other as is often done—as a result of incorrect upbringing? No. He returns home and sees that everything is very nicely cleaned (Arcady Arcadievich, you will certainly be hanging in our living room, that is, your full-length portrait, this evening it would be decorated with flowers). As if by the way she says, "Your bath is ready. I've already put out your linen. I've already taken mine." (Can you imagine that, sir?) How marvelous that she is happy and in anticipation of love has already prepared everything for it. He desires her, but she desires him too, and she gives him to understand this with no false modesty." You understand, sir? *desires* me, Veta *desires, desires,* with no false.... I understand, lad, I understand. But you haven't grasped my idea quite accurately. I had something else in mind. I was hinting not so much about the spiritual and physiological bases of your relationship, as at the material ones. More simply put, what do you intend to live on, what are the means, what is your income? Let's suppose within a short time Veta does consent to marry you, well, what then? do you intend to go to work or school? Bah! So that's what you are worried about, sir, though I did surmise that you would ask about that too.. But, you see, I will probably graduate from our specschool in a very short time, apparently as a correspondence student. And I will immediately enter one of the divisions of some engineering institute: like all of my classmates, I dream of becoming an engineer. I will quickly—if not to say *headlong*—become an engineer, buy a car and so forth. So don't worry, I would appreciate it if you accepted me as a potential student, no less. If you like, if you like, but in that case what of all your discussion of butterflies? You told me about a large collection, I was certain that a young colleague of promise was standing before me, and here it turns out that for the last hour I have been dealing with an engineer of the future. O, I made a mistake, sir, becoming an engineer is the dream of that *other* one, the one who isn't here now, although he may glance in here every minute or so. Me—not for anything, it would be better to do the humblest work, to be the apprentice of some bleak cobbler, to be a Negro of advanced age, but an engineer—no, not for anything, and don't even ask me to. I have decided resolutely: only to be a biologist, like you, like Veta Arcadievna, for my whole life—a biologist, and mainly in the area of butterflies. I have a little surprise for you, Arcady Arcadievich, in a day or so I intend to ship my collection off to the Academy entomology competition, several thousand butterflies. I've already prepared the letter. I trust that success will not make me wait long, and am confident that my future accomplishments will not leave you indifferent either, and that you will rejoice together with me. Sir, sir, just imagine, it's morning, one of the first mornings which find Veta and me together. Somewhere here, at the dacha—at yours or at ours, it makes no difference. Morning, full of hopes and happy premonitions, a morning which is marked by the news of my being awarded the Academy prize. The

morning which we will never forget, because—well, I
don't have to explain to you precisely why: can a scientist be allowed to forget the instant when he first tasted
fame! One of those mornings....

Student so-and-so, allow me, the author, to interrupt
you and tell how I imagine to myself the moment when
you receive the long-awaited letter from the Academy,
like you, I have a pretty good imagination, I think I can.
Of course, go ahead,—he says.

Let's suppose it's one such morning—let's suppose it's
one Saturday in July—the postman named Mikheev, or
perhaps Medvedev (he is rather old, obviously not under
seventy, he lives on his pension and also the half salary
he receives in the mail for distributing newspapers and
letters, for being deliverer of telegrams and various messages which, by the way, he carries not in the usual postman's bag, but in a bag extraordinary for a postman—his
bag—an ordinary shopping bag made of black leatherette
—not on a strap across his shoulder, but on the usual
handstrings, slipped over his bicycle handlebars), thus,
one Saturday morning in July postman Mikheev stops
his bicycle alongside your house and, oldmanishly, in a
pensioner's awkward way, hops off into the bitter roadside dust, the yellow roadside dust, the light and flying
dust of the road, and presses the rusty button of his bicycle bell. The bell strives to ring, but there is hardly
any sound, since the bell is virtually dead, because many
of its crucial internal gears are extremely worn down,
they've abraded each other in the course of long service,
and the tiny hammer fastened to the spring is virtually
immobilized by rust. But nevertheless, this morning as
you sit on the open veranda, which is enveloped in your

father's merrily chirping garden, you hear the croak of
this dying bell, or more accurately, you don't hear it,
but sense it. You go down the veranda steps, you stride
across the merry, bee-filled garden, you open the gate,
see Mikheev, and exchange greetings: hello, postman Mikheev (Medvedev). Hello, he says, I've brought you a
letter from the Academy. Here, thanks, you say, smiling,
although there is no point to your smile, since your
smile won't change anything either in your everyday relations or in the fate of the suntanned old postman, as it
hadn't been changed by thousands of other smiles, smiles
precisely like this, smiles which didn't oblige anyone to
anything, ones which he encountered every day at hun-
dreds of dacha and even non-dacha gates, doors, exits
and breaks in the fence. And you can't help agreeing
with me, you understand all this perfectly well yourself,
but the custom of polite gestures, which you have been
urged to observe since childhood in school and at home,
functions independently, apart from your consciousness:
saying to Mikheev, here, thanks,—you take a yellow envelope out of his aging, veined hand and—you smile.
During one moment of your brief meeting, your traditional, i.e., unnecessary dialogue, unnecessary to either
of you but somehow essential ("Hello, postman Mikheev," "Hello, I've brought you a letter from the Academy," "Here, thanks"), during one hour of merry,
light blue boats slipping, slipping across the river Lethe,
which is invisible from here, and across other invisible
rivers, his hand—blue and speckled with age and ugly
from birth—holds out a yellow envelope to you and
slightly touches your hand—young, dark from tan, and
essentially free of wrinkles. Can it be—you reflect during
that second—can it be that my hand will get like that
someday too? But you immediately set yourself at ease:

no, no, it won't after all I run conditioning wind sprints in school, Mikheev didn't. That's why his hands are like that—you conclude, smiling. "Here, thanks." "You're welcome," Mikheev (Medvedev) murmurs indistinctly and without a smile, suburban distributor of letters and telegrams, deliverer of messages and newspapers, an old man, pensioner-postman, somber bicyclist with the usual extraordinary bag on his handlebars, a pensive man, gloomy and bibulous. Not looking back at you or the garden full of bluebirds, and just as awkwardly as he had dismounted a minute ago, he mounts his bicycle and, clumsily pedaling, takes his, or rather others', letters in the direction of the rest home and watertower, in the direction of the settlement outskirts, flowering mead-ows, butterflies and silver hazelnut trees. He's slightly hung over, he should probably hurry up the delivery of the remaining literature and letters, even if they're all bad ones, and then head home, mix a small quantity of water and spirits—his old lady works as a janitress in the local hospital, and this substance never gets used up at home, though it is put to good use—and after snacking on a slightly salted tomato from an oaken tub (in the cellar where it stands there are spiders, cold, germinating pota-toes, and a smell of mould), go off somewhere among the pines, among the rowan trees, or among those hazel-nut trees beyond the watertower, and sleep in the shade till the sun stops parching. When a postman is past sev-enty there's no need for him to go riding around all day in heat like this, he's got to rest too! But there are still some letters in the bag: someone is writing someone, someone isn't too lazy to reply, even though they have to borrow an envelope from a neighbor every time, buy a stamp, remember an address and walk through the heat to find a box. Yes, there are still a few letters left, and they have to be delivered. And there he goes now, in the direction of the watertower. The path, barely marked out in the uncut grass, goes uphill, and Mikheev's feet, which are shod in black shoes with high heels, almost like women's, slip off the pedals now and then, and when this happens the handlebars stop submitting to the letter carrier, the front wheel tries to stand against the motion of the other parts of this uncomplex machine, the wheel gives a skid, during which its spokes cut off the tops of some dandelions—the white seed parachutes are swept up and slowly descend on Mikheev (Medvedev), bestrewing the old mailman as if they intended to impregnate his black felt and wool hat and side-buttoning shirt, which is no doubt very sticky in this kind of weather. The little parachutes also descend on his pants, which are made of rubberized cloth, and one leg of which—the right—is pinned above Mikheev's ankle by a light linden clothespin so that the material, contrary to expectation, won't get caught in the gear mechanism—chain, small sprocket connected to the back wheel by means of a bushing, large sprocket with pedal mechanisms welded to it,—otherwise Mikheev would immediately tumble into the grass and flowers, spilling all the letters as he did so. They would be caught up by the wind and taken across the river, into the backwater meadows: it had already happened, or it could happen, and therefore—it was as if it had happened—and what could an old mailman do then except take a boat from the ferryman and cross over, cross the river, capture and collect his, or more precisely, others', letters. Because somehow people do find time to write, there are still those who have the patience for this, but not to consider that all it takes is for Mikheev to fall off his bicycle one fine morning, and all their idiotic scribblings, all these congratulatory postcards and so-called urgent telegrams can go flying across the river—not a one of them ever thought about that even once, for each person tries not to fall himself, from his own bicycle, and then of course they don't care about an old letter carrier who hasn't known anything all his life except delivering their wretched scrawls from house to house. The wind,—Mikheev (Medvedev) tells himself in an undertone—the wind is just in the upper air somehow, nowhere else, it's blowing up a rain. But that's not true: there is no wind of either lofty or lowly sort. And it will be at least a week before rain pours down on the settlement, and all that time it will be fair and windless, and the daytime sky will be coated blue Whatman paper, and the night sky—black carnival silk studded with big glistening stars of multicolored foil. As for Mikheev—he's just deceiving himself now, he's just sick of this heat, these letters, this bicycle, these indifferently polite addressees who always smile when they greet him at the gates to their gardens with their throbbing, ripening apples, and he, Mikheev, wants to give himself hope of at least some change in this stiflingly hot, boring and monotonous dacha life which, it would seem, he belongs to, but in which he scarcely takes part, although everyone who has his house here or on the other side of the river knows Mikheev by sight; and when he comes on his ancient velocipede with the soundless bell, the dacha people he meets smile to Mikheev, but he looks them over, gloomily or sadly, or in an old man's pensive way, as if admiring them, and then rolls on silently—towards the station, or the wharf, or—as now—the watertower. Silently. Mikheev is nearsighted, he wears rimless glasses, from time to time he lets a beard grow and from time to time he shaves it off, or maybe, it is shaved off by the wind, but both with

the beard and without, in the minds of the dacha folk
he is a singular specimen—elderly dreamer, amateur of
bicycle riding, and master of postal manipulations. The
wind,—he continues lying to himself,—there'll certainly
be a storm by nightfall, a thunderstorm, it'll ruffle up all
the gardens, they'll be wet and ruffled, and the cats—
ruffled and wet: they'll hide in the cellars, under the
porches of the dachas, flood all these samovars boiling
on verandas along   with the smoky kerosene lamps, it
will flood the mailboxes on the fences, and all the letters
that are now lying in his sack, and which he will soon
distribute to the boxes, will turn into nothing, into empty sheets of paper, words washed away or turned into
gibberish, and the boats—these idiotic, rag-tag rowboats
used by the loafers from the rest home and the dacha
boaters—these boats, upside down, will float along in
the current to the sea itself. Yes,—muses Mikheev,—the
wind will turn this whole garden-samovar life upside
down and conquer the dust at least temporarily. "Dust,"
—the pensioner suddenly recalls something he once read
somewhere,—"the breeze will build silver keels out of
dust!" That's it, out of dust, Mikheev analyzes, and precisely, keels, that is, keels for boats, keeled boats, ergo,
and not flatbottomed ones—may they all be empty. If
only the wind would hurry up and come. "Wind in the
fields, wind in the poplars," Mikheev cited, again in his
mind, at the point where the path bends to the right and
goes a bit downhill. Now to the bridge itself, across the
ravine where burdock grows in abundance and snakes no
doubt live, one can leave the pedals alone and give one's
feet a rest: let the legs hang freely, jouncing on either
side of the frame, not touching the pedals, and let the
machine roll on by itself—to meet the wind. The Sender
of Wind?—you wonder of Mikheev. You no longer see

him, as they sometimes said, he's disappeared around a turn—melted in the July dacha heatwave. Bestrewn with the flying seeds of dandelions, risking with every meter of his bicycle's rush the loss of those summer postcards written from nothing to do, with his old man's veined hands, he is now rushing forward to meet that of which he has dreamed. He is full of cares and anxieties, he has virtually been thrown overboard from dacha life, and this he does not like. Poor Mikheev,—you think,—soon, soon your woes will leave you, and you yourself will become a metallic head-wind, a mountain dandelion, the ball of a six-year-old girl, the pedal of a highway bicycle, universal military service, the aluminum of aerodromes, the ashes of forest fires, you'll become smoke, the smoke of rhythmical food and textile factories, the screech of viaducts, the pebbles of the sea shores, the light of day and the pods of prickly acacias. Or—you'll become the road, part of the road, a stone of the road, a roadside bush, a shadow on the winter road you'll become, a bamboo shoot you'll become, you will be eternal. Happy Mikheev. Medvedev?

I think you told about our postman beautifully, dear author, and it wasn't a bad description of the morning when the letter was received, I certainly wouldn't have been able to do it so graphically, you're very talented, and I'm glad that it was you who took upon yourself the work of writing about me, about all of us, such an interesting story, I really don't know anyone else who could have done it so successfully, thanks. Student so-and-so, your high evaluation of my humble work pleases me very very much, you know, of late I have been trying hard, I write several hours a day, and the rest of the hours—when I'm not writing, that is—I meditate about how to write better the next day, how to write so that all future readers will like it, and, above all, naturally, you, the heroes of the book: Savl Petrovich, Veta Arcadievna, Arcady Arcadievich, you, the Nympheae, your parents, Mikheev (Medvedev), and even Perillo. But I fear that he, Nikolai Gorimirovich, won't like it: still and all he is, as they used to write in novels, *a little too* tired and gloomy. I suspect that if my book comes into his hands he'll call your father—as I recall, he and your father are old army buddies, they served together with Kutuzov himself—and he'll say: do you know, he'll say, about the pasquinade that's been made up about us? No, the prosecutor will say, what's it like? Anti-us, the director will say. And who's the author?—the prosecutor will ask curiously,—give me the author. Writer so-and-so,—the director will report. And I'm afraid that after that there will be great unpleasantnesses for me, up to and including the most unpleasant, I'm afraid they'll immediately ship me off *there*, to Doctor Zauze. That's right, dear author, that's precisely the area where our father works, the area of unpleasantnesses, but why do you insist on having your real name indicated on the title-page, why don't you take a *mynoduesp*? Then they wouldn't be able to find you even if you're right under their noses. Generally speaking, not a bad idea, I will probably do that, but then I will feel uncomfortable before Savl: daring and irreproachable, the geographer moved openly against everyone, infuriated. He might think badly of me, decide perhaps that I'm not good for anything—neither as a poet, nor as a citizen, and his opinion means a great deal to me. Student so-and-so, please advise me how to handle this. Dear author, it seems to me that though Savl Petrovich is not with us, and apparently is no longer thinking about us, nevertheless it would be better to act the way he himself, our teacher, would have acted in the analogous situation, he wouldn't have assumed a pseudonym. I see, and thank you, and now I want to find out your opinion about the name of the book... Everything would seem to indicate that our narrative is approaching its end, and it's time to decide what title we will put on the cover. Dear author, I would call your book A SCHOOL FOR FOOLS: you know, there is a School for Piano Playing, a School for Playing the Barracuda, and so let it be A SCHOOL FOR FOOLS, some readers will be surprised: it's called A SCHOOL, but the story is about only two or three students, and where, they'll argue, are the rest, where are all those youthful characters, astonishing in their variety, in which our schools today are so rich! Don't worry, dear author, let your readers know, yes, tell them bluntly that student so-and-so asked you to let them know that in the whole school, except for the two of us, and maybe Rosa Windova, there is absolutely nothing of interest, there is no astonishing variety in it, everyone there is an awful fool, say that Nymphea said that you can only write about him, because it is only about him that you should write, inasmuch as he is so much superior to and more intelligent than the rest, which even Perillo admits, so when speaking about the school for fools it's sufficient to tell about student so-and-so—and everything will instantaneously become clear, just pass that on, and in general why are you concerned about who says or thinks what out there, after all the book is yours, dear author, you've a right to do with us, the heroes and titles, as you like, so, as Savl Petrovich remarked, when we asked him about the torte — dig in: A SCHOOL FOR FOOLS. All right, I agree, but still, just in case, let's fill a few more pages with a chat about something related to the school, let's tell the readers about a botany lesson, for example, after all, they are conducted by Veta Arcadievna Acatova, for whom you have so long cherished these feelings. Yes, dear author, I'll be glad to, it pleases me so much, I suppose that it won't be long before everything will finally be resolved, our interrelations are becoming more and more sharply defined, as if they weren't relations, but a boat floating along the bemisted Lethe on an early morning when the fog is breaking up and the boat keeps getting closer, yes, let's write a few more pages about my Veta, but I, as so often happens, I can't figure out how to begin, with what words—prompt me. Student so-and-so, it seems to me it would be best to begin with the words: *and then.*

And then she came in. She came into the biology department office, where two skeletons stood in the corners. One was artificial, but the other—real. The school administration purchased them in a specialized store called SKELETONS, in the center of our city, moreover, the real ones there cost far more than the artificial ones —that's understandable, and it's hard to function outside this *efemoral* framework. One day, as we were passing SKELETONS together with our kind, beloved mother— this was shortly after the death of Savl Petrovich—we saw him standing in the show window, where samples of wares were displayed along with the hanging sign: *Skeletons from the Population Received Here.* You remember, autumn was setting in, the whole street was shrouded in long mousquetaire cloaks, and it had been splattered with mud by the wheels and hooves of frozen phaetons and disheveled drozhkys, and no one talked about

anything but the weather, regretting the lost summer.
And Savl Petrovich—unshaven and skinny—stood in the
showcase wearing just his sport shirt and sail pants,
turned up to his knees, and externally the only conces-
sion to autumn were the galoshes on his bare feet. Mama
saw the teacher and her hands flurried up in their black
knit gloves: Lord, Pavel Petrovich, what are you doing
here in such bad weather, you have no face on, all you're
wearing is a shirt and pants, you'll catch your death of
pneumonia, where's your nice warm good suit, and your
covert coat, the farewell gifts we gave you, and the hat
that we all took such a long time picking out together,
the entire parents' committee! Ah, dear mama,—replied
Savl, smiling—don't you worry, for Allah's sake, everything'll be all right with me, better take care of your
son, look, he's already got a runny nose, and as for the
clothes I have this to say: to hell with them, a pox on
them, I can't stand them, they choke me, they pull in
one place, they pinch and crush, don't you understand?
All of this stuff was alien, unearned, not purchased
with my own money—so I sold it. Careful,—Norvegov
took mama under the arm,—the omnibus will splatter
you, get away from the edge. And why,—she asked, trying to free herself from his touch as quickly as possible,
and she made this too obvious,—what are you doing
here, by such a strange store? I have just sold my skeleton,—said the teacher,—I sold it in advance, bequeathed
it. Tell Perillo, have him get a car and come, I bequeathed
my skeleton to our school. But why,—mama asks in surprise,—isn't *that* very costly to you? Very, dear mama,
very costly, but one has to earn one's daily bread somehow: if you want to go on living, you have to know how
to make do, isn't that so? You must know that I'm no
longer on the school payroll, and you won't make ends

meet for very long if you have to get by on just private lessons: just think about it—are there so many failures in my subject in today's schools? All right, all right,—said mama,—all right. And mama didn't say anything else, we turned around and walked on. Good-bye Savl Petrovich! When we get like you, that is, when we don't exist any more, we'll bequeath our skeletons to our beloved school too, and then whole generations of fools—straight A-students, B-students, and D-students—will study the structure of human bonery from our unmouldering remains. Dear Savl Petrovich, is that not the shortest route to the immortality for which we all so fervently yearn when we find ourselves alone with ambition! When she came in, we rose and stood in front of the skeletons, so that she couldn't see them, but when we sat down, the skeletons remained standing and she saw them again. That's right, they always stood—on black metal tripods. Admit it, you love them a little, especially that one, the real one. Well I'm not hiding the fact, I really did love them and I still do, to this time, after many years, I love them because they somehow exist on their own, they are independent and calm in all situations, especially the one in the left corner whom we call Savl. Listen, what were those incomprehensible words you just uttered—*to this time, after many years*—what do you mean, I don't understand, what are we—do you mean we aren't in the school any more, aren't we studying botany, running strengthening wind sprints, carrying white slippers in little bags, writing explanatory notes about lost faith? Perhaps not, perhaps we're not writing, not running and not studying, the school has been without us for a long time, either we graduated with honors, or we were expelled for stupidity—I don't remember now. Good, but then what did you and I do all those years after school? We worked. Oh-ho, but where, as what? O, in the most varied places. First we worked in the prosecutor's office with father, he took us on there as pencil sharpeners, and we sat in on many judicial hearings. In those days our father had initiated a case against the late Norvegov. But what was it, can the teacher have done something wrong? Yes, in spite of the new law about windvanes, prescribing the destruction of the same when located on roofs and in the yards of private houses, Savl didn't take down his windvane and our father demanded the court and lay assessors try the geographer under the most severe article. He was tried in absentia and sentenced to supreme punishment. Damn it, but why didn't anyone intercede for him? Here and there people learned about the Norvegov case, there were demonstrations, but the sentence remained in force. Then we worked as yardmen in the Ministry of Agitation, and one of the ministers often called us in to his office in order, over a cup of tea, to consult about the weather. They respected us, and we were in good repute and considered valuable members of the collective, for no one else in the Ministry had faces as frightened as ours. They were getting ready to promote us, transfer us to elevator duty, but at that point we made a certain declaration, at the wave of a wand, and on the recommendation of DoctorZauze we entered Leonardo's studio. We were students in his studio in the moat of the Milan fortress. We were only humble students, but how much that celebrated artist owed to us, students so-and-so! We helped him observe flying on four wings, we mixed clay, carried marble, built projectiles, but mainly we pasted cardboard boxes and guessed rebuses. And one day he asked us: youth, I am working on a certain woman's portrait right now and I've already finished painting it except the face; I'm in a quandary,

I'm old, my imagination refuses to work the way it used to, advise me, what, in your opinion, should the face be like. And we said: it should be the face of Veta Arcadievna Acatova, our favorite teacher, when she enters class for the day's lesson. That's an idea, said the old master, so describe her face for me, describe it, I want to see this person. And we describe it. Soon we quit Leonardo's: got bored, eternally having to grind colors, and there's nothing that would get your hands clean. Then we worked as controllers, conductors, switchmen, inspectors of railroad postal divisions, janitors, excavators, glaziers, night watchmen, ferrymen on the river, druggists, carpenters in the desert, haulers, stokers, as starters, or rather—captives, or more precisely, as sharpeners of pencils. We worked there and here, here and there—everywhere where there was a possibility of laying on, that is, using our hands. And wherever we came, people said of us: look, there they are—Those Who Came. Greedy for knowledge, daring lovers of truth, heirs of Savl, his principles and declarations, we were proud of each other. Our life all those years was extraordinarily interesting and full, but during all its vicissitudes we never forgot our special school and our teachers, especially Veta Arcadievna. We usually imagined her at the moment when she entered class, when we were standing looking at her, and everything that we knew about anything else before this became totally unnecessary, stupid, stripped of sense—and in an instant flies off like a husk, a rind, or a bird. Why don't you tell exactly what she looked like when she came in, why not give, as Vodokachka says, a letter-of-recommendation portrait? No, no, impossible, useless, that will just overburden our talk, we'll get tangled in definitions and subtleties. But you just reminded me of Leonardo's request.

Then, in his studio, we, it seems, did manage to describe Veta. Managed, but our description was laconic, for then too we could not say anything more than what we said: dear Leonardo, imagine a woman, she is so beautiful that when you look into her eyes you cannot say *no* to your joyous tears. And,—thanks, youth, thanks,—replied the artist,—that's sufficient, I already see that person. Good, but in that case at least describe the biology room and us, those who at first were standing, and then sat down, tell briefly about those of our classmates who were present at the lesson. The stuffed birds were there, the aquariums and terrariums were there, the portrait of the scientist Pavlov riding a bicycle at the age of ninety hung there, hanging, there were pots and boxes with grasses and flowers on the windowsills, including plants very ancient and distant, some from the Chalk Age. Moreover—a collection of butterflies and herbariums, gathered by the efforts of generations. And we were there, lost in the bushes, cushes and shoots, amid the microscopes, the falling leaves and colored plaster casts of human and inhuman innards—and we studied. Please enumerate the ships that were on the river rolls—or, to be more exact, now tell about us, those sitting there. Right now I don't recall many of the names, but I do recall that among us there was, for example, a boy who if challenged could eat several flies in a row, there was a girl who would suddenly stand up and strip naked because she thought she had a pretty figure—naked. There was a boy who kept his hand in his pocket for long periods of time, he couldn't help it, because he was weak-willed. There was a girl who wrote letters to herself and answered them herself. There was a boy with very small hands. And there was a girl with very large eyes, with a long black braid and long lashes, she was a straight-A student, but she died approximately in the tenth grade, soon after Norvegov, for whom she had joyous and tormenting feelings, and he, our Savl Petrovich, loved her too. They loved each other at his place in the dacha, on the shores of enchanting Lethe, and here, in school, on the discarded gym mats on the landings of the back stairs, to the thump of Perillo's methodical pendulum. And, possibly, it was precisely this girl that we and teacher Savl called Rosa Windova. Yes, possibly, but possibly such a girl never existed, and we invented her ourselves, just like everything else in the world. That's why when your patient mother asks you: and the girl, did she really die?—then: I don't know, about the girl I know nothing—is what you must answer. And then she walked in, our Veta Arcadievna. Up on the platform, she would open the class-register and call on someone: student so-and-so, tell us about rhododendrons. He would begin to say something, to talk, but no matter what he said and no matter what other people and scientific botany books said about the rhododendrons, no one could ever say the main things about rhododendrons—do you hear me, Veta Arcadievna?—the main thing: that they, the rhododendrons, growing every minute somewhere in Alpine meadows, are far happier than we, for they know neither love, nor hate, nor the Perillo slipper system, and they don't even die, since all nature, excepting man, is one undying, indestructible whole. If one tree somewhere in a forest perishes from old age, before dying, it gives the wind so many seeds, and so many new trees grow up around it on the land, near and far, that the old tree, especially the rhododendron—and a rhododendron, Veta Arcadievna, which is probably a huge tree with leaves the size of wash basins,—doesn't mind dying. And the tree is indifferent, it just grows there on the silvery hill, or the new one does, after it has grown up out of its seeds. No, the tree doesn't mind. Or the grass, or the dog, or the rain. Only man minds and feels bitter, burdened as he is with egotistical pity for himself. Remember, even Savl, who devoted himself entirely to science and its students, said, after dying, it's damned maddening.

Student so-and-so, allow me, the author, to interrupt your narrative again. The thing is that it's time to end the book: I'm out of paper. True, if you intend to add two or three more stories from your life, I'll run to the store and buy several more packages right now. With pleasure, dear author, I'd like to, but you won't believe it anyway. I could tell about our marriage to Veta Arcadievna, about our great happiness together, and also about what happened in our dacha settlement one day when The Sender finally got down to work: that day the river overflowed its banks, flooded all the dachas and carried off all the boats. Student so-and-so, that is extremely interesting and it strikes me as totally believable, so let's go get the paper together, and along the way you tell me everything in order and in detail. Let's go,—says Nymphea. Merrily gabbing and recounting pocket change, slapping each other on the shoulders and whistling foolish songs, we walk out into the polyped street and in some miraculous manner are transformed into passersby.